NICK'S HEART
(*In Your Arms* Series Book 2)

Charlotte S. Snead

This book is a work of fiction. Names, characters, businesses, organizations, places, events, and incidents portrayed in this book either are products of the author's imagination or are used fictitiously. Any resemblance to actual names, persons (living or dead), locales, or events is purely coincidental and is not intended by the author.

Published by Van Rye Publishing, LLC
www.vanryepublishing.com

Library of Congress Control Number: 2019904647
ISBN-13: 978-0-9982893-8-0
ISBN-10: 0-9982893-8-8

Dedication

This book is dedicated to wives and mothers,
especially all those mothers of preschoolers I have had the privilege
of mentoring for over twenty years.
You do the toughest job in the world, and I honor you.
I believe in the next generation, because of you!

Contents

CHAPTER 1

Conference Speaker

NICK COSTAS, PRODUCER for O'Malley Productions, met for a cup of coffee with his friend and mentor, Taylor Wilson, at their businessmen's conference several days after Missy O'Malley, gifted Christian singer, had finished a conference at the same hotel in Nashville. Nick had traveled there with her the previous week to produce her appearances as a worship leader. The entire musical O'Malley family had arrived for the closing concert, and they remained for Taylor's conference.

The prior summer, Taylor had approached Nick to speak at this Marketplace Ministries Summit that he led. Nick demurred—what did he know about business? Taylor and Ian O'Malley, Missy's dad and Nick's boss, laughed at him, pointing out that he single-handedly built O'Malley Productions. Nick said he was a producer, that all he had to do was put Missy O'Malley on digital sound, and that she and her talented father and brother made their success, not him.

"What I want you to share, Nick, is the making of a father," Taylor said at the time. "Your testimony is amazing, given the background of neglect and abuse you suffered. You can be an inspiration to many men out there who are struggling with the wounds of their past. Why don't you write a few things down and send them to me? We'll talk next month," Taylor said.

Nick began to write, and he roped his wife, Barb, into telling a bit of her side of their remarkable journey. He sent Taylor long emails, and they spoke often on the phone. By the date of the summit, Taylor presented him with a completed book, with Nick as author, ready for him to sign dedications for the thousands who would be in attendance. Nick didn't believe it was possible to complete a book in such a short time, but Taylor had editors who polished the book, titling it: *The Making of a Father*. Nick insisted the title must be *I Met a Woman* but that "The Making of a Father" could be a subtitle.

Nick was the keynote speaker at the first general session. Taylor strode confidently on stage. "Today, I'm going to introduce you to a remarkable man with a miraculous journey to share. I met him when he was looking for a house for his family. We had a house for sale that God had designed for his family. The more I heard their story, the more moved I was. The realtor was fascinated with this young man who'd never until then known the love of a family and yet was the most incredible father she'd ever met.

"Nick Jo Costas was taken from his mother due to neglect and abuse at the age of five. He had survived broken bones, starvation, burns, and neglect while his mother supported her addictions, and after months of surgery to repair what could be repaired, he was placed in foster care. The foster care system didn't treat him kindly. An energetic and intelligent boy, he rebelled time after time and drew some of the worst abusers in the system as so-called foster parents. By the age of seventeen, he ran away for the last time, joining the military as soon as he was of age.

"I traveled to West Virginia for a consulting job, and I was curious to meet the man who turned around a troubled teen, brought out his withdrawn, shy younger brother, and captured the heart of a fairy-tale princess whom he named Cinderella. I had a delightful evening with the Costas family, which by that time included his natural daughter and a newborn son, in addition to the three children he loves as his own. I watched his interactions with these five kids, and I was amazed. He'd never known a father's love, and yet he loved well.

"I asked Nick that night how he learned to be a father, and he handed me a handwritten journal. It simply contained Scripture verses referring to being a husband and father. He had carefully inscribed them, often in three or four different translations. 'When you don't know how to do something,' he said, 'you have to ask God every minute of every day. Barb and Robbie have been incredibly patient with this stumbling guy, and God has picked me up time after time.' When you read Barb's part of Nick's book, which is available for the first time at this summit, you'll see his humility.

"Without further delay, I want to introduce Nick Costas, producer for O'Malley Productions. The lyrics to the hit single 'In Your Arms,' by Ian O'Malley, are included in the front of Nick's book because the song played a large part in Nick and Barb's marriage. Come on out here, Nick." Taylor waved him onstage.

Nick, who had pushed Missy onstage for her part in the women's convention the week before, now realized what she had experienced as he walked out and looked into thousands of upturned faces. *What do I have to say to all these people? I am such a fraud!* Nick paused, and then he heard a familiar still, small voice whisper: "And they overcame by the word of their testimony and the blood of the Lamb."

Nick spoke: "God brought me here today through a circuitous journey and a road to healing because I met a woman—a remarkable and beautiful widow with three incredible kids who captured my heart. Although I had three strikes against me and all intentions of never being a parent because I didn't want to screw up the lives of innocent children, her love, faith, and unfailing confidence in me have made me a husband and a father. Where is she? Barb, stand up." The house lights swung around to her as she blushed and waved.

Nick began to share the words of his book: "When I met Barb, she'd lost her husband to the war in Iraq, and she didn't want to surrender her commission in the National Guard because she was 'needed for the mission.' Barb had been to Iraq once, and Bob died during his second deployment. Her oldest son was angry—angry with God and man, because his father had been taken from him. The year before I met them he had been suspended from school several times, and he resisted any attempts of men to influence his life. I lucked out. For some strange reason he liked me, and we hit it off. Alan, his younger brother, was into reading and far too compliant—certainly not the mischievous young man he is today! Ella turned two a few months after I began falling in love with this family. Her party was a Cinderella theme.

"I fought God over my attraction to this incredible woman, this wonderful mother. I got the idea she was interested in me, too, and I couldn't wrap my mind around that. I knew I had nothing to offer a lifelong Christian woman. I had come to know Christ a few short months earlier, and my knowledge of God and His Word was negligible, to say the least. I had quite a checkered past, so I told God I'd find out all the diseases I might give this saintly woman who was driving me crazy with her goodness and beauty, so that I wouldn't do so. I went to the doctor for tests. When Ian later got up in our church and sang the song he wrote for his wife—the song Taylor told you we included in the book—I had just found out all my tests came back clean. Two reprobates, Mike Green and myself, proposed that afternoon, and I've found God in Barb's arms ever since.

"Since then, she has given me two more children—a little Latina beauty, our Rosa . . ." a photo of Rosa flashed up on the big screens to the side of the stage, and the audience gave a collective gasp at her beauty. "And our son, Michael James." Another photo, of a husky toddler wobbling on sturdy legs, brought a wave of laughter. "But having children does not a father make. When I first met Robbie, I told him I didn't have a father, and the cocky teen informed me that was 'biologically impossible.'" The crowd laughed again.

Nick briefly outlined his childhood, skimming over the scars on his back but openly confiding the wounds on his soul, the anger and bitterness towards women that made him a user of women, and the depression that convinced him he was a no good loser and would never be anything else. "But I met a woman who refused to accept that image I had of myself. If I have stumbled into a more perfect way to love, to be a husband and a father, it is because of God's unfailing love and mercies and the love she and her children have poured into me. To borrow the words of Ian's song: 'In her arms, I feel God's love.' You know it?" The crowd applauded.

Nick went on to openly share about his mistakes: the night he walked out, the times he refused to become vulnerable, and his tantrums of silence. Then he gave the Scriptures that God had used in his life to correct and reprove him. Often the audience wept, occasionally they laughed, and by the time he finished, a long line of people looking to buy his book had formed at the table outside.

Nick sat at the table beside Barb, who found herself in conversations with women struggling with their husbands. "Nick makes me out to be a saint. All I did was love him, and he wasn't as difficult to love as he thinks he was. Of course, he *is* rather a hunk, don't you think?" and she leaned against him as he slipped an arm around her and rolled his eyes. The crowd gathered around them laughed.

After the table closed, the O'Malleys joined them for dinner. "I ordered dinner for all of us up in the room, Nick," Nick's boss, Ian O'Malley, said. "Alice is with all the kids, but Missy and Tim heard you, and I ordered a DVD, so we can see it later. Everyone's enthusiastic. You must have done a fine job, son."

"He did, Ian, except for making me out to be some kind of saint," Barb said.

"You are my personal saint, babe." Nick pulled her to his side and dropped a kiss on her cheek. "I hope God got the glory up there today."

"Oh, He did, Nick," Missy assured him, walking up beside him and linking her arm in his. "You gave all those Scriptures, and you told the story about Daddy's song in church. God did get all the glory. How did *you* feel, after you pushed me on stage for three days?"

"I'm sorry, Missy. I had no idea how difficult that would be! I hope I don't ever have to go on stage again."

Taylor walked up behind him, overhearing his remark. "Don't count on it. I have a dozen requests for you to consider. Ian tells me he's ordered enough food for Adelaide and me. May we join you?" Nick welcomed his mentor. "You did well. You're living proof of what God can do," Taylor added. "But I heard you speaking to women at the table, Barb, and you need to be a part of his presentation." Barb stared at him with alarm.

"You've got to be kidding! I told the women all I did was to love him. No one can change anyone, not even—maybe especially—your husband. Only the Holy Spirit can change someone."

"Have you read *The Man Whisperer*, by Rick Johnson? That's the thesis of his book. I'll check into his next presentation and make sure you touch base with him. You could write a sequel to Nick's book based on that concept."

"You are too much, Taylor! First, you get Nick to write a book, and now you want me to write one?"

"Honey, I didn't write that book," Nick said. "Taylor got a bunch of editors to do it."

"Nick, I saw the hours you put into that. I can't do that with five children."

"You tell me all the time how spoiled you are, and how you don't do anything, so do this, Barb. You have wisdom, and your knowledge of Scripture is incredible. I've been praying about what we're going to do with the revenue from my book and presentations, and I'm going to call Mother Joanna tomorrow about funding a boys' home. If we do this again, all the income from the books and presentations could fund a home in South L.A."

Barb's eyes filled with tears. "For that, I'd do anything. We could name it after your mother."

Taylor clapped Nick on the back and handed him a stack of papers. "That's entirely feasible. Look at all these requests for you to speak: Promise Keepers, Women of Faith, regional Marketplace Summits . . . even Celebrate Recovery out of Saddleback Church. I'll go fetch Adelaide."

"Please do, Taylor. We'd like that," Nick confirmed.

After supper, Nick and Barb decided to spend the evening with the kids. They went down to an indoor pool to give them time and activity. The older boys played games by themselves, but Missy's husband, Tim, and Nick were engaged in keeping the toddlers happy. Barb and Missy finally took pity on them and joined them in the pool. About nine, they headed upstairs.

Nick was glad the summit paid for a suite, because after they'd gotten the kids settled, he and Barb had a room to themselves. "This is a nice vacation for us and only a little work for me. I worked harder last week, producing Missy's performances. But this is a piece of cake, once I survived the stage fright. Are the kids all squared away?"

"You did a good job. Yes, the little ones are asleep. Robbie and Alan are playing video games at the O'Malleys', and Ella and Rosa and are asleep with Willow and Jeri. Only Michael's here. We'll have to sort our kids out before we go home." Barb was pulling her shirt over her head as she spoke, and when she threw it over a chair, she saw him looking at her and blushed at the intensity of his gaze.

Nick's lazy smile flashed across his face as his eyes swept over her. "You can't be blushing after all these years and the babies we've made." He crossed the room in two strides, taking her in his arms and kissing her breathless. He buried his face in her hair and nibbled down her neck. "God knows I missed you, Barb."

"I'd better shower. I've been traveling all day."

Nick grinned. "Sounds like fun. I'll join you." And he described all the places he would wash for her.

In the O'Malleys' suites, various older kids were playing video games. Alice read to some of the younger ones, leaving Missy and Tim, and her brother Jimmy and his wife Julie—who happened to be Missy's best friend—free to enjoy themselves. The O'Malley family had driven in for the end of Missy's conference, closing it with Jimmy and Ian joining Missy for a full concert.

Missy and Tim eventually headed to their room after wandering around the grounds. After she checked on the girls, she joined her husband in the living area. "Nick couldn't wait until Barb got here, Timothy. Didn't he do a good job today? God's done an amazing job in his life. Your family says you didn't laugh until you met me, and I never heard him laugh until he fell in love with Barb and her kids. Now he's the most contented guy, and a lot easier to work with! He has always been excellent, but he's really laid back now, and it's a joy to go to work on music with him."

Tim reached for her hand. "Singing is now a real job? God's changed your priorities."

"You saw how many lives God reached when I simply sang to touch His heart. It's simple, to sing for Him, and somehow the Holy Spirit works in His amazing way. Look how Nick simply told his story, and men were broken and put back together. I'll never stop wondering how God works and who He chooses. But it's kind of scary, you know."

"It's good to be scared, Missy. It keeps you dependent on Him. None of us can do anything in ourselves. We're simply conduits."

"Little did Barb know when she fell in love what would happen in a few short years."

"Nick wasn't an easy guy to love."

"Maybe not, but God gave her the love, and He used it to bring him to an amazing place," Missy said. "He's a fantastic father. We struggle to be good parents, and both of us had wonderful mothers. Our dads had some brokenness, but they loved us. Nick challenges me all the time, sharing the things God shows him. He reads the Bible and does it the best he can. I have a lot of respect for him. Barb says she had the Bible verses memorized, and he lives them out in front of her. I believe God gave him Barb because of her knowledge of the Word."

"Iron sharpens iron, God says. We sharpen one another, Missy. You've made me a much better person."

"Thank you, Timothy, and you are my strength. You gave me the confidence to do this conference. Your support and encouragement helped me to even think about singing for other people. And you know what? After all the grief I gave Daddy, I love it. I pray and stand back and watch God work. All I have to do is sing."

Tim took her in his arms. "You offer yourself, a willing vessel, and God fills you. I'm privileged to be married to you. I love you more every day."

"We sold over five hundred copies of the book Tiffany and I wrote. Do you realize how much that will help the pregnancy ministry and Hope House?" She reached for his hand. "I love you, too, Timothy, and God gave us Abby and Tiffany to free us for the next great adventures."

"Tiff is enjoying architecture, and she's a natural. She got several credits for her work as my intern last summer. And her romantic interest in Laura's son, who has taken a job at Elkins High, may be an incentive to bring her into the firm when she graduates."

Missy sat on the couch in their suite, her feet in Tim's lap. He loved to hold her feet, rubbing them idly as they talked together. He lifted his head off the back of the couch when she got on her knees and began to crawl towards him. Catching her in his arms, he drew her close. "Enough talk. We have the night ahead of us, and the kids are asleep," he whispered into her hair.

"My thoughts exactly, Timothy." Missy settled in his arms, lifting her face for his kisses.

"We couldn't be doing this without your mom and dad. God brought your dad back to us from Nashville at the right time," he said.

"Of course, if he hadn't come back, none of this would have happened, and your musical gift would've remained hidden under a bushel."

"Their love for the grandchildren gives us a lot of freedom, and the kids' love and total acceptance has brought Daddy healing. Isn't God efficient?"

"It would be efficient if we both took one shower. How about that for efficiency?" Tim asked.

Missy laughed. "I don't know. I envision a waste of water and time."

"I believe in that kind of waste. Let's get to it." Tim rose, offering her his hand.

CHAPTER 2

Breakfast with Family and Friends

S OMETIME IN THE MIDDLE of the night, Barb woke up, hearing a broken-hearted cry: "Mama, please don't leave me." She found Nick sobbing beside her and gently shook him, gathering him in her arms. "Nick, I'm here, It's Barb. Can you wake up?" Nick reached for her desperately. She freed an arm and swept the stray lock of black curl off his forehead. "Did you have the dream about your mother being taken away again?"

"Yeah." Nick tried to orient himself and went to the bathroom. He stuck his head under a stream of cold water and came back to the bedroom, toweling his hair. "I woke you up, babe. What time is it?"

"It's two. Let's go back to sleep." She patted the bed.

Nick sat, drew his legs up, and reached over to turn off the light. He curved himself around Barb, spooning her against his body. Her long legs stretched back and tangled with his. He breathed in the familiar lavender scent of her hair and felt his heart rate return to normal. He gave a half snort, half chuckle. "I cry all the time. I cry when you love me, I cry when the kids crawl into my lap, I even cry in my dreams."

"You had a lot of tears stored up, Nick."

He sighed, pulling her closer. "God knows I love you, *amada*."

"I love you, too, Nick. God wants to heal you so that you can minister to others. Last night, you touched many lives. You've given and given to me, and to our family. We must share you with all the people who need you."

"Um, I don't know about that."

She smiled and patted his arm, which was curved around her body. "Oh, I do, Nick. I do. I watched you. You had such compassion with those folks."

"Shh, Barb, you women talk too much."

* * *

The next morning, Barb was up with Michael, but Nick was asleep when Missy tapped on the door, saying she had their girls with her. "You guys want to go to breakfast with us?" Missy wondered. "Ella and Rosa wanted to find Mommy and Daddy."

Barb explained what happened during the night and said she'd keep the kids satisfied with fruit bars until Nick woke up and that their family would go to breakfast together then. Nick woke up later, when he heard another knock at the door. He heard Barb talking to Taylor and walked out of their bedroom.

"Daddy!" crowed Michael, running to Nick.

His daddy swung him into his arms, beaming and kissing his upturned face. "Good morning, buddy. Are you hungry? Morning, Taylor, what brings you here?"

"I heard you had a rough night, son. Are you all right?"

Nick frowned at Barb. "I told you women talk too much. Who did you tell and what?"

"Missy came by to bring the girls and wanted us to go to breakfast. I told her about your dream, but I didn't say that much."

Nick grinned at Taylor. "When you work for the O'Malleys, you become family. I'm okay. I dreamed about the night they took Mama away—the same dream I had after Rosa was born. Cried like a baby. Talking about all that stuff at the conference must have triggered some memories."

"God is bringing you healing, Nick."

"You gave me healing when you found Mama and I was able to see her before she died. I want to find a cop named Jesús. I owe him big time. He got me to the hospital after they took Mama, and he visited me for weeks until I was discharged."

"I can get somebody on that. Your health records and case files need to be a part of this story. Maybe your second book should be titled *A Boy Called Nickie*."

"You are nuts, you know that, Taylor?" Nick answered. "Nobody wants to know all this stuff about some Hispanic kid from South L.A." Barb exchanged glances with Taylor, and they smiled.

"I also came by because Dan Murphy wants to meet you. Can you guys join us for breakfast?" Taylor asked. Barb reminded him they would have to put up with the children, but they were all at least dressed and ready, except for Nick.

"Give me ten minutes," Nick suggested. And the men arranged to meet in one of the restaurants. "You know that Murphy guy is a shrink, don't you?" Nick continued after Taylor left. "You guys aren't ganging up on me and arranging a head-job, are you?"

Barb laughed. "No, I didn't know. He's one of the speakers, isn't he? Your head is perfect, Nick," and she pulled his face toward hers for a long and lingering kiss.

"Don't start that. We need to meet these guys in ten minutes. And we appear to have spectators." Michael stared at them and burst into a happy grin when they turned and looked at him. Nick gave him his hand, and he toddled behind his father. Nick shaved to a rapt audience and dressed quickly in a new pair of slacks and a sweater Barb had brought. When he walked out, her hazel eyes widened appreciatively.

"You look good, Nick. Be sure to tell all your adoring fans that you are spoken for."

"You do look nice, Daddy," Ella added. "We're ready to go. Rosa has her bright yellow dress on, and I have this dull old pink thing."

Nick squatted down, taking Ella in his arms.

"But you are beautiful in pink, my fair gringo girl. Your eyes are blue, and your blonde hair is like spun gold. Rosa needs yellow to give some color to her black eyes, but you are my perfect-in-pink Cinderella." Ella basked in his praise.

"Can you brush my hair, Daddy?"

"Ella, we've brushed your hair, and we need to go," Barb reminded her.

"Only takes a minute, Mommy," Nick said as he took Ella's hand, walking her into the second bedroom. He gave her fair curls a few quick strokes, kissed her on the cheek, and offered her his hand.

"Come on, Rosa. Are you girls ready to eat?" Barb asked. She had Michael on her hip.

Nick grabbed the diaper bag, and the girls ran ahead of them. "I guess the boys will find us?" he questioned Barb. "I feel like Mary and Joseph with our sons somewhere among the others. It's not hard to figure how they lost Jesus. Hey, girls, come back. Here's the elevator."

The Costas family arrived in the restaurant only a few minutes late. While Nick settled the girls in chairs and Michael in a high chair, Barb apologized and explained his negotiations with Ella to Dr. Dan Murphy and Taylor. Dan Murphy had no intention of offering therapy to Nick. Instead, he'd read Nick's book on the plane and wanted Nick's help with a workshop later in the day. A man came up to them at the table, interrupting their meal to speak to Nick, who stood, drew him aside, and leaned toward him, touching his arm.

"I really want to talk to you at some point," he assured the man, "but I'm having a family meal right this minute. I'm sure you understand. I'll be in Dr. Murphy's workshop at eleven today. Could you meet us there? I can't leave my wife stranded with three kids under the age of five. It could be a disaster!" Nick laughed, patting the guy on the arm. The man smiled and left, promising to look for them later.

"You handled that like a pro, Nick. You made him feel special while you drew your boundaries around your family," Dan praised.

"You do what you gotta do and treat people the way you want to be treated. No big deal," Nick replied as he took his seat.

Barb's eyes shone with pride as she leaned in toward Taylor. "You see what I mean? I know the Word, chapter and verse, but he simply lives it."

"He teaches me every time I'm around him," Taylor whispered back. "It took me years to get that kind of balance. Let me pick his brain. Nick, why did you put that guy off?" Taylor asked.

"Taylor, I was lost for thirty-five years before God got a hold of me. I never dreamed I'd marry again after striking out twice. God gave me this saint of a woman and five precious kids. They're the most important thing in my life. Ella will never be five again, and she's off to kindergarten in the fall. Rosa will never be two and a half, and Michael is our last baby. I need to be around them as much as possible, and I can't help that guy anyway. I'm not God. What is that Scripture, Barb, about a time for everything?" Barb quoted Ecclesiastes, and he grinned at her, saying, "She's my walking Bible, this one. She keeps me straight." Nick regarded her with love shining in his eyes. "God knows that guy, and he's the Holy Spirit's job, not mine."

"I like the way you think, Nick!" Dan said. "I'm glad you agreed to help me."

* * *

Later, after the workshop, Dan caught up with Taylor. "He is one put-together guy," Dan said. "I need to interview him. He's an interesting case study. Has he ever had therapy?"

"Didn't he mention some counseling in his book, when he was bounced around foster care? He stayed in a juvenile mental health hospital for several months, but he told me being married to Barb and being Robbie's stepfather brought him more healing in a year than years of therapy."

"His openness and honesty enable him to reach wounded souls. Barb must be a remarkable woman," Dan observed.

"God dropped a gift of love for him in her heart, she says. She never expected to remarry after her first husband died. Apparently, they were lifelong sweethearts. Her son, Robbie, told her to marry Nick. The boy told her God had given them a lot of love, and their family could teach Nick how to love because he never knew that kind of love—the love of a family. Nick had reached out to the boy because he was a troubled kid once himself. Robbie's a great kid—he helps Nick in the studio. He's a big boy, like his birth father, and towers over Nick now. But he has profound respect for him and loves him like crazy."

"Nick definitely will be an asset in this kind of ministry. I like him. He's personable and funny, with self-deprecating humor. I thoroughly enjoyed his book, and I like him in person even more."

"I learn from him every time I am around him," Taylor said. "He takes the Word literally and tries to do it. He doesn't get caught up in theology. He applies it practically. Did you hear he got to see his mother before she died?"

"Yes, he told that story in the workshop," Dan said.

Taylor chuckled. "Last night he told the crowd about his journey to forgiveness and had everyone in tears, and then he got us all laughing about handling a two-year-old on the plane. Look, the whole family is coming toward us."

"Is that Robbie?" Dan asked. "He *is* a big lad."

"Come on, I'll introduce you," Taylor said.

Robbie extended his hand to Taylor, and Alan gave Taylor a high five. "Hi, Mr. Wilson," Alan greeted him. Ella simply reached up her arms, with every expectation of being carried. Rosa grinned at Taylor, but regarded Dan Murphy with caution, peeping at him from behind her father's leg and looking up at him with solemn black eyes.

Dan squatted down to her level. "Are you Daddy's little rosebud? He told me about his Rosa."

She grinned. "Who are you?" she asked.

Laughing, Dan introduced himself to her. When Barb tried to apologize, he shook his head. "I've got grandchildren her age. Little ones are honest and quite refreshing. Jesus said we should all try to enter the kingdom like little children."

"We're going to lunch. Do you wanna come?" Ella invited. Dan looked at Nick, who shrugged.

"If you can put up with all of us—we're all together for the first time in days. The boys have been off with the O'Malley boys, I traveled here last week to produce the show for Missy, and Ian and Jimmy came in Saturday night to join her for a concert. They're an amazing family. I'm grateful to work for them."

"Nick told me when he gets to heaven he is going to ask God if he can work for the O'Malleys for eternity!" Robbie said. "Nick's good. Mr. O'Malley says Nick made O'Malley Productions."

Nick stopped Robbie. "You know how anointed they are, Robbie. All we do is turn the sound on and let God have His way. Do you guys already have plans for lunch?" Nick asked Dan and Taylor.

"I want pizza Daddy," Ella said.

"We had pizza last night, Ella. I want tacos," argued Rosa.

"Hmm, if we can't agree, we can't eat now, can we?" Nick mused. "Whatever should we do? Maybe we should go upstairs, take a nap, and think about it." All the kids clamored for food. They obviously would starve if they did not eat within the next few minutes. Nick laughed at them. "I have reservations at a buffet, so you can choose what you want. Is that good, Mommy?"

"Perfect, Nick."

Dan and Taylor joined them for the meal, but Nick spent the entire time pulling stories out of the children about what they did last week while he was gone. Ella had recited a poem in Sunday school, and she performed it proudly for them. Rosa had colored a Sunday school paper for him, and Barb pulled it out of her pocketbook. Alan had played a baseball game, and his team won. Robbie had worked in the studio, with Jimmy and Ian. Nick asked each child specific questions and listened carefully. Michael sat on his lap, patting his daddy and leaning his head on his chest. Occasionally, Nick looked over at Barb and winked.

"What an amazing mother you have. She got you to all these places. How many miles did you put on the car, Mommy? And how did you do all this by yourself?"

Barb smiled at him. "It was tough. Thank God Robbie has his license now. But we still couldn't do it without Sally. Thank you for making me keep her on as our nanny."

"I don't want you too tired for your night job, honey." Robbie and Alan exchanged looks and grinned.

"Mommy, do you go out to work at night?" Ella inquired.

"No, baby, Daddy is being silly. I stay home all night," Barb assured her.

Nick said, "She works at home, washing your clothes and doing your dishes, and—"

"And keeping Daddy very happy," Robbie interrupted, jabbing Alan with his elbow.

"Nick, I swear . . ." Barb blushed, unable to look at her older sons as they laughed with Nick, with Taylor and Dan joining in.

"Mommy, are you mad at Papa?" Rosa asked.

"No, Rosita, she's not mad. She never knows what to do when he teases her," Robbie assured his sister.

"Oh. Papa always teases us, Mommy. It's his way of loving us, he says."

"I know, Rosa, I know. And he loves us lots and lots, doesn't he?" Barb smiled at her beautiful Latina girl.

"I love Papa, Mama."

"I do, too, baby. I do too. Are you through eating?"

"Mommy, we haven't had dessert yet!" Nick protested. "Come on, kids, let's hit the dessert table." Nick herded the girls, placing their selections on a tray.

"He could eat everything in here and never gain a pound," Barb told Taylor.

Robbie overheard her remark. "It's 'cause he runs every day, rain or shine, Mom. I'm going to meet Jamie at the pool in an hour, so I'll swim mine off. Come on, Alan, are you going to get some dessert? Excuse us, please," he added, turning to Dan and Taylor. "And, Mom, don't be mad at Nick. Remember what I told you?" After he left, Dan asked Barb what Robbie had told her.

"You see how Nick is? He'll say anything, and he embarrasses me to tears sometimes. Once I fussed at him about a remark like that, and Robbie told me he loved Nick from the first because he treated him like a man. 'Nick knows how boys think, Mom,' he said. He said, 'We all think the same. Besides, he makes me treat my girlfriend with respect because I don't want to mess up anything. I want to have what you guys do.' I am trying to get used to Nick, I really am, because it works."

"Robbie's right. Boys need to learn how to love a woman, and the male gender is universally obsessed, so it's good to be open. I bet they ask Nick things that most boys would never ask their dad, and that's a good thing," Dan responded. Barb nodded in agreement.

Nick, balancing Michael on his shoulders and a tray of desserts in his hand, led his laughing girls to the table like a Pied Piper. Watching him, Barb said, "You didn't have much opportunity to visit with him, but he's missed the kids."

"I thoroughly enjoyed this meal, Barb. He's a good father," Dan said.

"He's the best, Dr. Murphy," Robbie enthused as he walked up, reaching for Michael and helping Nick get the girls in chairs.

"The best at what, Robbie?" Nick chimed in. "Drawing a great hand with five perfect kids and one perfect wife?" Nick pushed Rosa up to the table and retrieved a spoon for her. "Try to get most of it in your mouth,

Rosita. We don't have a washing machine at the hotel. Ella, you need a napkin?" She shook her head and lifted her napkin from beside her while she shoved ice cream in her mouth. "Now, don't worry, you don't have to eat all of that. Daddy will help you." Nick reached for his spoon and pretended to go for their desert. Both girls protested, giggling.

"You didn't get anything for yourself, honey?" Barb asked.

"I'm full, babe. My three girls are all the sweetness I need. You boys are off?"

"We're going to the pool in our wing, Daddy Nick," Alan informed him. "Mr. Jimmy will be there, and I have my cell phone charged, okay?"

Nick nodded at Alan and waved at Robbie. "Have fun guys. I'll see you at dinner. We're going to a movie with the Raines family, so look sharp and meet us at the room about five, okay?"

"Yes, sir," both boys chorused and charged off.

Barb shook her head. "Which is more exhausting, preschoolers or teenagers?" she asked Dan and Taylor.

"I find adult children keep me busy, too," Dan said, smiling at her. "Plus, now we have the grandchildren. But you wouldn't want it any other way, would you?"

"You girls about done? How about going up to our room for a rest?" Nick asked. "Daddy needs a nap. I had bad dreams, Cinderella, and you weren't there to calm me."

"I'm sorry, Daddy, but you can dance with your Cinderella now. Want to?"

"That would make me feel much better! And if my little rosebud would sleep beside me, that would make it perfect."

Rosa's beautiful face curved into a wide smile. "I will, Daddy. I missed our snuggles when you were gone. Don't ever leave us again."

Nick gently caressed her silken curls. "I never left you in my heart, Rosita. You know that, don't you?" She nodded. "Sorry to make you wait in line, Mommy, but two beautiful women are demanding my attention." Nick caressed Barb with his chocolate eyes, and she smiled.

"I wouldn't dare interfere. These girls have missed their daddy terribly. I was surprised they stayed with Jeri and Willow last night."

"I felled asleep, Mommy, when Gram Alice was reading," Rosa explained.

"And I had to stay with Rosa," Ella added.

"Good girl, to look after your sister, Ella," Barb praised as she rose from the table and excused the family.

Dan and Taylor signaled the waiter for another round of coffee. When they asked for their bill later, Nick had already paid.

"Nick reminds me once again to keep my priorities straight. I need to find Adelaide," Taylor said.

"Sorry, buddy, she's off shopping with Caroline," Dan told him.

"Our wives can get expensive on these trips!" Taylor laughed. "But it sure is more fun when they come along. I bet they're buying for the grandchildren."

* * *

Nick did fall asleep with the girls on the king bed in their bedroom. Barb was reading her Bible when he walked into the living area and dropped on the couch beside her. He pulled her into his arms, rubbing her back. She tipped her face up to his kiss.

"You know what your chocolate eyes do to me, Nick?"

"Mmm. I know I have no resistance when you look at me with your hazel ones. I fought those eyes for months!"

"I couldn't fight your eyes, or the electricity I felt when you touched me."

Nick grinned, caressing her until she moaned. "Still feel it, babe, after two kids?" he whispered, running kisses down her neck.

"If I hadn't had the tubal, we'd have another one coming along by now," Barb said. "Quit that, Nick."

"Quit what?"

"The way you caress me with your eyes. I can't stand it."

"Can you take it lying down?" Taking her hand, he led her into the second bedroom. "Shh, we don't want to wake Michael. Can you be quiet, for once?" he teased. "You've gotten kind of noisy since we moved all the kids upstairs."

"The boys will be coming in," she whispered.

"In two hours, though. I can make this a short one."

"Lord, help me!" Barb replied, but she clung to his hand as she followed him. "I put the Do Not Disturb sign on the door."

"You wicked woman!"

"I didn't want anyone to wake the children," she protested.

"Can we stop talking about the children, *mi amor*?" Lowering his mouth to cover hers, Nick cut off any response she might make, and she offered no resistance as they sank onto the bed.

After Barb was asleep, Nick brought a robe and laid it quietly beside her, closing the door behind him. He went into the living area, slipped out his cell phone, and punched in a number. After a series of connections, he spoke to Mother Joanna in L.A., describing what was going on in his life and presenting his dream of funding a group home for boys. "Do you think that is feasible? Could you staff such a place, and would you be interested?"

"Nick, this is an answer to prayer. The sisters and I have been talking about nothing else since you were here. Your life would have been different if we could have brought you here with your mother. We'll continue to lift this up to the throne."

"I'll come out there soon to discuss it further. Let me get some projections, and I'll get back with you."

"Please bring Barbara and the children with you, Nickie."

"I couldn't come without Rosa. She talks about Madre constantly, and she calls me 'Papa' now."

Mother Joanna laughed. "Your mama is smiling because she touched your family forever."

"The older ones call me Nick, but Ella goes back and forth between Daddy and Papa. I dreamed about Mama last night." He described his dream.

"Nick, we tried to get your mother to find you, but she was afraid. She said you could never forgive her. Can you understand that?"

Nick told her about Ian's struggle to reunite with his family. "I watched him. If God hadn't boxed him in, I doubt he would've ever found the courage. So, yeah, I understand. I'm just glad I got there in time."

"Oh, we are, too. She died in peace, Nick. Come see us, please. You always have a family here."

"I'll call you soon, Madre." Nick leaned his head back on the sofa, quietly praising God for his many families: the sisters, the whole O'Malley clan, the Wilsons, and of course Barb and the children.

Barb dressed, made up the bed, and walked into the living room. She found Nick with his eyes closed and his lips moving. "Were you on the phone?" Noticing the tears running down his face, she crossed the room and sunk down beside him. "Are you okay, sweetheart?"

Nick put his arm around her. "I am thanking God for all the family He's given this lost child."

"Jesus said, 'Give and it shall be given unto you, full measure, pressed down and running over shall men press into your bosom.' You gave Ella and my boys a father, and God has returned it to you. I heard Ian call you 'Son,' and Taylor, too."

"For a kid with no dad, I have some great ones now, don't I? Jeez, I'm turning into a regular waterworks."

"Let me get you a Coke." Barb rose and went to the refrigerator, returning with a soda. "Who were you talking to?" She asked as she sat beside him.

"I called Mother Joanna. She loved the idea of a group home for boys and said she and the sisters had been praying about how to serve the children since I was out there. We need to start raising some serious money, because anything we do needs to be done right—no cinderblock dorm, but a nice homey place, with sports centers and living areas. Do you think this is crazy, Barb?"

"No, Nick. God's been waiting for someone to do this for His lost children in South L.A. If God has called us to this, He'll see it done, and when Taylor gets a hold of something, he sees it through. This is going to be fun."

A grin spread across Nick's face. "I can envision a whole chain of homes. Maybe even one in Elkins, how about?"

"Let's start with one. What are you thinking now about speaking? You said you didn't want to go on stage ever again."

"I feel like Missy. Once over the stage fright, I see God moving, and it's exciting to be used that way. But I can't abandon my responsibilities at O'Malley Productions, so it'll be a challenge."

"Missy limits her trips and maintains a balance. You can do that, and you can apprentice someone and retain oversight. Look how much Robbie can do now."

"Yeah, but he has his own life. We need to preserve his choices. Maybe he'll want to follow his dad into the military."

"Maybe he'll want to follow his stepfather into God's Army."

"But he needs to make that choice, Barb, so let's don't put any pressure on him."

Barb scooted down and leaned against him. "God gave you to us, Nick, and I'm glad."

"Me, too."

They heard the click of a key in the door. Barb started to sit up, but he held her there. The boys came in with Missy and Tim's son, Todd Raines. "Tim said they'd be ready to go in half an hour," Robbie reported. "Are the little ones still asleep?" Rosa heard the boys and ran up to Robbie with her arms up. He laughed and swung her in the air. "Where's Ella, Rosa?" Robbie asked.

"She's coming. She went pee-pee and poopie."

"Ugh, TMI, Rosa," Alan groaned. "I hear Michael. I'll go get him."

"The nice thing about big families is I don't have to parent the little ones."

"Yeah, sure, Barb," Nick said.

"You watch, Nick. Alan will change Michael before he brings him out," Barb assured him. As they listened, Alan herded Michael into the bathroom and challenged him to do pee-pees in the potty. They heard a tinkle and a shout of celebration.

"Good job, Mikey. Wow! That's terrific. Soon you can get Mommy to buy you some Spiderman underpants."

Barb chuckled. "I'm still needed to do the buying, I guess."

Robbie came in from the boys' bedroom and tossed the robe to his mother. "Nick will always have something he needs you to do, Mom." He grinned at her and walked back into their room to get dressed. Barb's face flamed, but Nick laughed.

"Come on. Let's get these kids dressed and go." Nick held out his hand and pulled Barb up.

CHAPTER 3

Nick's Heart

A S THE TWO FAMILIES headed home to West Virginia in the tour bus that Ian and Jimmy had driven to get to Nashville for Missy's conference, Nick seemed to deflate. He slept most of the way home. Barb was concerned, because he wasn't his usual cocky self, full of teasing laughter. But Missy brushed her worries aside, telling her how hard he had worked. When they stopped to eat, Nick held Barb's hand but conversed minimally, which was also unlike him. She checked him for a fever covertly, thinking his color was off, but he assured her he was fine.

When they got home, Ian suggested a couple of days off, and Nick offered no protest. He loved his work, saying it was a joy to work with godly, talented people, but he was content to laze around the house with the kids.

"Mom, has Nick already run today?" Robbie asked. "I wanted to go with him."

"No, he never mentioned it," Barb replied.

"Strange. He hasn't run in several days." Robbie reached into the refrigerator and pulled out some eggs. "You guys eat already?"

"We had English muffins and yogurt, but the girls haven't eaten."

"I'll make enough for everyone." Robbie busied himself with preparations but put his hand on his mother's arm when she turned to go.

"What's up with Nick? Is he upset?"

A frown creased Barb's brow. "You noticed, too? He tells me nothing, but he's not up to his old tricks, is he?"

"Something is wrong," Robbie replied.

"I need to get him to the doctor."

"Good luck with that, Mom. You know how he is."

Barb walked into the family room where Nick was lounging on the recliner. The newspaper had slipped out of his hand, and his eyes were closed. He looked terribly still and gray. She crossed quickly and knelt before him. Nick opened his eyes and smiled at her. "What's up?"

"I'm worried about you."

He pulled her down, and his fingers tangled in her hair as his gaze caressed her face. She didn't shudder as she usually did at his look, and he wasn't sending those messages either. He definitely wasn't himself. They hadn't made love since they got home.

"I love you," Barb whispered.

His lips curved into a broad smile. "I love you, too. You're the best thing that ever happened to me."

"*Do* you love me, Nick?"

"Of course."

"If you love me, you will do something for me?"

"What?"

She leaned forward and put her arms around him, resting her head on his shoulder. "Go to the doctor, Nick. I want you to go to the doctor." She could see irritation cross his face. "Please. If you love me, you will do this."

"Fine, worrywart, I'll go. But you're making too much of a fuss. I'm tired."

"Thank you," Barb said as she stood. She went into the kitchen, and Robbie handed her the phone.

"Barb, this is Ian," the voice on the line said. "Alice and I have been talking about Nick. He's off his game, and Alice thinks you need to get him to a doctor. I know that won't be easy."

"I just got him to agree. It wasn't easy, but he says he'll go. Where should we go?"

Ian consulted with Alice and returned to the phone. "Alice will pave the way. I'll call you back with a time." Later, they called back and told Barb 1:00 p.m.

Nick grumbled all the way to the doctor's office. The internist examined him briefly and did an EKG. The internist stepped out of the examination room and returned with another doctor.

"Mr. Costas, I'm Dr. White. I'm a cardiologist, and these tests require a life-flight to the medical center in Pittsburgh. You'll be departing as soon as it arrives."

"Now wait a second, doc," Nick protested.

"You haven't a second to wait." Dr. White turned to Barb. "Mrs. Costas, if you want to have your husband around for a while, you must make him go."

Within hours, Nick was hospitalized in the heart unit at United Presbyterian Medical Center, and, even lying flat on his back, he was exhausted. Tests were run, monitors were humming, and he lay with his eyes closed. Barb sat beside his bed holding his hand and praying. Her phone rang, and she slipped out.

"I've been trying to call you," Taylor said. "When I couldn't reach Nick by cell, and no one answered the house phone, I called Ian. He told me he's in the hospital, after you dragged him to the doctor and they life-flighted him to Pittsburgh almost immediately. And they want to operate? Something about his heart?"

"It's a congenital something, Taylor," Barb said. "Of course, he knows nothing about his genetics from his father's side."

"Let me have his physician's name, Barb. May I call him?"

She agreed and took a few moments to call the boys and talk to them. Barb looked up when she saw a hospital aide looking for her. "Please come quickly, Mrs. Costas. Your husband is upset."

Barb hurried after her. Nick's doctor was in the room. Barb put her hand on her heart and sent a silent plea heavenward as she hurried to the bedside. Nick saw her, and peace descended like a blanket. He smiled and reached out his hand. She took it, and the doctor watched energy and strength flow into his patient's body. Barb leaned and kissed Nick. "Where were you?" he asked.

"Taylor's been looking for you. I spoke to him, and then I called and talked to the boys a while."

"Would that be Taylor Wilson?" the doctor asked.

"Why yes. Do you know him?" Barb asked.

"Not exactly, but I just spoke to him on the phone."

"He didn't waste any time," Barb said.

The surgeon chuckled. "No, he didn't. He told the CEO of the hospital that we'd get a $100,000 donation if he could speak to me within five minutes. They pulled me out of surgery."

"Oh, my," Barb said.

"It's fine. I have an excellent chief resident who is closing. This Wilson guy is a personal friend of Dr. Jonah Marshall—have you heard of him?" Barb shook her head. "He's a world-class heart surgeon. He's invented procedures we do here, and he's done things we don't attempt. Wilson's arranging for you to fly out to the medical center in Houston, Texas in his private jet. He's a good man to have on your side. I'm sending a resident with you. He says he'll fly him back. You'll be in the best hands in the world, and your chances have gone up. I'll make the arrangements on our end."

Taylor sent the big jet, knowing Nick would recover faster if he had his family around him. Jimmy got Robbie and the kids and drove them to meet the jet at the Pittsburgh airport. Nick and Barb arrived by helicopter from the hospital. Nick was heavily sedated, and the resident settled him in a bedroom on the plane. Robbie and Alan carried the little ones, and Ella trailed along big-eyed, clinging tightly to the hand of their nanny, Sally. "What's wrong with Papa, Mommy?" she whispered.

"Papa is very sick, Ella, and we need to pray for him. Something is wrong in his heart, and Mr. Wilson sent this plane to take him to the best doctor in the world to take care of him." She gathered the children around her as the plane prepared for takeoff. "Rosa, do you remember flying to see your *abuela*?" Rosa nodded. "We will be on the plane almost that long. We are going to Houston, Texas. Can you children be very good for Mommy? That's what you can do to help Papa get well."

Robbie came up to the group clustered around his mother. "Mrs. Wilson is used to traveling on this plane with grandchildren. I've found lots of books, girls. Come with me, and I'll read to you."

Sally took Michael in search of some snacks. Relieved, Barb sank on the seat beside Alan. "I don't even have an overnight bag. What am I going to do?"

"Mr. Wilson said the plane is stocked with personal items," Alan reassured her. "We left in a hurry to meet you, but Missy is going to pack and overnight some things to the hotel. Da O'Malley gave us some money to buy what we need to tide us over. How're you doing, Mom?" Alan put his arm around his mother's shoulder, and she leaned her head on him. When did her boy come into this maturity? Tears dripped on his shoulder. "God is in control, Mom." Alan quietly prayed, and Barb felt the knots in her stomach unravel.

"Mrs. Costas?" Barb looked up and saw the resident. "He's resting comfortably. I'll be with him. If he needs you, I'll let you know. In the meantime, why don't you try to rest?"

Barb nodded. A steward approached her with pillows and a blanket, and Alan eased her down, clicking her seat belt around her. "I'll make sure the kids are secured, Mom."

"Everyone is belted," the steward said. "We are lining up for takeoff."

CHAPTER 4

Taylor's Son

AFTER EVERYTHING WAS COMPLETED on Taylor's end and he had nothing more to do, he sat beside his wife, Adelaide, put his head in his hands, and started to weep. "If we lose him, it would be a tragedy—for Barb and those kids, for the kids in South L.A., and for me and us, Adelaide. Nick is God's replacement for John." Taylor and Adelaide had lost their first child to cancer when he was seven.

"Did you know he was born on John's birthday? Nick is exactly the same age," Adelaide said. Taylor nodded miserably. "This is accomplishing nothing. Let's pray!" she said. The couple held hands and prayed.

"We'll meet them out there," Taylor said, decisively. He rose. "Barb will need help with the little ones. I told her to bring their nanny along, but I want to be there, too. I'll call my secretary and cancel everything. We're going to Houston."

"Of course we are, Taylor, and I'm sending out an email prayer chain right now."

A few hours later, the Wilsons were settled in a room adjoining the suite where Taylor had booked Barb and the kids. Nick was taken directly to the hospital, and Barb was with him. The children settled with the nanny, but they wanted Taylor to hold and reassure them. He was patient, but he extricated himself as quickly as possible to go see

Nick for himself. Adelaide had brought toys and books for all the ages.

Robbie wanted to go to the hospital with Taylor. "This all happened so quickly, Mr. Wilson," he said on the taxi ride there. "Mom made Nick go to the doctor. He never complained, but he wasn't himself. He was quiet for one thing, and he didn't take his daily runs. I was worried, too. Mom told him, 'If you love me, you'll do this.' They never let him come home. I don't know what it will do to Mom if she loses him. I don't know what it will do to all of us." Robbie's voice broke, and Taylor put his arm around his shoulders.

"When I couldn't get you guys on the phone, I called Ian. All we can do now is pray," Taylor said. "Nick's a special guy. The sisters are praying, we've sent out a prayer alert, and donations are pouring in for the boys' home. I have some blueprints for it to go over with Nick."

"He wants Tim to do the blueprints, Mr. Wilson, because he can work with him right there in Elkins." Robbie started to cry.

"Look, son, first, you need to call me Pop, or Gramps, or Uncle Taylor and cut this 'Mr.' stuff. We're going to get through this together, okay?" Taylor drew the boy to his chest. Their driver pulled into the hospital entrance.

When they walked into Nick's room, he looked at Taylor. "You shouldn't make this such a big deal, Taylor."

Barb looked at Nick, eyes glistening as she blinked rapidly and shook her head.

"I shouldn't, huh?" Taylor questioned. "That's why they insisted a doctor be on the flight with you. My friend, Jonah, says he's operating at seven in the morning. Guess he's making too much of this, too?" Nick shrugged. "Listen, pal, Adelaide and I realized you were God's gift when we saw your birthdate. You were born on the same day as our oldest. John died of cancer when he was seven, and God gave you to us. Get this through your thick skull: you're like a son to me, Nick, and I want you around for a long, long time. We have some blueprints for the boys' home to review. Tim sent me his, and we added a couple of things. You need to call the convent by the end of the week, so they can call off the prayer vigil. Get over it, bask in the attention, and get well, you hear?"

Nick's eyes swam with tears, and he nodded. "I'll do the best I can. I love you, too, Taylor." Barb got up suddenly and left the room. Robbie followed behind her. "Go to her, Taylor," Nick urged him. "She won't let me see her cry, but it's harder on her than it is on me."

"I'm on it," Taylor replied, rising and walking after them.

Soon, Robbie came back and sat beside Nick. "You'd better not die on me, Nick. You're supposed to take care of Mom, remember? And losing two dads would really suck!"

Nick grinned and reached out his hand. "I'll try to keep that in mind, kid." Robbie leaned over the bed and hugged him. "I love you, Robbie. I couldn't love you more if you were my natural born son."

"I know, Nick. You've been a wonderful father to me and to all of us. And I expect you to continue to be."

Nick winked at him and then watched Barb come back into the room with a nurse trailing behind her. "Here comes the lady with the shot. I'm supposed to get a good night's rest, so they'll be in here every hour with another shot," he teased. Barb gave him a wobbly smile.

"Barb, I'll be here by 6:30 in the morning. Love you, sweetie." Taylor hugged her as Nick mouthed his thanks.

"I'm staying with Mom tonight," Robbie said.

Taylor nodded and left. But the phone beside his bed rang a little after 2:00 a.m. "Grandpa Taylor, Dad flatlined! They got him back, but Mom's a basket case and your doctor friend is on his way in," Robbie reported. "Can you come?"

"I'll be there." Taylor called for a taxi and was dressed and downstairs before it arrived. He gave the driver an extra fifty dollars to get him to the hospital in record time.

When Taylor got up to the waiting area where Barb and Robbie were, Jonah told them his team was taking Nick to surgery immediately. He looked over at Taylor. "If he makes it, Barb saved his life by getting him medical care when she did."

"Go in there and do your best, Jonah. The world needs more folks like him. He's too young to die," Taylor said.

Jonah nodded solemnly. "I'll do my best. You pray! In fact, let's pray together." Holding hands, Jonah, Robbie, and Taylor prayed out loud while Barb clung to them. Jonah strode toward surgery.

"Taylor, I . . . I . . . Thank you for coming. Thank you for everything. Oh, God, what will I do without him? How can those two precious girls survive without their daddy? And Michael, poor baby. How can *I* live without him?" Taylor took her in his arms and let her sob, praying quietly under his breath.

"Dr. Marshall said it will be a long surgery, even if all goes well. It's going to be a long night," Robbie said. "I wish the doctor could've gotten a good night's sleep."

"We're surrounded by prayer. Adelaide was calling the sisters when I left, and the O'Malleys. She'll update the prayer chain online. God, be with Jonah's hands, and the hands of all who labor with him." Seeing the concern in Robbie's eyes as he watched his mother, Taylor assured him she needed to cry.

"Mom, do you want the nurse to get you a sedative? Dr. Marshall left an order for you."

Barb shook her head. "I'm going to the chapel. They gave me a beeper, Taylor." They walked beside her and sat quietly in the row behind her. Taylor listened in amazement as verses and whole chapters of Scripture poured out of her. She looked up, seemed to listen, and smiled quietly. Verses of reassurance and faith followed. She looked at her watch. "It's six. The cafeteria's open. Do you want something to eat?" Barb asked.

"That's a good idea. We need our strength for him, right?" Taylor agreed.

Barb stood, walking steadily, although Robbie hovered at her side.

"God has never failed or forsaken us, Robbie."

Taylor put his arm around the teen's shoulders, and Robbie looked at him gratefully. Taylor knew exactly what the boy was thinking: *Maybe He has never failed us or forsaken us, but he let one father die already.* The boy took a deep breath and looked resolved, biting his lip. Taylor read his mind: *I'm not going to say that. I'm not.* Robbie saw the compassion in Taylor's eyes and knew he understood his thoughts. The older man squeezed the teenager's shoulder.

When Barb slipped into the ladies' room, they stood in the hall to wait for her. "It's no sin to doubt, Robbie," Taylor reassured him. "We all struggle sometimes. Even your Mom was afraid yesterday, and she knows more Scripture than anyone I've ever met."

"Yeah, I know, but I love Nick so much."

"I know you do, and what's even better, he knows that, too."

Robbie's phone beeped with a message. Barb joined them and told him the cafeteria had an exterior door where he could step out and check the message. Taylor and Barb went through the line while Robbie talked on the phone. "That was Angela, Mom," Robbie said when he returned. "The whole church is praying. They have a sign-up sheet, and people are praying around the clock. She said at 3:00 a.m., over a dozen people woke up and started warring in the Spirit. That's cool, huh?"

Barb smiled and laid her hand on his arm. "That's very cool and very encouraging, don't you think?" He nodded and went to get his plate.

"I told you Nick is special to God, Barb," Taylor reaffirmed.

"God knows he's special to me, too," she responded.

They passed on occasional updates to those who were checking in from home, and around nine, Jonah joined them in the waiting room. "He's holding his own. Other than this congenital defect, he's healthy as a horse. Once he recovers, he should live a normal life. You saved him, Barb. He's a fortunate man." She nodded, unable to speak, and took his hand. He squeezed it. "You'll think of questions later, but I'm going home. That guy robbed me of my rest last night. Did you use the sedative, Barb?" She shook her head.

"Can you get her to the hotel to sleep, Taylor?" Jonah went on. "Look, Barb, you have your beeper. He'll be in a drug-induced coma for at least one full day. The best thing you can do for him is to rest. Take that pill. I don't want him worrying about you when he wakes." He shook his head as she started to protest. "I don't want you to even see him now. It's not a pretty sight. I promise we'll call you if anything changes, any little thing, and you can call the nurses' station 24/7. Go rest. You can't do anything right now."

Barb looked up at Taylor, who offered her his arm. "We could all use some shut-eye, and the children will feel more secure when they see you," he said.

Barb stood, and Robbie moved close to her. She swayed, and his arm surrounded her waist. "Will you lie down as soon as we get to the hotel, Mom?"

"As soon as I spend some time with the children. You've talked to Alan?"

"Yes, ma'am, and the others, too."

"I'll get us a taxi," Taylor said as he hurried ahead. Dialing the hotel, he reached his wife. "We're bringing her back, but she's determined to visit with the children. I don't know when she slept last, but she's dead on her feet. . . . They are? That's perfect, if we can get her to lie down before they wake up."

Taylor had the taxi when Barb got to the door, and they did get her to sleep by promising to wake her when the children got up. But the children were content seeing her lying down in her room, so Sally took them downstairs to eat. Robbie and Taylor slept for five hours and woke up hungry. "Should we call the nurses' station?" Taylor asked when he roused.

"Barb has spoken to them twice," Adelaide said. "She's with Sally and the kids at the restaurant. Do you want to join them for dinner?"

Adelaide picked up her pocketbook and headed after her husband, who was hurrying out the door.

"Come on, Robbie. I could eat a whole side of beef."

"Right behind you, Grandpa Taylor."

Adelaide looked quickly at her husband, smiling. He grinned back at her. "A few more grandkids are fine with you, aren't they, Grammy A?"

"The more the merrier, Taylor," she said, squeezing his arm against her body.

* * *

The next day, Alan went with them to the hospital, but they didn't see Nick. Barb slipped in and kissed him gently, but Jonah wanted to keep him under. He was doing fine but was in a lot of pain and restless, so the doctor felt it best to keep him sedated. "If you're sure," Barb said.

"I'm sure. I'd square with you, Barb. He's going to be fine. Give us time."

Barb straightened her shoulders and rejoined the three in the waiting room, explaining that they could return to the hotel and maybe even do something fun with the children to give Sally and Adelaide a break.

"Adelaide's in grandmother heaven. Don't fret about her," Taylor assured her. "Who is Robbie talking to?"

"He's giving his girlfriend an update. She passes it on to all those praying in Elkins. I can feel the prayers. Once, Tim Raines told me he couldn't pray after Missy's accident, and others' prayers carried him. I understand that now."

When they got to the hotel, Taylor called Adelaide And reported to Barb that, "They're in the restaurant, and we're to meet them there."

"Sounds good. I could eat," Barb said.

When their mother walked into the restaurant, the girls left their chairs and ran to her. Michael banged his spoon on the table. "Mommy," they chorused. Barb smiled and gathered them to her.

"Is Papa awake yet?" Rosa asked. Barb tried to explain to them as they hung on every word.

"Will Daddy dance with me again?" Ella asked.

Taylor touched her fair curls. "Dr. Marshall says he'll be good as new, but you must be patient for a while."

"I miss my Papa," Rosa sighed.

Barb pushed her food around the plate. They waited for Taylor and Robbie to finish, and everyone went upstairs together. Barb called the nurses' station every two hours. Even though they had repeatedly promised her they'd call with any minor change, they were unfailingly kind with her.

At about 6:30 a.m., two days post-surgery, the beeper went off. Barb grabbed it, pushing buttons frantically. Robbie, who was sleeping in the same room, extricated it from her hand and retrieved a number, which he punched into his cell phone. She seized it.

"Barb, this is Jonah. We're going to bring him up, and I'd like you to be here. Can you make it by 7:30?"

"I'm on my way."

The adults in the suite slept lightly, and a tap on the door announced Adelaide's arrival. "Is everything okay?" she asked Barb.

"Yes. They're going to wake him, and I need to go."

"Taylor's getting dressed. He'll have a car waiting."

Robbie emerged from the bathroom fully dressed.

"I'll be ready in a minute," Barb said. She had laid out clothes for immediate departure. She dressed quickly and looked put-together after brushing her hair. They arrived at the hospital at 7:15.

CHAPTER 5

Sleeping Beauty

JONAH WAS MAKING ROUNDS on the floor, and he walked toward them with a big smile. "Are you ready for Sleeping Beauty to awake? I'll bring Barb in. This is Intensive Care, so only five minutes every two hours, but Barb, you can stay. We'll turn off the drip, and he should begin to come around in fifteen minutes or so."

Barb nodded, clutched her pocketbook, and followed him in, casting a frantic glance at Robbie and Taylor, who mimed praying hands. While Jonah watched, his stethoscope on Nick's chest, a nurse pulled a medicine vial off the IV flow and studied the doctor's face. He smiled and nodded. The nurse pulled a chair up beside the bed and settled Barb where she could take Nick's hand.

"He's doing fine. I'll be back every few minutes." Jonah rose and patted Barb's shoulder. She kept her eyes focused on Nick, but her lips moved in quiet prayer. He began to stir and opened his eyes. His glance rested on her, and he smiled.

"Hey, babe. I told you, you made too much of a big deal out of this. I love you."

"It's good to see your eyes, Nick. I love you, too."

"You can't stand a couple of hours without my eyes on you?"

"A couple of days, Nick. It's been over two days."

"For real?" She nodded. "Come here, babe." Barb leaned down and kissed him. He lifted his hand with the IV needle in it and stroked her cheek. "Do you know what I want?" He caressed her with his eyes, and she smiled.

"Anything, Nick. I'll get you anything you want."

"I want to make love to you."

"Nick!"

"I do. You're beautiful. I want to kiss down your long, elegant neck, and kiss your beautiful breasts, and bury myself in your softness."

"Nick!" she protested again. "Don't you remember after Michael? You wouldn't touch me for six weeks. This surgery is far worse than a C-section, for heaven's sake!"

"Do you know how hard that was, Barb? I can't wait." The door opened, and Jonah peeked in. "Come in, doc. I need to ask you something."

"Nick," Barb interrupted.

"What do you need to know? I'll give you the best answer I can."

"No, Nick, please . . ." Barb said quickly. "Would you just shut up for once in your life?" Seeing he had no intentions of keeping quiet, she buried her face in her hands.

"When can I make love to my beautiful wife? Isn't she beautiful?"

Jonah started to laugh and couldn't stop himself.

Raising her flaming face, Barb fumed. "If you weren't so sick, I'd smack you."

"Baby, I can't help it. I love you," Nick insisted.

Jonah gathered himself together, his eyes merry. "You're the first patient to ask me that at this stage of the game. Can we get you out of ICU first, Nick?"

"You mean, we can't have conjugal visits on the floor? Get me out of here!"

Jonah sat. He laughed so hard he had to wipe his eyes.

"What meds do you have him on?" Barb asked.

"Nothing that's ever acted like an aphrodisiac before, I assure you."

"Nick never needs an aphrodisiac. He needs something to keep his mouth shut."

Still chuckling, Jonah said, "We'll cut back on his happy juice and get him something to eat. That should help." Patting him on the shoulder, Jonah added: "Hold off on that thought, stud. You'll be good as new, but you need to give it some time." Shaking his head, he went out the door, laughing.

"Nick Jo Costas, I'll never forgive you for this!"

Nick's eyes filled. "God knows I love you, Barb. Forgive me. Can you just forgive me?"

She shook her head and smiled. "Waiting will be hard for me, too, but remember what you told me?" Barb reminded him. "We'll make up for lost time when I'm sure it won't hurt you."

"It won't hurt me. What are a few popped stitches?"

An aide came in, bearing a tray. "Dr. Marshall says you need to eat right away. Do you want to help him, Mrs. Costas?"

"I will," Barb assured her. She scooted her chair closer as the aide arranged the bed. Nick winced when they moved him and put more pillows behind his head. Barb carefully spooned in Jell-O and yogurt.

"That's enough. I want to sleep. Hold me." Barb leaned over and held him until he dropped off, then she lowered the bed and went into the hall, searching for her son.

"Jonah was out here laughing his head off. Guess Nick's his old self," Taylor said when they saw her.

"I hope he didn't tell you what he said."

"Every word. He thought it was priceless."

Barb blushed furiously. "I don't know what to do with him!"

"Just love him. He's one of a kind, and God gave him to us." Then Taylor decided it was a good time to change the subject. "Dan Murphy's in Austin, Barb. He wants to come by later in the week." Dan, a Christian psychologist, had met Nick at the conference and wanted him to collaborate on an upcoming book.

"Jonah said Nick should be in a regular room in a few days," Barb informed him. "He can have visitors then. You guys can see him today. Hopefully, he'll be sobered up by then." She shook her head, and Taylor put his arm around her shoulders.

"Jonah said he's never seen a man more in love with his wife, and it'll give Nick a great incentive to work hard to recover."

"Nick will recover, Grandpa Taylor," Robbie asserted. "He's strong as an ox, and he loves all of us, not just Mom. He'll be dancing with Cinderella and Rosa before you know it." Barb smiled her agreement.

A nurse came out to the waiting area. "Mrs. Costas? He's asking for you." Barb moved as fast as she could.

"Where did you go, Barb?" Nicked asked her.

"I went to reassure Robbie and Taylor about you. They'll tell the others. Last night the girls wanted to know when they could see Papa, plus folks from Elkins are praying around the clock, and so are the sisters. You're loved by many, Nick."

"Please stay. Can you stay?" he pleaded.

"I'll be right here. You sleep. I only stepped out to the waiting room." She took his hand and brought it to her lips. He smiled and closed his eyes. But about an hour later, he groaned and opened them.

"I'm right here," Barb said.

"God, help me. Somebody parked a semi on my chest."

Barb reached for the call bell, but a nurse walked in. "Mr. Costas, you're ready for some pain relief." She stepped up to his IV line and plunged a needle into it.

"How do you know?" Barb inquired.

"He's on a lot of monitors. We know every move he makes." She patted his shoulder. "You should feel better soon, but Dr. Marshall made us cut back. You were a little out of your head this morning."

"I was very much in my head, thank you, ma'am! I know what I want." Merriment danced in the nurse's eyes, and Barb realized Nick's earlier comments had made it around the floor. She blushed furiously as the nurse grinned at her and winked.

"Must be nice to be loved, Mrs. Costas."

Barb smiled back at her. "Yes, it is. Nick loves me more than I deserve."

"No, *mi amor*, I can never love you enough." Nick continued in Spanish, but the nurse interrupted him.

"Mr. Costas, this is Houston. Almost everyone can understand you—what you would like to do with your wife." She chuckled. "Maybe I shouldn't tell him. It might be entertaining to hear more." Barb noticed her name tag, Lisa Martinez. She lowered her eyes, and Nick grinned.

Nick dozed most of the day, but each time his eyes opened, he sought Barb before he relaxed. Taylor and Adelaide came in for five minutes and brought Barb some reading material. When Alan and Robbie tiptoed in, Nick opened his eyes. "Hey, guys, you won't take advantage of the old man while he's down now, will you?"

Alan's eyes flooded. "Jeez, Daddy Nick, you scared us. Don't ever do that again!"

Nick winked at him. "I didn't exactly plan this, kid. Come here." Nick put his unfettered arm around the boy and hugged him. "I love you. You know that?"

"Yeah, I love you, too, Dad. We're helping Mom. The girls cry for you, and Mikey goes around saying, 'Papa? Papa?' But we hold him and tell him you'll be home soon. Missy called last night and sang him to sleep," Alan said.

Robbie touched his brother's shoulder. "We need to go. See ya, Nick. You behave now. Mom nearly blushed to death this morning." He grinned at Nick and gave him a wave. Nick winked.

* * *

Later, during the afternoon, Barb heard a commotion at the door. "You are not keeping me out of there, young lady. I flew all the way from

Los Angeles to see that boy. He's the closest thing to a son I have."

Nick looked at Barb. "That would be Mother Joanna. Can we get her in?" Barb stepped out and spoke to the aide, and the nurse was called. At Barb's request, the nun was able to see Nick.

"All the sisters wanted me to come personally and bring back a report. You must be Barbara," the nun turned to Barb. "He certainly loves you!" Mother Joanna said. "How is Rosa?"

"She's fine. She talks about you constantly. She heard Nick talking about going to L.A. to discuss the Home, and she insisted she was going to see you."

"I told Nickie to bring all of you. I want to meet your boys."

"Do me a favor, Madre?" Nick asked.

"Whatever I can," she said.

"They're all here at a hotel nearby. Could you go see Rosita?" Nick asked. "She's scared. This all happened suddenly, and the children are confused. It would mean a lot to her."

Mother Joanna looked at Barb, who agreed. "Taylor Wilson is here, with his wife," Barb informed her. "He'll take you."

"I'm staying at a sister house, but my flight back isn't until tomorrow evening. I would love to see the children. Now, Nick, I will bless you. But first, tell me how you are? Will this change your life?"

"Doc says not, Madre. It was some congenital abnormality, and they repaired it. He says I'll be good as new. Did you hear they gave me a pig valve? I'm stubborn as an ox, and now I have a pig heart."

Her face exploded into a smile. "This is the best news. The sisters will be very happy."

"Taylor has blueprints he wants to go over with Nick. He'll show them to you at the hotel, Mother Joanna. I hate to rush you, but no one's allowed in here more than five minutes. But if you could stay another day, Nick might be in a regular room."

"Maybe I can change those reservations." Mother Joanna turned to Nick, made the sign of the cross over him, and prayed.

Barb felt a sweet peace flow over her. Strength surged into her body. She opened her eyes and hugged the nun. "Thank you. We've felt your prayers, leaned on them, and drawn strength from them. I couldn't have made it without them."

"I know, my child." The nun kissed her cheek and leaned down to kiss Nick. "You be good, Nick. Do what they tell you. We need you. The children of South L.A. need you. I need you, son. Your mama is proud."

"She told me to come back and finish the Home," he said.

Barb's eyes widened. "Nick flatlined Sunday night. They rushed him to surgery in the middle of the night."

"Around midnight our time, in L.A., was it?"

"Yes. Just after 2:00 a.m. here."

The nun nodded. "We all awakened at the same time. We prayed earnestly for about an hour and established a 24-hour vigil. You see, Nick, God isn't through with you."

Nick nodded, his eyes swimming. When the nun swept out of the door, he reached for Barb's hand. "She is a force to be reckoned with. What a lady!" Barb said.

Nick grinned. "I love her, and I hardly know her. But some people come into our lives that way, for eternity. Rosa will be happy to see her."

When Taylor returned, he told them that Mother Joanna was with the children, and Rosa asked the nun if she would be her *abuela* on earth since hers had moved to heaven. The nun took her into her lap and promised she would try hard, but she didn't know how. Ella told her that was okay because their family taught her daddy to be a father, and they could teach her how to be a grandmother.

"You and our family keep on giving, *amada*," Nick said to Barb.

"Jonah said maybe you could move tomorrow, and Mother Joanna changed her reservations, so we can go over those blueprints," Taylor suggested. "Mind your manners, son, so you can get to work."

When Nick got into a regular room, they brought the girls in for a short visit, but he reserved his strength to discuss the Sister Marie Teresa Home for Boys. Barb struggled when she sent the children back to the hotel without her, but Adelaide gently took them from her embrace and led them away to the awaiting nanny. Alan helped, taking the girls by the hand while Sally carried Michael.

As Nick unrolled the blueprints, Taylor informed him he'd diverted everyone who asked about sending flowers into sending donations for the Home instead. When Nick heard the amount that had been raised, he was astounded. "Maybe I should die, and we could raise it in no time, at that rate."

Barb looked horrified. "That's not a joke, Nick. Please." She began to cry.

Adelaide took her by the arm and led her out. They walked to the chapel, and Barb sobbed in her arms. "We're on the downhill slide, Barb. The worst is over." Adelaide held her close.

Barb nodded. "I'm tired. My poor babies—I've abandoned them."

"Mike Green has sent a ton of toys. It's like Disney World. Taylor hired some help for Sally. They go to the pool twice a day, and they're spoiled rotten. You'll have your hands full when we get out of here."

Barb gathered herself together, and they went back upstairs. Nick searched her face as she came through the door. "I'm sorry, babe. That was a rotten joke. Are you okay?" Nick held out his arms, and she moved into them. He whispered into her hair and rubbed her back. "I'll never leave you. You're stuck with me."

"Promise?" she whispered back. She cradled his face with her hands.

"I promise." He kissed her hungrily but gently while the others made a great pretense of looking at the drawings.

"Are you happy with the plans?" Barb asked when she stood.

"We need a few minor changes," Taylor said, "But the basic concept is solid. Don't you think, Mother? You didn't have much to add.

Do we have too many rooms, enough study space, recreation areas? You're adding a lot of work to your convent. Tell us what you need."

The nun stared at the blueprints. "Ever since we met Nick, when he came to see his mama and we heard his story, the sisters and I have prayed about ministering to the poor children of our area. We thought perhaps a tutoring program, maybe a feeding program. We dreamed of housing the homeless, but we never dreamed this grand." She lifted her eyes to Nick. "Thank you, my son."

"What was meant for evil, God has used for good, to save much people alive," Barb quoted. "God has a way of working His redemptive plans through our pain."

"Amen, Barbara, well said!" Mother Joanna agreed. "Could I get a copy of these blueprints to take back? We must present them to the bishop and get some fundraising going in our Diocese."

Taylor stood, rolled them up, and put them in a tube. "Let us make these final changes and we'll FedEx two copies to you, one for the Mother House and one for the Bishop. Would that work?"

"Yes, excellent. Now, I must leave for the airport. Nick, behave."

"I understand I have two *abuelas* watching over me, right?" he replied.

She beamed. "Imagine, a nun with grandchildren! Ah, Nick, you have done us all proud. To God be the glory. And you, Barbara, thank you and your family for watching over our boy. Taylor, you brought him in time to send Sister Marie Teresa to her grave in peace. Thank you. Now," she said abruptly, clearing her throat, "I will say a blessing and be gone." Afterward, she leaned down, kissed Nick briefly, blinked her eyes rapidly, and nodded to Barb, who reached out and embraced her fiercely.

"Thank you for coming. It meant the world to him, and to me."

"Humph, he'd better not think he can get away without bringing your precious family to L.A."

Barb smiled. "Rosa won't let us forget, Madre."

"You are a good girl, Barbara. Nickie is blessed to have you." She patted Barb, adding, "I will tell the sisters all of you are coming."

CHAPTER 6

Betsy and Jonah

BETSY HEARD THE HUGE solid oak door open in the grand foyer of her and Jonah's home. Who could be coming into our house at this hour? The alarm didn't sound, the kids are in school, and Jonah couldn't be home now. She hurriedly settled the trim skirt of her new designer suit and hastened down the wide staircase. Jonah was there, staring up at her as she stood on the landing. The light flooding in through the floor-to-ceiling windows behind her surrounded her.

Jonah looked up at his wife, haloed like a statue in a lighted alcove of a cathedral. Always lovely, she took his breath away. Betsy, a former Miss Virginia, was gorgeous. Her blonde hair rolled in an elegant coif at the base of her beautiful neck. Jonah couldn't believe she had borne two children. She was as slender as the day he met her, and the round-ness of her curves made her even more desirable. His heart caught in his throat as he stared up at her.

"Jonah? What are you doing here now? Are you ill?" She moved quickly toward him, gently placing her hand on his forehead in the way of all mothers.

"Are you going somewhere? You look lovely in your pink suit. Is that new?"

"Jonah, answer my question: are you sick? You don't have a fever." She looked up into his eyes, concern flooding her face.

"I'm not sick. I wanted to come home, to be with you. Are you going out?"

"Luncheon at the club—a planning meeting for the charity ball."

"Do you have to go? I took off from the hospital. I realize I didn't give you any notice. It was kind of a spur of the moment thing. I asked Charlie to conduct presentations today." He took her into his arms. "I suddenly realized we haven't had much one-on-one time in God knows how long. I've missed you, Betsy."

Tears sprung to Betsy's eyes, and her arms tightened around his waist. Jonah lifted her chin with his long, slender fingers, and caressed her cheek. Her eyes closed as she savored his touch. Her lips were slightly parted as she tried to catch her breath. Gently, he leaned and kissed her in a way they had not kissed in longer than she cared to remember. He could feel her smile under his lips. "What's funny? Have I forgotten how?"

"Both of us are doing quite well. I guess it's like riding a bicycle. Oh, Jonah, I've missed you, too."

"Will you blow off this lunch and spend the afternoon with your long-lost husband?"

"What do you want to do? Are you hungry? Do you want to go to lunch, eat here?"

Jonah lifted her bodily and started slowly up the stairs. "I'm hungry, but not for food."

Betsy laid her head on his chest, feeling warmth flood her belly and joy coursing through her entire body. She kicked off her shoes on the landing, and they landed soundlessly on the plush carpet. Jonah strode toward their bedroom, setting her on their king size bed and ripping off his tie.

"Let me," Betsy said, as she unbuttoned his shirt slowly. Jonah took a deep breath, steeling himself to slow down as they undressed one another. Later, resting her head on her husband's shoulder, Betsy asked: "What happened?"

Jonah laughed. "Do I have to explain it to you, Mrs. Marshall? It's been too long. God knows I love you, but I wonder if you know it."

Betsy's fingers traced his long, lean torso, and she was thoughtful. "I do, but sometimes I have to remind myself—take it by faith, I guess. I know you belong to more people than just me."

"Oh, Betsy, I'm sorry. You deserve more than I give you. You're a wonderful wife, a perfect mother, and I couldn't do what I do without you in my corner." Holding her back, he saw tears glistening on her lashes. He leaned and softly kissed them away. She sighed. "You never complain. When I was driving like a NASCAR driver to get home to you, I realized how many of the other doctors are divorced, and you'd be justified. I miss the kids' important functions. I wasn't with you when Rachel had her tonsils out or Jacob had his broken arm repaired. I've missed dinners, dates—"

Betsy interrupted him. "Jonah, I was a scrub nurse when I met you at Johns Hopkins. You were already a legend as a hotshot resident. You shared your calling with me, and I watched Dr. Carson. I knew it wasn't going to be an easy life, and I prayed long and hard. I asked God for grace to enable you to fulfill your calling. I try to explain it to the kids. Sometimes they understand, and sometimes it's harder for them, but we're all very proud of you." This time the tears sprung to Jonah's dark eyes. Feeling his silence, she rose up, her honey-colored long hair spilling around her shoulders. She leaned over and gently kissed him, and he smiled as her curls tickled his chest.

When Jonah collected himself, he settled Betsy close to his side. "I mean it, Betsy. I could never do it without you. I'm confident you manage things well—the kids thrive in your care, and our affairs run smoothly. I don't even think about things that worry most husbands. If I have any success, if anyone lives today because of these feeble hands, it's thanks to you—and God, of course."

"You wouldn't know how to pay the first bill if anything happened to me." She propped up and smiled at him. "Tell me, what started all this deep thought?"

"Remember the guy I took to surgery in the middle of the night? Taylor Wilson's friend, the guy from West Virginia who works for the O'Malley Family? Nick loves his wife like crazy. He woke up from his coma, and the first question out of his mouth was: 'When can I make love to my beautiful wife, doc?' I had to laugh. I'd never heard that question at that stage of recovery. He said, 'But she's beautiful, doc. Isn't she beautiful?' Funny thing is, she's not beautiful. She's attractive and sweet, but not a real beauty. When I looked over at her, she blushed furiously and fussed at him. For an instant, I saw her with his eyes, his love washing over her, and she *was* beautiful.

"They're an amazing couple. She never left his side except when I made her go to the hotel and sleep when we put him in the coma. You'd be there for me like that, Betsy, but that kind of love is rare. Love made her beautiful. I haven't treasured you as I should or made you glow like that. But you're a natural beauty. You don't look beautiful in my eyes; you *are* beautiful. I wonder how many men covet my wife. Men who'd be easier to love, better dads, handier around the house, more attentive lovers."

Betsy, rumpled and glowing from their love-making, never looked lovelier. "Jonah, hush. I've never loved or wanted anyone but you. You're fishing for compliments."

"I regret the life I've given you, the way I've taken you for granted and never told you how much I need and appreciate you."

"I confess, it's nice to hear. Thanks for taking the afternoon off." Betsy sat up and stretched like a cat, and she almost purred.

"I'm starving! I have worked up quite an appetite with all this exercise. Let's find something to eat," Jonah said.

She headed for the bathroom as he slipped on a pair of running pants. "Jonah?" she called out. "Would you get my robe? It's in the blue bedroom."

"Sure," he responded and walked across the hall. He saw the robe on the unmade bed and noticed her reading glasses on the nightstand and her Bible and a current novel beside it. He returned to their room and followed her into the bathroom.

"You've been sleeping in there, Betsy? Why haven't you been sleeping in our bed?"

Standing naked before him, she looked so vulnerable that his heart wrenched. "I don't know. I'm not as lonely in there. I don't miss you as much in that bed. We haven't slept together in there. When you aren't here, I get lonely. I try to give it up to God as my sacrifice, but I miss you . . ." Her voice trailed off, and her eyelashes fluttered down.

"Oh, Betsy," Jonah whispered. "Oh, honey, I wish you knew how I miss you, how often my thoughts turn to you and the kids. God knows I'm sorry." He gathered her naked body into his arms and found himself wanting her again. Feeling him against her, she put her hands on his chest and backed him across the bedroom. Both laughing like kids, they tore at his pants and tumbled together on the bed, tangling arms and legs, hands everywhere on each other's bodies.

Later, when Betsy looked up, she was startled again to see Jonah home, looking down at her in the middle of the day. She smiled, with a contented, satisfied glow on her face. "Did I fall asleep?"

He grinned. "You might say that. It's been a long time since we did that."

"I've never denied you."

"No, you never have, good wife that you are. But we haven't taken the time to be so . . . thorough in a while. It was good, Betsy."

She blushed. "You're telling me, stud!"

He laughed. "That's what I told Nick: 'Hold that thought, stud. Give us time.' But he kept on about how beautiful Barb is. Poor woman was humiliated, but I thought of the *Song of Solomon* and God's plan for man and woman. You need to meet those two, Betsy, they're amazing people." Jonah stood. "I'm really hungry now, woman. Let's go find something to eat." Giggling, they gathered their clothes and headed down to the kitchen. Betsy, having abandoned her pink suit, had slipped on blue jeans.

Maria, busy with dinner preparations in the kitchen, looked up, surprised to see Dr. Marshall home in the middle of the day. Quickly giving them the once-over, she smiled knowingly. "Good afternoon, doctor. Have you had lunch? Mrs. Marshall, you no go to the Club?"

"I, uh, Jonah came home, and I, uh, didn't go. Do we have any leftovers? We're both hungry."

Maria's round brown face creased into another smile. "*Empanadas es bueno, si*?"

"Perfect, Maria." Jonah leaned down to place a kiss on her cheek. This kind woman watched his children, kept his home, and prepared his food. She had lived in the house since shortly after Rachel was born, and he couldn't imagine life without her. She scurried about, opening the refrigerator, shooing them into the breakfast nook, and pouring them cups of rich, dark coffee laden with cream and sugar before she popped the stuffed pastries into the microwave.

"*Café con leche*," Jonah observed, and he inhaled the scent before taking a sip from the steaming cup. "*Gracias, Maria. Delicioso*! How do you happen to have *empanadas*? They take some time to prepare."

"Ah, Jacob, he love my *empanadas*. I keep in freezer. He warm anytime. He eats them all the time. He's healthy boy!"

"That's why he runs all the time and doesn't get skinny as a rail. Yes, Maria, you feed us all well."

"I bake them, Dr. Marshall, not fried." She placed the tasty, meat-rich baked sandwiches in front of them and slipped out.

"Remind me to give you a raise, Maria. These are wonderful!" Jonah called after her.

She stuck her smiling brown face back through the door. "No, you too good to Maria. When my Mario died, you get me legal, give me work and a home. No, I am blessed. And anything taste wonderful to you now, señor doctor. You eat mud now and be happy!" Her eyes merry, she disappeared into the kitchen.

Shaking his head, Jonah glanced at Betsy, who was flushed. "She's right, you know. If I look anything like you do, we're pretty obvious. But these are good."

"You look quite . . . uh, satisfied."

"You were a bit noisy upstairs. I hope she didn't hear us." Betsy flushed again but smiled at him with a dazzle he felt to his toes. "You'd better not look at me like that!" he warned. "What's on your agenda for the rest of the day?"

She glanced at her watch. "Pick up Jacob and take him to soccer practice. Rachel's going home with Suzanne to study for an algebra test."

"What do you do while he practices?"

"Sometimes I run to the store for pick-ups. But mostly I sit in the van and read, or I talk to the other parents."

"I could call off the rest of the day, and we could neck in the back."

"Jonah Marshall! What's gotten into you?"

"Nick Costas. His love for his wife made me realize what I've missed. I must spend more time with you and the children. Let's go to Galveston for the weekend."

"I couldn't have you make me that noisy on the same floor of a hotel with the kids. Besides, Jacob has a game. Nick Costas? He's the one who had heart surgery?"

"You've heard of him?"

"I bought his book yesterday. It's right there." She pointed.

Jonah rose to cross the room and picked up the book on the gleaming, polished oak sideboard. He flipped the pages. "This sounds like him. I want to read this." He picked up their dishes and headed into the kitchen to put them in the sink.

"*Gracias*, doctor," Maria said, smiling her rosy smile.

"*De nada, Maria.* Thank you." He patted her shoulder and reached for Betsy's hand. "Let me call in." He fished in his pocket for his cell phone and pushed speed dial 1. "Charlie, how's it going? . . . His head's so big it won't fit through the door, and he's headed for a big crash. I hope the hospital is spared the fallout and some poor patient doesn't die. If he gives you any trouble, dial me and hand him the phone. I'm taking the rest of the day off. Check in on 412 for me, will you? . . . Yeah, it's been good." He looked at Betsy and winked. She slipped her arm around him. "See you in the morning—but you're in charge, Charlie. Don't let him buffalo you. . . . Good man, thanks."

"Do you need to go back, Jonah?" Betsy stepped away, as if to release him.

"If I go back there, I'll be sucked in. I choose to spend this day with you. Now, does the back seat of the van make into a bed?"

Betsy laughed and threw her arms around him. "What am I going to do with you?"

"You already have done something." Looking down into her face, he took a deep breath. "God knows you are beautiful. I can't believe you fell in love with an Ichabod Crane like me."

"You're not so bad-looking. I had to fight the entire cadre of the nursing staff—not to mention that vamp from the social work department."

"We've been married seventeen years, and you still look like you're in your twenties. Look at all this gray." Jonah ran his fingers through his hair.

"You look very distinguished, Doctor Marshall. Are you really going to the field with me, or do you want to study?"

"I want to study *you*. I'm showing all those fathers that you have a real, live husband, who loves you like crazy. My car or the van?"

"I give several boys rides. We need to take the van. Do you want to drive?" She handed him the keys, but he shook his head.

"I'm not sure I could find the field."

CHAPTER 7

Jonah's Children

WHEN JACOB CLIMBED into the van with four friends, Jonah caught the incredulous look on his face. "Dad, are you sick?" Jonah's heart squeezed. "No, son, I chose to spend this afternoon with your mother and you. Who are all these fine boys?"

Jacob introduced his friends. Their usual bubbly chatter was subdued in the presence of the great heart surgeon, but when they arrived at the field, Jonah piled out of the van with them and kicked the soccer ball around until practice began.

"He's cool, Jake," he heard one of the boys say as they ran over to the beckoning coach.

"You haven't lost your magic," Betsy said as she leaned against the maroon van.

"We haven't lost our magic either, Betts." His knuckles grazed her cheek, and her knees felt weak.

"No, we haven't, have we?" She stepped into his arms. Keeping one arm securely around her, Jonah steered her to the bleachers on the side of the field, where several moms and a few dads eyed them curiously. Betsy introduced him around.

"Wasn't Millie supposed to bring the drinks today?" she asked.

"Toby's sick, so she didn't come," one of the mothers replied.

"Let's see what I have in the back," Betsy offered. She waved

Jonah over to the van. "I probably have enough snacks, but we need to go get some drinks." The world-famous Dr. Jonah Marshall climbed into a soccer-mom van to fetch drinks for his boy's team, feeling more content and at peace than he had in a long time.

After practice, they dropped the other boys off and swung by to pick up Rachel. "Dad! What are you doing home? Are you okay?" she asked, as she climbed into the van.

"He chose to spend the afternoon with Mom and us, Rach. Isn't that cool?" Jacob informed her.

"Way cool, Dad. Everything all right? You didn't get fired or anything?"

Jonah shook his head. "I realized how much I miss you guys, so I took the day off."

"I didn't think you could do that," Rachel said.

"He can't do it often, guys, so let's enjoy the rest of our day, all right?" Betsy replied as she pulled onto the road.

Studying her profile, Jonah sighed. "I'm going to take more time off. Your Mom's incredible, but I need to be around more. You two will be grown and gone before we know it."

"Dad, I'm only a freshman!" Rachel protested.

"Yeah, and you were in kindergarten last year. When did you get so beautiful, by the way? You look like your mother. Tell me about this algebra. Are you ready for your test? Your old dad wasn't too bad in math and science."

"I've memorized the problems, but I don't understand it. You and Jacob make me crazy."

"Math's a cinch, Rach. It's all logical," Jacob said.

Jonah laughed. "She's better in history and English, Jake. Women can always out-talk us, buddy. Better keep on her good side. You might need her someday."

"My favorite subject is Spanish. Maria helps me all the time. I love languages! I'm taking French Two now, and next year I'm going to take Japanese," Rachel said.

Jonah looked at Betsy. "She's kidding, right?"

Betsy glanced over at him and smiled. "No, she's in honors Spanish and has a 12th-grade equivalency. She needs to go to the college campus next fall."

"I mean about the Japanese?"

"They're offering it via satellite. We'll see how it works next year." He shook his head. "Your son has never made less than a 115 percent average in math," Betsy added.

"How can he get more than 100 percent?"

"He answers all the extra point questions, Dad. I tell you, I hate him!" Rachel complained. "Can we go out to eat?"

"Maria has spent the day preparing enchiladas. She'd be crushed," Betsy said. Neither child wanted to forgo Maria's enchiladas, and so they turned toward home.

After dinner, Jonah patiently explained the concepts behind the math problems for his daughter. Every time she grasped something, her eyes widened, and Jonah felt rewarded. He played a round of video games with Jacob, and Betsy and Rachel laughed as his son crushed him. Leaning his head back on the couch, Jonah joined the laughter at his own expense and hugged Jacob. "I can't remember when I've had as much fun! What time is the game Saturday?"

"It's a tournament; our first game is at nine. The next one depends on whether we win or lose. They're a good team."

"It's an all-day affair?"

"It's an all weekend affair, Jonah," Betsy told him. Seeing the look of disappointment cross his face, she added: "It ends the season. No more soccer till fall. But I want to see him play." Turning to the kids, she said, "Dad wanted to take us somewhere for the weekend. Maybe we can do that next weekend."

"I have plans to go shop with Suzanne and her mom next weekend, Mom," Rachel informed her.

Maria carried out a tray of chocolate-dipped pastries and said: "You go, Señora Marshall. I stay with kids. Okay? You two go."

Jonah studied his children. Both shrugged. "Jacob, you don't want to go to the beach? Maybe deep sea fishing?" Jonah asked.

"Some other time, Dad. The guys want to get together after the season."

Maria patted Jonah's arm. "You go. Have fun. We are fine, no?"

"Yes, Maria, *si*. We'll be fine," Rachel said.

"I want to plan a family trip, though—and sooner rather than later," Jonah insisted.

"Theese time is about you and the señora, Señor Doctor." Maria nodded knowingly.

"Thank you, Maria. But we'll go to the tournament. When do you go to San Antonio for your niece's First Communion?" Betsy asked.

"*Junio, señora—Junio quinze*." She turned to Jacob and slapped his hand. "No more!"

Jacob grinned, reaching for one more. "*Deliscioso, Maria. Una mas, por favor*." His eyes begged her, and she relented.

"*Si, solamente una, chico!*"

Jonah ran his hand through his son's hair. "Upstairs, kids, time for bed anyway. *Gracias*, Maria."

"Yeah, thanks, Maria. It was fabulous!" Jacob added.

Betsy led the way up the stairs, with Jonah enjoying the view as he followed directly behind her. "I'll be in your rooms to pray in a minute," Jonah told them. "After your showers."

"Dad, could we have a read in y'all's room? Sit around the bed and read and pray together? We haven't done that in forever."

Jonah's eyes misted as he turned to reply to his daughter. "Sure, I'd like that. See you in a few."

In short order, two freshly-scrubbed youngsters piled on his bed, each with a Bible. They all turned to the same chapter and verse. "I like the daily Bibles you gave us, Daddy. When you can't be home, I know what you're reading, and I pretend I'm reading it with you," Rachel told him.

"Me, too, Dad. Sometimes we read with Mom," Jacob said. "She always prays with us, though, and asks us about the reading to check on us."

Betsy grinned. "I don't catch you often." She looked at Jonah expectantly, and he began to read in the firm, quiet voice of authority she loved. As he finished, he looked up and asked a few questions. After the discussion satisfied him they'd understood, he took their hands beside him, and they prayed. His daughter's legs were crossed in front of her, his son hung off the bed, his wife was propped up against the headboard, and he led his family in prayer.

"Thanks, Dad. It's been a great day!" Rachel leaned forward and kissed her father, knocking him over. Jacob leaped into the fray, and they tussled on the bed.

"Enough, children," Betsy fussed fondly. "Go to your rooms."

Each youngster kissed her, with a hug. "'Night, Mom," they called back, leaving the room.

Jonah scooted against the headboard and took Betsy's hand. "You've done a marvelous job with them, Betsy. They're good kids."

"Oh, Jonah, you haven't been altogether an absent father. You have had a lot of influence on them. They're very proud of you."

He shook his head. "You're the heart of this family, Betts, and my anchor. No matter what I face, knowing I have you to come home to makes it survivable. I love you, sweetheart." His thumb rubbed across her knuckles as he looked tenderly at her.

"I love you, too. Always have, always will."

"God, how can I thank You enough for a good woman? She's your best gift to me, and I'm eternally grateful." He pulled her into his arms. "What a perfect day! Do we have enough for me to retire?"

"We have enough to raise and educate the children if I have to do it alone, but you have a calling and a gift. You can't forsake it, and after a time you'd be lost if you tried. I know you. I love you. This is the life we chose together."

"Do you regret leaving your career? You're an excellent nurse."

"Do I regret having you and these beautiful children? Not once have I looked back." She rested her head on his shoulder. Smoothing her hand across the spread, she realized that at some point in the day Maria had come up and changed the sheets. She giggled.

"What?"

"We left this bed a mess!"

He looked down, surprised. "Maria must've made it up while we were at the field. Do you think she's happy?"

"She loves these children, and she's the only grandparent they have." Betsy patted his hand. "It works. She loved her husband. She's happy as she can be without Mario."

"Mrs. Marshall, would you care to take a shower with your husband?" He rose and extended his hand to her. She smiled and followed him.

* * *

The next day, when Jonah dismissed Nick from the hospital, he told Robbie about the soccer tournament and asked if he and Alan would like to join them at practice that afternoon. He arranged to pick them up at the hotel. After they spent the day at the field, Jacob invited the Westfall boys to spend the night.

"Thanks, Jake, but this is Nick's first night," Robbie responded. "Mom might need a hand with the little ones."

"I'll drive you boys back to the hotel," Jonah said. "I thought the O'Malleys were there. Your mother isn't alone, is she?" Jonah was concerned.

"They are. Grandpa Taylor didn't leave until they got here, and Missy's little girl, Jeri, and Rosa are the same age, so she's staying in their rooms with Ella. Maybe Mom and Nick would rather be alone, but

I'd feel better seeing how it's going. This was fun, though, and I'd like to come with you tomorrow. You're an amazing player, Jake. You've got a terrific kick!" Jacob grinned in response to Robbie's praise.

"We'll pick you up about 8:30 then," Jonah said as he pulled under the hotel canopy.

"Glad you made it, Dr. Marshall," Robbie replied. "Thanks, we'll see you then."

As Jonah and Jacob pulled away, Jacob said, "They're nice. They go to public schools, but they're Christians."

"Public schools in West Virginia are a lot different than public schools in Houston, Jacob."

"Yeah, they see drugs and girls get pregnant, but they have Christian activities in the schools and mostly Christian teachers. I like Lakeland Academy, Dad, but it's expensive, and you work too hard."

"You, Rachel, and your mom are my best investments. I have no expensive vices. What better to spend my money on?"

"Could you be home more?"

Jonah's jaw twitched, and his grip tightened on the wheel. "Not really, son. I don't work for money. I work to save lives and to help people. But, I'll try to spend more time at home with you guys. I'm bad at delegating."

"Mom says you care about people, and you have a hard time letting go because somebody else wouldn't care as much."

"There's some truth to that, but basically I'm a control freak, I guess."

Jacob pondered. He looked at his father quizzically. "Is that something we can pray about?" Jonah laughed until tears ran down his cheeks. "What, Dad? Is that a stupid question?"

"No, son, it's a brilliant question, and the answer is yes. We can definitely pray about it."

"I know it's God's will for you to spend more time with us, but Mom says God called you and gifted you for a special work not many people can do, and we help Him when we free you to do it. And you love us lots."

Turning into the driveway, Jonah stopped and looked at his son. "Your Mother's a remarkable woman. Do you know she was an outstanding nurse at Johns Hopkins when I met her? She's right. I could never do this job without her support, without her management skills, without her watch-care over you kids. She's my strength. Remember that when you choose a wife. It's the most important decision you'll ever make in life, after making the decision to follow Christ."

"I want someone who loves me like she loves you," Jacob said, pulling on the door handle.

"Good plan, Jakie."

Betsy met them at the door. She'd arrived home ahead of them because they'd dropped Barb's boys off at the hotel. "Come on in, guys." She tiptoed up for Jonah's kiss, which lingered a bit. She smiled.

"Do we have a snack?" Jacob asked. "I'm starved!"

"Teenage boys are always starved. It's a life fact," Betsy assured Jonah.

He laughed. "I could eat, too, and I haven't run all over a soccer field all day."

"No, and you haven't stuffed yourself with hot dogs and chili, nachos and cheese, and snacks and Twinkies all day, either. Come on guys, steak's on."

"Red meat? What can I tell my patients?"

"Tell them we eat red meat two or three times a month and what your cholesterol levels are. That should shut them up. Tell them you go to the gym four times a week. Tell them—"

"I get it! Steak is good—with baked potato, even better. I'm a Texan, after all."

After the blessing, Betsy served each plate and said, "Missy O'Malley called and invited us to eat with them tomorrow, after the tournament."

"Mom, you mean *the* Missy O'Malley—"Recovered and Free," "When I Am in Your Arms"—*that* Missy O'Malley? Why would she call us?" Rachel was squealing. Jacob rolled his eyes.

"I operated on their producer last week. They came down to be with him. How would this work? I don't want Nick going to the restaurant."

"They'll order room service," Betsy proposed.

"How can they fit so many people in a hotel room?" Jacob asked.

"They have two suites, each with two bedrooms and a large shared living room," Betsy explained.

"Oh, Daddy, can we go? Can we? How cool!"

Jonah smiled at his excited daughter while simultaneously catching Betsy's eyes across the table. Betsy nodded at him, keeping her own excitement at bay.

"Are there any downsides to this?" he teased.

"No!" both kids protested. "Please, please," they begged. Chuckling, Jonah nodded his consent.

"But tonight's an early night." Betsy cautioned. "Jacob faces the best—the second best—team in the league tomorrow. And you are going with us tomorrow, Rachel?" Rachel nodded.

"I'm tired, Dad. I'm ready for bed now." Jacob stood up, stretching and yawning.

"How about chocolate brownie sundaes first?" his mother asked.

Jacob immediately sat back down.

"You can go ahead and clear the table, son," Jonah instructed him.

"Yes, sir."

Jonah watched him proudly. He and Betsy were determined the children wouldn't be spoiled. They would do chores and respect Maria. He rose to his feet and gathered plates and platters himself, waving Betsy to sit.

"Hold the door for Maria, Rachel," Jonah directed. She jumped to her feet.

"Wow, Maria, that looks yummy!" Rachel exclaimed. Maria swept into the dining room bearing a tray of sundaes.

"None for me, Maria, thank you," Betsy said with a smile.

"You can afford half of one, honey. Split one with me. You ran up and down the sidelines all day," Jonah urged.

"Well, maybe a half."

Jonah carefully cut a brownie, placing a half portion in front of each of them. "You're perfect, Betts. I can't have my beautiful wife getting all skinny on me."

"Mom and I walk three or four times a week, Dad," Rachel told him.

"That's the best exercise," he informed her. But you're on the volleyball team still, aren't you?"

"Yes, sir, but I don't get much court time."

Jonah looked at Betsy with a question in his eyes.

"She's a freshman. She plays on a team with juniors and seniors."

"How much taller will I get, Dad?"

"Not much, sweetie. Most of your growing taller is behind you. But you get more beautiful every day, doesn't she, Mommy?"

Rachel glowed under his compliment, her shoulders squared, and she stood gracefully. "I'll help Maria get these things in the dishwasher."

"May I go take a shower?" Jacob asked. At his father's nod, he took off for the stairs.

Rachel asked, "What's on our agenda tonight, Mom?"

Betsy sighed contently. "I couldn't add another thing to this perfect weekend."

"Maybe we could have more of the same?" Jonah raised his eyebrows.

"Jonah, what has gotten into you?"

Lifting her out of her chair and spinning her in his arms, he sang, "I've got you under my skin." She laughed, snaking her arms up around his neck. He leaned down and covered her luscious lips with his own.

"Oops, bad timing," Rachel murmured as she backed into the kitchen. They heard her whispering: "I totally walked in on them, Maria!

Yikes, they need to take it to the bedroom."

"They have done that, too, *chica*!" Maria replied with a merry chuckle. "Yes, a lot of *amor* around here. *Es bueno*, Rach."

"Yeah, it's great to have parents that love each other. Even in our Christian school, several of the kids live with divorce. You wanna watch a movie, Maria? Jake's going to bed, and I don't think they want me hanging around."

"Your mama and papa love you, *bambina*."

"I know, but they deserve some time alone. Let's go see what's on TV."

"You get your jammies on and come spend the night with Maria, *si*?"

Looking out of the door carefully, Rachel ran for the stairs.

"Do you want to come in here with us?" Betsy called out to her when she heard her upstairs.

"No, thanks, Mom. I'm going to watch a movie with Maria."

"That will be fun, sweetie."

Rachel smiled and thought, *Not as much fun as you're going to have, I bet!*

CHAPTER 8

Rachel, Meet Alan

WALKING ACROSS THE FIELD the next day, Betsy waved at Jonah as he walked toward her and Rachel with two boys. "Are those boys O'Malleys, Mom?" Rachel patted her hair and tugged at her shirt, straightening herself up.

"No, those are Nick's stepsons. They'll be with us tonight, too. You look fine, honey. Relax. Smile, Rach . . . No, smile like you mean it."

"You didn't tell me they are cute, Mom. I thought they were from West Virginia."

"They are. Do you think all West Virginians are toothless hillbillies, or what?" Betsy laughed at her daughter's stressing.

Jonah walked toward his waving wife and watched the interaction, noting his daughter's anxious tugging at her clothes. *Dear God, help me with this young woman my daughter is becoming. How did this happen? I only looked away for a moment.* "Rachel, this is Robbie and Alan Westfall," Jonah said. "Boys, my daughter, Rachel."

Robbie gave a polite response, but Alan was completely tongue-tied. Robbie looked at his brother and grinned, jabbing him with his elbow. "Hi," Alan managed to stammer. "Uh, your brother plays good."

"Oh, you were here yesterday, weren't you? He is good. We're proud of him. Do you play soccer?"

"No, my brother plays football, but I'm into baseball," Alan said.

"Did you bring the book, Betsy?" Jonah asked. Reaching into her large pocketbook, Betsy pulled it out and handed it to him.

"That's Nick's book," Robbie noticed. "Do you like it? That's a loaded question, sorry."

"No, it's fine. I love it. It's terrific," Jonah replied. "It's life-changing. I'm going to order it for the men of our church."

"I think it has a discussion guide with each chapter," Robbie said.

"Do you guys want to go to church with us tomorrow?" Jonah asked.

"We'll ask Mom tonight and let you know. She'll probably stay with Nick."

"That's a good plan at this stage. How's he doing?"

"He doesn't complain, but he hurts. He hates to take pain pills. He hates to get dopey. They make him sleepy."

"Nothing wrong with giving his body a rest after the trauma of open heart surgery, Robbie. I'll talk to him."

"Nick's tough, Dr. Marshall. He's come up hard."

"I get that. He's the most stoic patient I've ever encountered. I can't believe him!" The whistle blew, and all heads swiveled to the field. Betsy jumped to her feet.

"My mom's the same way when Robbie plays, Rachel," Alan assured her, and they quickly got into watching the game themselves. Soon, however, Alan and Rachel got involved in a side conversation. They walked over to the concession stand, brought back snacks for everyone, and pulled their chairs off to the side, leaning their heads together to converse. After Jacob's team won its round, the group took off for the ice cream stand, while Robbie stayed behind, flipping his phone open.

"Hi, Robbie, having a good time?" his mother answered.

"Yeah, but I thought I'd call to give you a heads-up."

"About what?"

"The Marshalls are having dinner with us tonight, right?" She confirmed that they were. "Alan likes their daughter, Rachel."

"Well, that's nice. I'm glad. Is she cute?"

"Not exactly cute. She's drop-dead gorgeous, like her mother. But she's nice, not stuck-up or anything. But listen, Mom, he *likes* her—really likes her, like I like Angela, okay?" Barb was silent on the other end. "What I mean is, don't embarrass him. Don't do anything cutsie, you know?" He heard his mother take in a breath. "Talk to Nick, okay?"

"But isn't he young? I mean, to have a crush?"

"Mom! That's exactly what I mean! I met Angela in middle school, and we're getting married. I have a feeling about Alan and Rachel. It might just be the real thing for them."

"You and Angela have talked about marriage?"

"Not getting married *now*, Mom. After college, when we can afford it. We aren't stupid."

"But that's a long time, you know, to be serious—*that* serious ."

"Don't worry, Mom. Dad has talked to me about respecting her and all. If we don't get married, she'll be someone's wife, and she'll be pure. I promise."

"Dad talked to you?"

"I mean Nick has."

"Oh, well, I'll talk to him about . . . being cutsie, okay?"

"Do that, Mom, promise? Because, if this is the real deal, we don't want to mess it up." When she assured him she would, he hung up, watching Rachel and Alan approach. He eagerly took the nachos they offered him, catching a yellow drip with his tongue. "Hey, guys, what's up?"

"Rachel is like a linguist, Robbie. She speaks Spanish as good as Nick. She's taking French, and this year she wants to take Japanese."

"That's awesome, Rachel. Learning other languages is a real gift. I hear if you can learn one, you can learn lots of other things, too. I struggle with Spanish, even with Nick around, but Rosa chatters away in both languages."

"Ella's pretty good, too," Alan added.

"Maybe it's because they're younger. I was bilingual as a baby. Maria, the lady who lives with us, is Hispanic. I've been exposed to it all my life."

"Is she your nanny?" Alan asked.

"No, she lives with us. She's more like a grandma, but she does help take care of us and the house, and Daddy pays her." Rachel was thoughtful. "I never thought . . . I guess she is a nanny, of sorts. She's just Maria. When her husband, he was our landscaper, died—it was sudden, a tree fell on him—she moved in with us, and she's been there ever since. But she's always taken care of me and Jacob. I love her. She's terrific, and she cooks great—all these Mexican foods, and American foods, too."

Robbie excused himself to call Angela.

"Angela's his girl," Alan explained. "They've been together since middle school. She's a Christian, too. That's important in a relationship. I couldn't be with anyone who didn't love the Lord."

"Mom and Dad say it takes three to make a marriage work. You've got to have God. I go to a Christian school, though, and I see divorces there. But Mom and Dad are, like, in love. I walked in on them last night in a lip-lock. It was embarrassing—but cool, you know?"

"Yeah, Mom and Nick are like that, too. Makes you feel . . . I don't know, secure, I guess." The teens talked together about their parents and what makes a good home, hardly noticing the game.

Jonah's phone chirped, and Rachel rolled her eyes.

"What is it?" Alan asked.

"Daddy has to go. It's the hospital. He always needs to go. He had to leave in the middle of my dance recital," Rachel complained.

"He came in at two in the morning and saved Nick's life. I'm very grateful. We all are. We'll pray for him the rest of our lives. But it must be hard on your family," Alan said.

Rachel watched her father walk away from the noise, to the far sidelines. She blinked back tears. "Thanks for giving me some perspective, Alan. I never get to see the other side—the patient's side, and the patient's family's side. Your dad means a lot to my dad. He really likes him."

"Nick is a special guy."

"Oh, that's right. He's your stepdad, isn't he? Are your folks divorced?"

"No, my first dad died in Iraq when I was six. Nick's been great. Robbie was in big trouble when Nick came into our lives, and I was shy as a rabbit. Mom's all lit up inside, and Ella follows him like a shadow."

"You have two siblings?"

"Mom and Dad had three kids, and God has given us Rosa and Michael. They're Mom and Nick's kids."

"Your mom has *five* kids?" Rachel gasped.

"We do. She's a good mom. Nick never intended to have kids, so he is really happy." Alan outlined Nick's childhood briefly and then added, "Your dad's coming back."

Rachel stood up and slipped her arms around her father. "You have to go, Daddy?"

"No, sweetheart, that was Nick's heart doctor in Pittsburgh, wanting to know how he's doing."

Robbie walked up and joined the conversation. "I think he's doing great, Dr. Marshall. And you let him out of the hospital. So, I guess you think he's doing all right."

Jonah heard the questions behind the teen's comments. He put his hand on Robbie's arm. "He's amazing. He's recovering faster than anyone I've ever seen, and I fully expect he will make a complete recovery. I told Dr. Oster that Nick's family, especially the love of his wife, had a tremendous part to play—although he was already healthy as an ox other than this heart problem."

"Nick loves Mom and all of us. He's been a great dad. I was really scared. I didn't know how any of us would make it without him. I got bitter after I lost my first dad. Nick pulled me out of that. He taught me to be grateful for a father like my dad. Have you seen the scars on Nick's back?"

"I asked him about them when I did the examination. He brushed it off." Jonah sat down beside Barb's boys, and Rachel pulled their chairs closer. Robbie told them about the first time he'd seen those scars and what Nick had shared about his abuse. Rachel blinked back tears. "You get that some, from his book, but he doesn't go into it a lot," Jonah said.

"He doesn't talk about it much. He says he needs to forgive and not dwell on it. Did you see the deep hole?"

"When I put the stethoscope on his back, I asked him about it. He said it was an old childhood injury."

"It came from the wrong end of a belt," Robbie informed him. "His foster father was beating him with the buckle end, and it caught in his back and tore. They didn't take him to the hospital for stitches because they didn't want to lose their income." Rachel gasped. "I think another boy bought some antibiotic cream and put bandages on it when it started oozing," Robbie added.

"Jesus, help him get this boys' home established," Jonah prayed.

"Yeah, I guess he's living for that, too," Robbie said. "Did you hear that his mother told him to come back to L.A. to start the Home?"

"What?" Rachel exclaimed. "I thought she was dead." Robbie told them Nick said he'd seen his mother in heaven when he flatlined.

"We had a code blue on him," Jonah said. "He was literally dead momentarily. That's a great story. In my line of work, I've heard a few, but that's among the neatest."

Betsy shouted. She was jumping up and down. "Your son just scored, in case you didn't notice," she said. Jonah stood and walked over to her, hugging her close to his side.

"Your dad certainly has had an impact on those two. Jeez, they are so lovey-dovey these days," Rachel said.

"Have you heard the O'Malley song 'In Your Arms?' Nick says love is contagious." Robbie went on to share about the day Nick proposed to his mom.

The game ended in a decisive win, and Robbie, Alan, and Rachel joined the fans rejoicing on the sidelines. "Now we have a final playoff?" Jonah asked his wife.

"Yes, after the other teams play for second place. We can go get something to eat, but first, tell me what your call was all about. I'm glad you didn't have to go," Betsy said.

"It was Nick's doctor from Pittsburgh, Dr. Oster, wanting to know how he was doing. When I told him about Barb and Nick's remarkable connection, he said he saw it, too. He said Nick was extremely agitated—that happens to heart patients. Barb had left the room, and an aide ran to get her because Nick was beside himself, hollering for her. Dr. Oster said the minute Nick saw her, he became calm, and when she leaned and kissed him, he could almost see energy and a life-force flow into him." Jonah gave a half-laugh. "That's not something we surgeons say, but it opened the door for me to share Christ with Dr. Oster. He was profoundly moved. I told him I'd send him Nick's book, and he promised to read it."

Robbie reached out for his brother's hand and dropped his head. "Father, we pray for Dr. Oster right now. May Dr. Marshall's words and Nick's life and love for Mom demonstrate Christ's love and draw Dr. Oster into your kingdom."

Jonah added a few words to the prayer, and said, "You know I get far too much credit. Everyone thinks I'm such a hotshot doctor, but I depend on God, and I know He Alone is the Healer. I worked with Dr. Ben Carson in Baltimore—have you ever heard of him?" he asked. When the boys shook their heads, he said, "Read *Gifted Hands*. It's his autobiography. He has separated many conjoined twins. He's done remarkable work, but he gives all the glory to God. He taught me a lot about partnering with God."

"You gave me that book, Daddy, but I never read it. I will now. In fact, I'll use it for my summer reading elective book report," Rachel said.

"It'd be a good one," her father said.

Alan was typing into his phone. *"Gifted Hands*, you said?"

"Yeah." Jonah stood. "Who wants to go with me to get some real food? I don't think hot dogs and nachos are going to do it for me for the rest of the afternoon."

Robbie stood. "I'll go, Dr. Marshall." As they walked to the van, he said, "Nick's life keeps giving and giving. Mom said after he spoke at Grandpa Taylor's conference, she knew he'd be speaking a lot more. Lots of people from that conference were saved and touched. I was helping with the kids, so I missed it. But we have the DVD, and I can't wait to see it."

"I can imagine. I'd like to see it, too. I went to a conference like that once, but I've been too busy lately. Nick has changed my priorities. God help me to never let that hospital consume me again."

"I read in Nehemiah the other day, doc, where the prophet said he couldn't come down from the wall because he was doing a great work. God has called you, and you are doing a great work, sir. Our family is grateful."

Stopped at a red light, Jonah turned and looked at Robbie. "That is remarkable, and I receive it as a word from the Lord, but rearing children and loving my wife is a great work, too." The light changed, and Jonah urged the van forward. "I have to find some balance somehow," and he told Robbie about his conversation with Jacob on the way home from the field after practice. "Rachel is growing up fast, and so is my son. They'll never be this age again."

"I'm really fortunate. I've been working with Nick in the studio ever since I was in middle school. God restored the fathering that the locusts had eaten. You know that promise?"

Jonah smiled. "I do. You certainly know the Word for a young man your age."

"Nick says my mom is a walking Bible. She quotes whole chapters, even whole epistles. She's an amazing woman. I'm really blessed to have her for a mom."

"That's what Taylor says. Let's pick up some chicken. KFC has got baked now." He turned in to the restaurant, and after they selected their meal, they returned to the field.

CHAPTER 9

The Marshalls Meet the O'Malleys

L ATE INTO THE SECOND HALF of Jacobs's last game, Betsy screamed. Jonah put his arm around her shoulders. "He'll be okay. Worst case scenario, his leg's broken."

"He has a broken leg? Oh, God!"

"Maybe. Stay here. You'll embarrass him." Jonah held her to his side, and they watched their boy limp to the sidelines, draped on the shoulders of two of his teammates.

"Aren't they going to call that? Obviously that bully fouled him! Oh, Jonah, go check. You're a doctor. Go see."

"Are you all right, Betsy?"

"Go!" Betsy had her fist in her mouth, and she was gnawing her knuckles. The teens joined her, anxiously watching until Jonah walked back.

"Greg Anderson is here, and his office isn't far away. He's going to run to get him some crutches and a leg immobilizer. He doesn't think it's broken, but he wants him to stay off it for a few days. I'll run him by the office after the game for an X-ray, but he's definitely out of play."

"Is he in pain?" Betsy asked.

"I gave him some Tylenol. Don't fret, Betts. He's a boy. Boys get hurt." She sighed and stepped into his arms. He held her, and she leaned

77

her head on his chest. Rachel hung on to her father's hand.

"Man, I'm glad Mom has Nick," Alan commented.

"You can say that again, bro. I called her and had to tell her to talk to him."

"What about?"

"I told her about Rachel—how drop-dead gorgeous she is, and what a nice girl."

"I thought you and Angela . . ." Alan eyed him warily.

"You doofus, I'm talking about you. I told Mom *you* like Rachel and that she'd better not embarrass you, and that's the thanks I get?"

"Oh, sorry. Thanks, that was a good idea. She *is* nice, and smart."

"She'd have to be brainy. She'd never get past first base with you if she wasn't. Now you are in for the old Nick talk, though. I see it coming. He's cool. He talks real straight, and you can ask him anything. He won't get upset or act weird." Alan colored. "I've told you, he knows what it's like to be a teenage boy."

* * *

Back at the hotel, Barb sat on the couch, staring into space. Hearing the bedroom door open, she turned and saw Nick coming toward her, pain tugging at the corners of his eyes. Usually rich milk chocolate, they were lighter, faded somehow. "You need some pain medicine, Nick. I'll get it for you." Seeing him ready to protest, she said, "We're having the Marshalls for dinner. You need to get the medicine working so you'll feel better when company gets here."

Nick shrugged, waved his hand in assent, and dutifully swallowed the pill she presented him.

Barb sat beside him. "Robbie says I need to talk to you." His brown eyes rested on her, brimming with love, and she smiled at him. "I do love you. I hope you know that."

He returned her smile. "For the life of me, I'll never understand it, but I do know it, and I'm eternally grateful. What does Robbie want?"

"He called to give me a heads-up. Seems Alan 'likes' Rachel Marshall, and he told me he had a feeling it could be the 'real deal' for Alan, and I'm not to act 'cutsie' and blow it."

Despite the ebbing pain, Nick chuckled and reached out for her hand. "He's a good big brother. Robbie's a great kid, Barb."

"What does that mean? I told him Alan and Rachel are too young for a crush, and he told me he and Angela knew they'd get married when they were in middle school. He said you'd given him 'The Talk' and that they wouldn't be stupid." She waited while Nick grinned. "Did you know they were so . . . serious?"

"Sure, Barb. Robbie and Angela have been crazy about each other for years. They're compatible, they pray together, and they make a good couple. When did you know Bob was the one? I thought you were betrothed in kindergarten."

"Oh. I guess that's true."

"You guess? Either it's true or it's not."

"It's true." She looked miserable.

"When did you first talk about marriage?"

"Gee . . . sixth or seventh grade, I think."

"When did you start making out?"

"Making out?"

"You know, necking, kissing, petting." Nick looked at her. "Oh, let me guess—after marriage, right?"

"We kissed goodnight."

He shook his head. "But you were serious in middle school. Are these kids different? Why does Robbie think it's the real deal? Because it probably is, you know? Alan's always been a serious kid and goal-directed."

"But they are so young. It's . . . risky. What did you tell Robbie? He said you talked to him about respecting a girl, and he knew to keep her pure. Nick, how do you know my boys better than I do?"

"Honey, I've been a teenage boy. You see them as your baby boys.

I see them as the lusty young men that they are."

"They're . . . 'lusty' young men?"

"They're teenage boys. The testosterone is at astronomical levels. Their voices are deep, they're hairy, and they have wet dreams."

"They do?"

He laughed. Bringing her hand up to his lips, he kissed it.

Tim knocked gently and pushed the door open. "What are you laughing about, Nick?" Tim asked.

"Tim, are all teenage boys 'lusty?' I mean, at Alan's age?" Barb demanded to know.

Tim's eyes sparkled as he pretended to look thoughtful. "Maybe not 'all'—only the normal, healthy ones." He and Nick laughed. "I tell Missy you women have no appreciation for the male mind. We think about sex, oh, about 90 percent of the time."

"How do you get anything done?"

The men both laughed. "It's tough, baby. Especially when I look at you," Nick said.

"You are all perverts? Are the girls being good? Do you need me to get Rosa for this conversation?"

"The girls are playing dolls, but Michael needs a nap. I resent being called a pervert, Barb. I only desire my wife. Although a good-looking woman can make my thoughts turn to her."

"I'll never understand men."

"We men are simple. It's you females that are complicated," Tim rejoined.

Missy appeared at the doorway, with Michael rooting around her breast. "He needs his Mommy," she announced the obvious, laughing, and carried him over to Barb.

"I thought with me gone so much he'd wean, but he seems to need me even more."

"He's making up for that time," Missy said. "He'll outgrow it soon enough. What's complicated?"

"These guys tell me all normal teenage boys are 'lusty,' Missy. Did you know that?"

"Barb, all *men* are lusty. You know that. They're males, aren't they?"

"But, they're boys."

"Let's see, do they have hairy armpits? And Alan's voice has changed. Get a grip, Barb."

Barb groaned, settling a sleepy Michael on her breast. "No wonder Robbie said I should talk to Nick." She shook her head. "He told me Alan 'likes' Rachel Marshall and that I shouldn't be 'cutsie' and embarrass him.

"Good advice," Tim said. He looked at Nick. "I assume you've had 'The Talk,' huh?"

"With Robbie, and I've left it open with Alan, but he's in for it now."

"What do you say in this 'Talk,' Nick?" Barb asked.

"Bottom line: keep it in your pants, kid."

"Nick!"

"You don't want Angela pregnant, do you?" Missy and Tim were doubled over. "Look, I read the Scripture about keeping a virgin. I tell them real men respect women. I tell them they are walking powder kegs and not to get into tempting situations because even the best intentions can fail. I told him how I had to keep from being alone with you until after we were married."

Barbara's face flamed. "You talked to him about us?"

"I sure didn't want to talk to him about me and other women. Do you think he doesn't know we have sex? We have two kids, and they didn't arrive by magic. Let me amend that—it *was* rather magical. Look, Barb, I'm teaching them to be men of honor, to be husbands."

"God knows I couldn't have raised these boys alone." Barb groaned.

"That's why two are better than one. Kids need both parents. Imagine if Nick and I raised Rosa and Jeri without you gals?" Tim said, looking at Nick. "You want to tell your daughters about their periods?" Nick shuddered.

"I never could've raised boys by myself!" Barb agreed.

The Marshalls arrived a little later, and Jacob was on crutches. They gave a vivid description of the games before room service arrived with the meal. After they left, Nick disappeared with the boys. He was gone for about an hour. When he came back into their room, Barb chuckled. "How did 'The Talk' go?" she asked.

Nick stretched out on the bed beside her. "Easier than with Robbie. His brother had already talked to him. He's good, Barb, but I agree with Robbie that Rachel might be the one for Alan."

"Why do you think that?" Barb snuggled up to him.

"The things they've talked about: ideas, goals, issues. They're both praying teens. They fit."

"You're amazing, Nick. How do you get this kind of information?"

"It's not hard. It's what you want others to do for you. You take what they say seriously, ask questions to understand more, and listen. Honey, would you take your clothes off and lie here beside me?"

"I thought we—"

"It's the old King David thing. I want the comfort of your body, even if I can't do anything. This stupid pain medicine kills my libido. I'm glad Jonah is doing a stress test this week. This is getting old, fast."

Barb giggled as she checked the lock on the door and shucked her clothes. Lying down beside Nick, she put her arms around his waist and cuddled his back. He sighed. "It was old the minute you woke up from surgery, you sex fiend," she said.

He smiled into the semi-darkness. "I'll be glad to get home, away from all these lights and sirens and back to the peace and quiet of our mountain home."

"Me, too, but I'm most glad you'll be coming back with me." She kissed his shoulder.

CHAPTER 10

Betsy's News

NICK AND BARB HAD BEEN back home in West Virginia for a month. Betsy called Barb and Missy at least once a week, surprised by what good friends they had become. When Betsy realized she had missed a period, maybe two, she made an appointment with her GYN. Her mother had died when she was fourteen, and she didn't know much about her female history. Before she went to the doctor, however, she noticed her breasts were tender, and she was tired and queasy. She bought a home pregnancy test.

Betsy sat on the edge of the bathtub, staring at the test. *I'm pregnant. Thirty-nine years old and I'm pregnant. What will Jonah say?* She smiled. *It shouldn't be any great surprise. He hasn't been able to keep his hands off me since he met Nick. Not that I mind.* She stood and dressed quickly. Jonah had left earlier, and she had to get the kids to school. She woke them and went to put on her makeup, planning how she would give the news to her husband.

Jonah had been making every effort to get home at a reasonable hour and eat with his family, but he called to say he was delayed—tonight, of all nights. Betsy was determined to wait up for him. She put on her prettiest gown and took a book to bed. She propped up against the headboard but couldn't resist what she now knew was pregnancy fatigue. The book slipped out of her hands as she surrendered to sleep.

Jonah walked in at about one in the morning, surprised to see the light on. He smiled as he looked at Betsy's beautiful golden hair spilling around her long, elegant neck. He noticed the blue gown, and suddenly his body leaped into action. *She was waiting up for me. Whoa, stud. She's asleep.* He threw his jacket on the chair and tugged at his tie.

Betsy stirred, and her eyes fluttered open. She raised her arms to him. "You're home. What time is it?"

Jonah crawled across the bed and pulled her close. "You're beautiful. You know that? I still can't believe you love me. Were you waiting up?"

"Mmm," she mumbled, eagerly responding to his kisses. "I need to tell you something."

He tugged the straps of her gown down and kissed her breasts, thinking how lush they were. She moaned and reached for his belt buckle.

Later, with her tucked into his arm, Jonah asked. "What were you going to tell me?"

She pulled back. "Oh. Well, it should come as no surprise . . . but it *was* a surprise to me."

"What?"

"I did a home pregnancy test this morning. It was positive."

A flash of surprise crossed Jonah's face, and a slow grin split it as he stared at her in wonder. "You're pregnant?"

She smiled. "You're happy?"

"I'm going to be a father again, at forty-three? How about that?" He pulled her close.

"I'm going to be a mother again, at thirty-nine."

"We'll get more help in the house. We aren't just starting out this time. I'm established in my practice. We're well off. You're to take it easy this time. You can spend the entire time on a chaise lounge if you want."

"Are you crazy, or do you want to drive me insane?"

"How do you feel?"

"I haven't had a period in a while, so I made an appointment with Sam Brown. I thought maybe I was entering into early menopause, you know? But I realized I'd been tired and queasy and that my breasts are tender."

"Did I hurt you?" His hand cupped her breast tenderly. "I noticed they were rather lush."

"You never hurt me when you love me, Jonah."

"God, thank you for this woman, my wife." He tucked her closer to his side and brushed his lips in her hair. "I love you."

"I love you, too, Daddy." She giggled, and her hand strayed across his chest.

"I came home exhausted, dead on my feet, and I saw you in that blue gown, your glorious hair spilled across the pillow. Suddenly, my body sprang into action, and I wasn't the least bit tired."

"You mean, like this?" she reached down and took him in her hand. He groaned. "You quit that."

"You don't really want me to quit," Betsy murmured as his body responded to her continued touch.

"You realize twice in one night is a bit much for a man my age. We aren't youngsters on a honeymoon, you know."

"You seem quite up to it."

Jonah rolled onto her and slowly, gently they made love again. This time they both fell into a deep sleep.

Before too long, the eastern sun shone into their window. Kissing her brow softly, Jonah rose, hearing the children in the hall.

"You guys overslept," Rachel said when he came out. "Where's Mom?"

"Shh, she's sleeping. I got in about one, and I'm not going to wake her. Get dressed. I'll take you to school on my way to the hospital."

"I need my pink blouse. I have to ask her where it is."

"Go find something else. You're not waking her up."

"Jeez, Dad, what's wrong with you? I need my pink blouse. It goes with this skirt," Rachel's voice raised in anger. She started to push past him into the bedroom where her mother lay naked under the sheets.

He grabbed her arms and held her firmly. "You listen to me. You are not going in there and disturbing her. Go find something else to wear."

Rachel stared up at him and furiously turned on her heel. "I can't believe you," she spat back.

Jacob watched, big-eyed. "Is Mom sick, Dad?"

"No, she's fine, just tired. We're going to have to all help out around here for the next few months."

"What's wrong?"

"Nothing's wrong, son. You get dressed, and I'll take you to school. Thanks for getting up on time. You did a good job. I'll see if Maria has our breakfast."

Jonah went downstairs, and Maria greeted him with his coffee. He noticed she had tea at Betsy's place at the table and told her he was letting Betsy sleep in. Maria nodded sagely. Jacob scooted in to the table, and after prayer, he dug into his food in typical teenage-boy fashion.

"Maria, I don't think Rachel will make it to breakfast. Would you mind fixing her a protein shake?" Jonah requested.

Rachel flounced down the stairs and headed for the door. "Because I had to pick out a whole new outfit. We need to go, or we'll be late," she said. Jonah offered her the shake, and she grimaced. "I don't want that old thing."

Her father opened a car door for her, and she climbed in. He handed the shake to her. "Drink it, Rachel. It's not my fault you missed breakfast, and you need it." Pouting, she took it from his hands and set it in the cup holder in the console. When he got in on his side, he glanced at it. He backed out of the garage. "Drink the shake, Rachel, or I won't drop you off at school." Jacob looked back and forth between them, watching the struggle of wills.

"What is *wrong* with you, Daddy?" Rachel picked up the shake and sucked on the straw noisily. "There. I hope I throw up."

Jonah sighed. "Thank you, sweetie."

Jacob sat back in his seat without a word.

"I'll be home early tonight. Sorry I was late last night," Jonah said as they piled out of his car.

"See you later, Dad. Thanks for the ride," Jacob said.

Rachel slammed the door and marched off without so much as a goodbye.

Jacob looked at his dad. "She gets like that sometimes. Mom says it's teenage girls."

"Have a good day, son."

"I will, Dad. You, too."

Jonah smiled and waved at his boy as he pulled off.

* * *

Betsy woke up about ten, shocked that she had slept that late. She rose quickly but sat back down as a wave of nausea swept over her. When her stomach settled, she went downstairs, seeking Maria. "Good morning, Señora," Maria said when she came into the kitchen. "Are you ready for breakfast?" Betsy paled, and her hand flew to her tummy. "You sit. Maria will fix you ginger tea. You will feel better."

Betsy sat at the counter. After taking a few sips, she said, "Thanks, Maria, this does help."

"You feel like a poached egg? It is better for the baby to eat."

"You knew I was pregnant? I only found out yesterday myself."

Maria chuckled. "It happens when you love much, Señora." She patted her on the arm.

Betsy blushed. "I will have a poached egg. Thank you."

"You have been tired, no?" Maria bustled about the kitchen prepar-

87

ing Betsy's breakfast. Betsy nodded. "And you didn't want the coffee. Maria knew. When we have this baby?"

"I'm not sure. I didn't even realize. It's been a while. I have an appointment with my OB on Tuesday."

"Our doctor—he knows?"

"I told him last night, but I don't know what the kids will say."

"Maybe they need time, but they get used to the idea," Maria assured her.

"I'm not sure how Rachel will take it." Betsy rubbed her hands over her face. Maria was kneading bread dough when the phone rang, so Betsy stood to answer. Hearing Jonah's voice, she smiled.

"How's the little mama this morning? You looked beautiful lying there. I couldn't wake you. We didn't get much sleep last night." He chuckled. "Not that I minded."

"How are you? You are the one who had to go to work. Thanks for taking the kids."

"Adrenalin is keeping me going. And love. My feet haven't touched the ground yet, gorgeous. I'll be home early tonight, and we can tell the children together." He paused. "I saw a side of Rachel this morning. She was quite . . . selfish. We had a run-in, I'm afraid."

Betsy sighed and carried the phone into the family room, sinking into the big chair there. "I've felt sorry for her. You were gone a lot. I guess I've spoiled her. I've done her a disservice, Jonah, and I'm sorry for that."

"It's as much my fault. We'll have to pray for her and get her through this. I'll see you tonight. Have you gotten a doctor's appointment yet?"

"Tuesday, 9:00 a.m."

"Okay. I'll arrange to be off and go with you."

"You don't have to do that."

"I want to," he said. "See you about six. Can you get the kids?"

"I can. I'm fine. Maria fixed me ginger tea and a poached egg."

"You told her?"

"She knew. How did she know before I did?"

"How did she know before your own husband did? I love you, Betts."

"Love you, too."

When Jonah walked into the house later, the delicious smells of dinner greeted him. Betsy was sitting in front of the news. She looked up. Jonah thought, *I can't believe I didn't notice the darkness under her eyes.* He crossed over the family room and knelt in front of her. "How do you feel?" he asked, touching her cheek and pushing her golden hair back off her face. It was thicker. He wondered how long she'd been pregnant.

"I'm good."

Jacob for once in his life came down the stairs soundlessly. "What's up? I knew it. Something's wrong with Mom."

Jonah stood and put his arm around his son's shoulder. "Mom's fine. Would you get your sister?"

Jacob, unconvinced, trudged up the stairs and called his sister to dinner.

Maria peeked in. "I serve now?"

"In just a minute, Maria. We need to tell the children," Jonah said. "Thank you for taking care of Betsy."

Maria beamed. "Is good, doctor."

He grinned back. "Yeah, it is."

"What's good?" Rachel demanded.

"Sit a minute, kids. Your mother and I have some good news for you." They looked at him expectantly. "We're going to have another baby," he said with a smile.

Rachel's eyes widened, and she turned toward her mother. "Is this true?" Betsy nodded. "How could you do this to me? I can't believe this. *Good* news? I'll be the laughing stock of the school." She spun around and glared at Jonah.

"I think it's cool," Jacob said, smiling at his mom.

"Cool? You think it's *cool*? I think it's humiliating!" Rachel swiped at her eyes. "I'll never forgive you two for this! What are you going to do about it?"

Jonah regarded her sadly. "What do you intend for us to do, Rachel? We will welcome this baby with all the love we welcomed you and Jacob with."

"Well, I won't. It's obscene, that's what!"

"Rachel, go to your room and talk to God about this. And don't talk to your mother like that again. Get your attitude straight, young lady." She ran up the stairs, crying.

Jacob sat beside his mom and put his arm around her. "I think it's cool, Mom, and I'll help any way I can. She'll get over this. You tell me it's the girl hormones, remember?"

Betsy smiled through her tears and patted him. "Thanks, Jakie." She looked up at Jonah, who took her hand.

"Feel like eating, Betts?" he asked her. He led her to the dinner table. Maria was quietly setting the dishes on the table, and Jacob went to help her.

"We need to stop calling him 'Jakie,' don't we? He's not a little boy anymore. He was more mature than his older sister," Betsy said as Jonah slid her chair under her.

He patted her shoulder. "He was. We'll pray for Rachel." When he said the blessing, he added a prayer for his daughter to rejoice in the addition to their family.

"And help her get over herself, God," Jacob added.

Betsy giggled, but Jonah noted a touch of hysteria. He took her hand and squeezed it. "God's never failed us yet." He forked pieces of baked chicken onto a plate and passed it to his son before he spooned mashed potatoes onto Betsy's plate and his own.

Maria entered the dining room with steaming hot homemade rolls. "You like the salad, Jacob?"

"Mmm," he said, through his full mouth. He swallowed. "Cherry Jell-O and fresh fruit—it's great! Thanks, Maria. Can you pass the green beans, Dad?" With a chuckle, Jonah complied.

CHAPTER 11

The Power of Peers

NICK AND HIS FAMILY HAD BEEN back home in West Virginia for several months, and Rachel and Alan were still burning up the email and text lines back and forth between their states. If Barb expected the ardor to diminish, she was sadly mistaken. Nick watched, bemused, whenever the unflappable Alan was late making or receiving communication from Texas.

Alan smiled happily when he saw the phone number on his phone, and he walked quickly into his room, picking up the call. "Rach? Hey, I can't believe you called. I was looking for your email."

"I needed to talk to you, Alan." Rachel was crying and almost hysterical.

"What's wrong? Hold on. I can't help unless you tell me. You need me to call your Mom?"

"No! I don't ever want to talk to her again. I can't believe she did this to me."

"What did she do? You can't mean that."

"She is *pregnant*, Alan. I'm a freshman in high school, and Jake's in seventh grade. How could she do this to me?" Silence fell between them. "Alan, are you there? Did I lose you?"

"I'm here. I'm trying to think what to say."

"I know. It's awful. I'm so embarrassed."

"Why are you embarrassed, Rachel? Children are a blessing, and parents who love each other are wonderful. Every teenager should be so lucky. I thank God every day for the love Nick and Mom share. I hope one day to love like they do."

"But my folks are *old*, and in four years I'll be in *college*."

"When Rosa was born, Robbie was a freshman. You do remember Rosa and Michael? My baby sister and brother?"

"Of course, I remember them! They are adorable. But—"

"But what, Rachel? But they're *my* family and not yours?"

"I . . . I thought. I don't know what I thought. Are you mad at me? You sound mad."

"I'm not angry, Rachel, I'm . . . disappointed. You are totally ruining your mom's joy. She and your dad must be happy, and you're messing that up. Unless you haven't told them how you feel."

"No . . . I mean, yes. I've been pretty nasty to them."

"Oh, Rach. I can't tell you how much fun I've had being a big brother to Rosa and Michael. They're the joy of our lives, and Mom and Nick are happy to have them."

"But they are newlyweds, and your mom is young."

"My mother is forty-four, Rachel. She was forty-one when Rosa was born."

"Oh, she's older than my Mom. How old is Nick?"

"I think he'll be thirty-nine. Maybe thirty-eight. He's got a birthday coming up."

"Wow, he's *younger* than your mom?"

"Yeah, a lot younger. So, don't talk to me about embarrassing. My grandmother thought he was some sort of predator, out to get my dad's benefits. At least she did until he saved her life. Now she tries to get along with him."

"He saved her life? You do have the most interesting family. Tell me about it."

Alan told her about the investigation their family had faced because of Nonna's report to the Department of Health and Human Services. Then he described the details of the day Nick and Robbie saved Nonna's life, and how his stepfather drove his grandfather across the state later that night to the hospital in Charleston.

"He lived out a lot of forgiveness that night," Alan said. "Now Nonna and Gramps are both saved and serving God. Nick's older than his years. Robbie says he has a lot of life experience, you know? He's a wise person and a great dad. He didn't even want to be a father because he had such an awful childhood, but God made him into the best dad ever. We're blessed to have him, and I'm glad he has Rosa and Michael. They're God's blessings, and they've been good for him and for all of us. Grow up, Rach."

"Thank you, Alan. I'm glad I called. You've given me a lot to think about. It takes a special friend to bring correction. In our youth group, we talked about friends who hold you accountable. Thanks for doing that—for listening to my stupidity and straightening me out."

"I'm glad you called, too, Rachel. It's nice to hear your voice. I hope I helped some."

"Oh, you did, Alan! I must apologize. Would you pray with me?"

"Sure."

Rachel began hesitantly, weeping as she confessed her cruel and thoughtless words. Alan listened to her earnest and humble confession and prayed for God to help her go to her parents. He encouraged her to do that immediately. "And did you have permission to call me? Don't tell me your dad won't notice the bill, Rachel. You need to tell him."

"You don't cut me any breaks, do you, Alan?" Rachel laughed. "Okay, I'll tell him first thing. It will bring up our conversation, and I can tell them you straightened out my bad thinking and gave me a better understanding."

"Rachel, you've got to give your mom lots of support right now. Pregnant women are emotional, you know? And you've put them through it. Besides, it's even harder because she's older."

"How do you know all this?"

He laughed. "I lived it, remember? I'll pray for you to get excited about your new baby and to truly welcome him, okay?"

"I think I can do that now. I feel . . . different. Thanks so much, Alan. I don't want to hang up. It's good to talk to you. I miss you."

"I miss you, too, Rach. Are you guys going to the fundraiser for Nick's home for boys? I could see you then."

"I'll make my parents go and bring us, Alan. When is it?"

Alan gave her the website information. "I hope we see you next fall. The construction has already begun in L.A. Nick and Tim are flying out there next week. By the way, congratulations on winning that Spanish award. You did great!"

"Thanks, Alan. I love . . . uh, talking to you. See you online, okay?"

After Rachel hung up, she prayed again, took a deep breath, and walked to her parents' room. She stood a moment, and then she lifted her hand to knock softly.

"Come in," her mother called. Looking at her calmly, but holding her breath, her mother smiled tentatively. Shame flooded Rachel as her glance flitted around the room, taking in the soft green drapes and seeing her mother's gracious hand in the tasteful, homey space. Beyond the bedroom's appearance, Rachel felt love here and realized she'd always taken it for granted.

"Is Daddy here?" Jonah heard her voice and walked in from the bathroom, eyeing her warily. "I called Alan. We talked a while, and he told me I had to tell you to expect the bill."

"Thanks for letting me know," her father replied and waited.

Rachel nervously shifted from foot to foot, eyes cast down. Taking a breath, she looked up, willing herself to face them. "He was wonderful. In youth group, we talked about real friends—friends who hold you accountable. He did that for me. I owe you guys an apology. I was awful, and I'm really sorry. Did you know Barb was forty-one when Rosa was born? And Robbie was a freshman. Those babies, Rosa and

Michael, are precious. Why did I think our baby wouldn't be precious, too? He or she will be my brother or sister, for heaven's sake! I don't know why I was awful. Please forgive me."

"Oh, honey!" Betsy held out her arms, and Rachel ran into them. She cried and threw herself onto their bed, crawling into her mother's embrace.

"It takes a lot of maturity to correct your course, Rachel. I'm proud of you. I'll pay the phone bill with pleasure," Jonah said. "Alan's a good friend, and you're blessed to have him."

"I know, Daddy," she sniffed. "He didn't cut me any slack. I felt foolish. I've been selfish and stupid! Please forgive me."

Betsy rubbed her back, held her, and wiped her hair back from her eyes. Cupping her hands around Rachel's face, she lifted it up and kissed her gently. "Of course, we forgive you, honey. And you'll be the best big sister in the world."

"Ella is a good big sister, and she's only six! She really takes care of those babies, doesn't she?" They laughed together.

"You've got a few years on her," her mother said. "You'll be lots more help. I'll need you these next few months."

"Alan told me that, too. I'll try, Mom, I really will. I promise. Daddy, I'm sorry." Jonah held out his arms, and she scooted off the bed and ran to him, crying again.

"It's okay, baby. We'll never love you less, you know. You're our firstborn—the child of our youth." He rocked her from side to side as she clung to him. "Are you all right, now? Do you want me to take you to your room?"

"And pray with me, Daddy? I'd like that." Tucking her under his arm, Jonah pulled her close to his side and walked her down the hall. Betsy smiled as she watched his dark head from its vast height lean down to catch her daughter's words. As blonde as she, Rachel shared her mother's tall, slender build, but Jonah was six inches over six feet and dwarfed them both.

"You missed supper, sweetie. Do you want to get a bite to eat?" Jonah asked his daughter. When they went into the kitchen, they noticed Maria had left a plate of dinner covered in wrap sitting to the side for her. Rachel carried it over to the counter while her dad poured her a glass of milk. He sat beside her, and they chatted quietly while she ate. Jonah thought about mentioning her behavior from that morning, but he realized she'd come a long way in a short time, and he trusted God to complete the work. He loved this precious replica of her mother, and he knew God was working in her.

When he returned to his and Betsy's room, Betsy was propped up on the headboard with her eyes closed. "You all right, Betts?"

"I am now. God has done it again, hasn't He? You made sure she ate dinner, didn't you?" She held out her arms, and he came into them. Sitting on the edge of the bed, he enfolded her in an embrace.

"I've been thanking Him," Betsy said. "Thanking Him for her wonderful father and Alan's wisdom and friendship."

"How do you feel tonight?"

"Good. Did you bring me my crackers for in the morning? That was a good tip Barb gave me. It helps."

"How good do you feel?" he asked, running his fingers down her arm.

She looked at him and grinned. "Good enough, big guy. Why? Do you want more of what got you in so much trouble with your daughter?"

"We might as well. We can't get any more pregnant, can we?" Laughing, he pulled her down. "I love you, Betts."

"I know, and you love me very well, too," she replied and lifted her face for his eager kisses.

She fell sound asleep, and he curved his arm around her, resting his hand gently on her still-flat belly. Soon, he would feel his baby growing inside. Once again, he thought of the sacrifices she had made to give him his family. He kissed her softly on her bare shoulder and drifted off, contented and very much in love.

CHAPTER 12

Welcome, Baby

ON TUESDAY, BETSY convinced Jonah she could drive herself to her doctor's appointment, but he insisted on meeting her there. He arrived a bit breathless and found her in the waiting room. He collapsed on the seat beside her. "It's just nine o'clock. Did you run up six flights of stairs, silly?" she teased him.

"I wanted to go in with you," he said.

She laughed. "You'll learn to be on the other end and wait for the doctor." She hardly had the words out of her mouth when the nurse called, and Jonah followed her down the hall.

Sam Brown was surprised to see Jonah. "I don't often see husbands at OB exams. Are you having trouble? Worried about something?"

Jonah shook the other doctor's outstretched hand. "According to a home test, we're pregnant. I understand they are pretty reliable."

Sam grinned. "They are. Aren't you a bit old for another go-round?" He sat and swiveled his chair toward Betsy. "How do you feel about this?"

"Surprised. Excited. I asked God if He truly wants me to do this again, but it's pretty obvious He does."

Sam looked down at her chart. "Thirty-nine. Are you wanting amnio?"

"No," Jonah said. "We wouldn't terminate under any circumstances."

"That's kinda what I figured, knowing you two. Okay, Betsy, how long has it been?"

"I'm really not sure. A while. I made an appointment to see if I was going into menopause, but then I realized I was having symptoms, and so I bought the test."

"What kind of symptoms?"

"Breast tenderness, fatigue, low-grade nausea, and some dizziness if I get up too fast."

"No problem there," Sam said. "Let's have a look."

After he checked her, he said, "Your cervix is blue, and you're definitely pregnant. We can better estimate once we have a sonogram. Can you remember anything about when you might have had your last period?"

Jonah grinned. "It's been a couple of months, I'd say."

Betsy blushed, realizing he was thinking the same thing she was. They hadn't had a week off in a long time. "Probably about . . . When did Nick have his surgery, Jonah?"

Jonah looked at Betsy. "May. Remember his kids took their finals online?"

"I guess May," Betsy said. I remember I had a period when Rachel had her dance recital. That was May 7th."

"That gives us something to go on. This is the end of July. You think you've been pregnant that long?" Sam asked.

"I've been tired for weeks."

"I'd say," her doctor said. "You'll be through with this stage and starting to show soon."

She shrugged. "It's exhausting keeping up with teenagers. I thought . . ."

"Looks like you'll be keeping up with teenagers *and* late-night feedings, Mom. If we're that far along, let's go ahead with a sonogram. You got time? I'll roll the portable in here."

Betsy looked at Jonah. He took her hand, his eyes dancing. "Sure.

Let's see this kid." When Dr. Brown left, Jonah leaned over the exam table and kissed his wife's lips. "This is the real deal, honey," he said. Her eyes swam with tears. "Are you okay? Any second thoughts?"

"Too late for that, lover boy. You play, you pay."

"You'll pay a lot more than I, Betsy. I've done my part, and it was pure pleasure. You've got the raw end of this deal."

"That's where you're wrong. I'll feel this little guy moving and growing under my heart. It's magic, mystical. I'm having a baby."

"I love you, Mrs. Marshall." He kissed her softly.

After a light tap on the door, a technician rolled the machine into the room and began hooking it up. "You've done this before, right?" she asked. The paper rustled as Betsy lifted her gown. Jonah drew his chair up to where he could peer at the screen. He squeezed her hand. She sighed, and he glanced at her. A dreamy expression fluttered across her face. The image flickered on the screen, and soon their baby appeared. The tech began to point out the obvious: spine, arms, and legs. She looked up. "This is your first appointment? You've been pregnant for a while."

"Yeah," Betsy replied. "Guess it's not menopause, huh?"

The tech laughed. "Nope, definitely not."

Jonah couldn't tear his eyes off the screen. "He looks good, honey."

"Is it a he?" she asked.

"We can't tell for sure, but it looks like a healthy pregnancy. I shouldn't say anything, but you're a medical doctor, right Dr. Marshall?"

"I'm a heart surgeon, and I like the looks of that strong, healthy heart."

Another tap on the door and Sam entered. "Got him up already, do you?" He smiled. "Go ahead and do the measurements, but he's definitely two months along. Looks fine." He sat. "Now, tell me who this Nick guy you mentioned is."

Jonah told him about Nick Costas and Nick's love for his wife,

Barb. "Nick straightened out my priorities, starting one day when I came home from the hospital in the middle of the day."

Sam chuckled. "In the middle of the day *and* in the middle of her cycle, right?"

"Guess so," Jonah said.

"I'm right here, gentlemen. Please quit talking over me," Betsy said. "Can you print out a picture from that machine?" she asked the tech.

"Oh, Mrs. Marshall, you'll want to wait until we get our 4D shots. They are really amazing!"

"But these are our very first. That's all we had with our other two."

"This isn't your first child?" she asked.

Sam chuckled. "They have teenagers. Can you imagine starting over with teenagers?"

"I didn't dream of it. God surprised us," Jonah said.

Sam stood. "It's not like you didn't know where babies come from, Jonah." He looked at Betsy. "Another appointment in a month, unless you have any problems. You call me if you do."

The tech handed them a grainy photo. "This shows the most. Something to take home to the kids, right? Wait till they see the 4D. You've got a daughter?"

"Sixteen."

"She'll go ape." The technician rolled the machine out of the room. "You can get dressed and make your next appointment. Need anything else?"

"We're good," Jonah said and helped his wife sit. He reached out to help her down.

"Wait just a minute, okay?" Betsy said, stopping him.

"You dizzy?"

"A little." She dropped her hand to her tummy.

"Sick?" Jonah asked.

"Not really. It's just . . . He's in there, Jonah. Your love is growing in me."

Tears sprung to Jonah's eyes. "Oh, Betsy, what hath God wrought?"

"We'll see, won't we?" She smiled up at him.

"I have never loved you more, Betts."

She stood up in his arms. "I love you, too, Jonah Marshall."

Jonah and Betsy walked down the hall hand in hand. She made the appointment, and they rode down in the elevator together. He held the door, and they walked out into the Houston sunshine and heat. He asked if she wanted him to take her home.

"No, I'm fine."

"Where's your car?"

"In the parking garage. You go on now. I know you need to get back to work."

"I'll walk you to the van," he said, and he did. After tucking her in, he leaned in the window for one last lingering kiss. "You be careful. See you tonight. I may be late, but I wouldn't have missed this for anything. Don't you show those kids the picture until I get home." She smiled up at him and waved as she pulled off, and he whistled while walking to his car.

Betsy was in her pajamas but sitting up watching a news show when Jonah got home about nine. "Why aren't you in bed?" He asked as he crossed the room. "You need your rest." He looked under her eyes. "I felt terrible when I realized I hadn't noticed the darkness under your eyes. What a miserable husband you married."

Betsy laughed. "Don't fret, Jonah. I can't deal with this hovering for nine months."

"Seven months," he corrected.

"Seven months. You told me I couldn't show the kids the photo until you got home."

He grinned and bellowed up the stairs, "Kids, come here."

Jacob came bounding down the stairs. "What, Daddy?" Rachel

called down.

"Your mom has something to show you."

When both children were standing in front of their mother, she opened her purse and pulled out the sonogram photo.

"Oh, wow, Dad. Is that our baby?" Rachel said.

"Lemme see, Rach." Jacob crowded next to her, and they looked at it together. "Okay, Dad, what am I seeing here?" he asked. Jonah pointed out the prominent spine and the oversized head, tiny arms, and legs. "Gosh, Mom, how far along are you?"

"Two months."

"You've been pregnant for two months, and you've been taking care of all of us that whole time?" Rachel asked.

"She's a pretty great mom, isn't she?" Jonah asked. Both kids agreed.

"Well, I'm not so good a wife, Jonah. Have you had supper?"

Like a mother goose, Betsy led the way into the kitchen, her family trailing behind her. She got Jonah's dinner out of the warmer and set it on the counter. "You kids want some fruit? Yogurt?"

"Yogurt would be good, Mom, but you sit here by Dad. I'll get it. You want anything, Jake?"

"Could I have some of Maria's gingerbread cookies, Mom?" Jacob reached for the tin.

Rachel saddled up on the stool next to her mother and gently reached out to put her hand on her mother's tummy. "Welcome, baby. Welcome to the Marshall family." Her eyes glistened. Her mother smiled and hugged her. "Soon as I finish this," Rachel waved her spoon, "I'm getting online with Alan."

CHAPTER 13

Los Angeles

ABOUT FOUR MONTHS LATER, a young curate met the Costas family at the airport in Los Angeles. He and Robbie loaded the luggage into the back of a dark van. "Mother Joanna had to battle the sisters. They all want to meet you. She solved it by delegating me to bring you straightaway. But if you're too tired, we could drop you at the hotel for a nap and call them."

"I want to see Mother Joanna and Sister Brigit," Rosa demanded.

"Me, too," Ella voted. The older boys agreed. Michael slept in his mother's arms, but Robbie strapped his car seat in the van, and he hardly stirred when Nick settled him.

"Do we call you Father?" Nick asked.

"Brother Dean will work. I read your book. It's a remarkable story. I'd like to know more—the extent of the surgeries, and how you managed to become whole emotionally."

"It's all in the title: *I Met a Woman*. Of course, I met God first, but she undid me—she and her precious kids," Nick said.

Dean looked in the rear-view mirror, spotting Ella. "I bet you're Daddy's Cinderella."

She smiled. "I am, and she's Papa's little rosebud." Ella pointed to Rosa.

"Sister Brigit's eager to see you, Rosa."

"Are we there yet, Brother Dean?"

"Not too much farther, Rosa. Do you see the Cross over there? That's the Cathedral beside the convent." Dean slowed, took a right turn, and pulled into the parking lot. A flock of flapping black skirts descended upon the van as the sisters pulled open doors on either side, all talking at the same time.

"Sister Brigit!" Rosa cried, holding her arms out.

"Do you remember me, Rosita?"

"Do you have food for us, Sister Brigit?" The sisters laughed and urged them to come in and eat.

The family stayed in L.A. for five days, visiting the construction site for the boys' home to cut a ribbon for the Chamber and the Press and talk to the bishop. The local papers and TV stations gave excellent coverage, and word about the fundraising dinner spread throughout the surrounding area. All too soon, the night of the event arrived. "This shirt is wrong. It doesn't have any buttons," Nick complained, tugging at his sleeves.

"Come here, silly," Barb fastened his cufflinks. Nick started to fuss. "Hush, Nick, you look incredible. If you knew how sexy you look, you'd stop complaining." She helped him into his jacket.

"Why don't you take this jacket off and prove to me how sexy I look?"

"Because you'd mess up my hair, and we don't have time. Zip me." Barb turned her back. Nick's fingers moved around her back and inched around her waist. He buried his face in her hair. "Nick, cut that out." She shivered. "Please, zip me." He paused, sighing. "Please, honey?" She stood, waiting patiently. "Nick, do I have to get Missy to zip me? Look, I'll make it up to you later, I promise."

Nick zipped her up, and then he spun her around in his arms and devoured her lips. "It isn't fair. You're gorgeous. I'll hold you to that, and I'll be thinking about it all night." He looked down her modest cleavage and grinned. She shoved him away gently. "Don't you forget, now, promise?" He ran a lingering finger down her neckline.

She laughed. "I promise. Now let me repair my makeup."

"You don't need makeup, Barb. You don't even need clothes. In fact, I like you better without them, but that dress is incredible. What color is that? Your eyes look green tonight."

"Rose. It's called rose—kind of a pinky-red. Missy and Julie helped me pick it out. Come on, the reception is starting." They hurried out the door. Feeling Nick's hand on her waist as they walked down the hall, Barb caught her breath.

"I'm scared to death you know, Barb," he confessed, pushing the button for the elevator.

"You've worked on your speech for days. We've prayed and prayed. You've prayed with Taylor and Ian. Do you think God brought you to this place to fail?"

He shrugged. "Do you think He brought me to this place?"

The elevator dinged, and the doors slid open, revealing a car full of people. Barb waved it on and waited until it lumbered down. "Yes, Nick. I *know* God brought you here. Mother Joanna knows He brought you here. The boys of South L.A. need you. You can do this, Nick, by the power of God. I'll be right beside you."

Nick reached out and pushed the down button again, listening to the hum in the shaft as a car drew nearer. "Yeah, you're right. I wouldn't be here if I didn't think that, but I don't feel it."

"That's when we walk by faith, Nick. Walk and reach for His hand, and He will hold your hand, immediately. Remember Missy's song?"

The door slid open, and Missy faced the people in the car, smiling. "Which song is that?" she asked.

"'Immediately,'" Barb replied.

Missy began to sing, and Nick felt the tension let go of his neck and back. Barb squeezed his hand, and he smiled at her. "You look gorgeous, Barb. I told you that scooped neckline would show off your beautiful neck," Missy said. Nick groaned, and Tim laughed. The two women rolled their eyes. "Jimmy and Daddy are waiting upstairs for a bit, until the end of the cocktail hour," Missy informed them.

"Taylor said these Catholics insist, and it'll make money for the Home," Nick answered.

The doors slid open to a lobby full of chattering people in evening attire—women in gowns with furs draped around their shoulders, men in tuxedos, and waiters weaving around the crowd with trays of drinks and appetizers. Nick slipped his hand in Barb's.

Mother Joanna bore down on them. "Here you are, Nickie. I want you to meet some people." She skillfully worked the crowds, knowing the wealthy people who supported her many and varied charities. Nick swallowed, putting his arm around Barb's waist and holding her tightly to his side. Before long, he loosened his grip, chatting amiably with first one man and then another as Barb spoke with women who would have considered her first little house a slum dwelling.

Barb spotted Mike. "Look, Nick. Mike and Clare are here."

Nick's face split into a wide grin as Mike made his way through the crowd like a salmon swimming upstream. "Hey, buddy," Mike slapped his back. "What a good crowd you've got here." Leaning in, he whispered, "Looks like the kind of people who can make this happen, Nick. And they put their pants on one leg at a time, remember."

Nick laughed and visibly relaxed. Barb mouthed "thanks," smiling at Mike. "You look right at home, Clare," she said.

"New York, Los Angeles, Washington—same people, same game. You gotta do what you gotta do, Barb. We're proud to be here. At least this is a cause we believe in—a cause we can get behind. It's going to be a good night. We prayed, and God gave us such peace. Nick's going to hit these people like a bomb!"

"That's what I'm afraid of." Barb giggled. "I never know what he'll say."

"Most of the time, he says exactly what God puts in his mouth. You know Amos didn't sound like Isaiah, and Peter didn't sound like Paul.

God uses all of us as He created us," Mike said.

"Spoken like someone who has never been embarrassed to tears by that man," Barb complained good-naturedly.

"Ah, but you love him just the way he is," Clare responded, laughing and pulling her into a hug. "You look gorgeous, by the way. I'm surprised you made it down here with every hair in place and your makeup perfect."

"It was a battle, and it took repairs, believe me!"

"And a promise for later, right?" Clare said. Barb nodded, her eyes shining. "Me, too. Isn't it great?" Clare whispered.

The doors to the dining room swung open, and the crowd surged forward. Barb looked around. Taylor made his way toward them, taking her arm and steering her off to the side where his wife, Adelaide, waited with a serene smile. "You look lovely, honey," Adelaide said. "We can go through this side door up to the head table." The Wilsons led the way, moving quickly.

God, please don't let me fall and make a fool of myself or shame Nick in front of all these people, Barb pleaded. *I won't be beside Missy, Julie, or even Clare.*

As if he read her thoughts, Nick stopped and came back to her side. "After me, love," he said, placing his hand on her waist and steering her forward. He winked. "You okay?" She nodded mutely, following Taylor's confident stride and straightening her spine. "Take a deep breath."

She obeyed. "Are you good, Nick?" Barb asked.

"Walking on water, holding His hand," he replied. "These aren't my kind of people either, Barb."

"Like Mike said, they put their pants on one leg at a time," she said, adding, "Doesn't Clare look ravishing?"

"She doesn't hold a candle to you, babe." Barb rolled her eyes, and Nick chuckled. "It's true, wife!"

Barb felt beautiful, basking in the glow of his adoring eyes. "Missy said the Marshalls arrived about five," she said.

"I bet Alan's floating five feet off the ground," Nick said. When Barb realized where she was, Nick was holding her chair, and she faced a grand ballroom full of people. She sucked in her breath, and he patted her shoulder.

Taylor leaned over to Nick, and they whispered about plans and timing. The waiters stood at the ready, and after the Bishop rose to give an invocation and said the grace before the meal, they moved swiftly into action. Servers smoothly set prime rib, steaming roast potatoes, and delicately-flavored grilled vegetables in front of them. "I hope this cow doesn't moo when I cut it," Nick whispered.

Barb put a napkin to her lips to cover a smile. "It's tender," she replied.

He grunted. "Should be. It cost an arm and a leg."

After the meal, Taylor took to the podium to introduce Nick. Nick squirmed under Taylor's compliments and shrugged, rolling his eyes at Barb. She smiled and took his hand under the table, playing with his fingers. He stood, and Taylor hugged him, patting his shoulder. "Go get 'em, tiger. Do it for the boys," Taylor whispered. Mother Joanna bowed her head quietly and fingered her rosary in her lap, under the table. Barb strained to see her friends, but the lights shone into her eyes, making the faces in the audience a blur.

Nick gave no indication of any hesitation, launching into his prepared speech with calm conviction. He had agonized for weeks over his remarks, going over them again and again. He discussed them over the phone with Jonah, not wanting Ian, Mike, or Taylor to hear what he would say about them. Nick moved the audience to tears and laughter. He made off-the-cuff comments that charmed everyone, flashing that one-of-a-kind persona. And he radiated the love of God.

When Nick sat back down, Barb stood and moved to the podium, waiting as Taylor adjusted the microphone. Since she and Nick were about the same height, he didn't change it much and simply patted her shoulder and grinned at a surprised Nick, holding his hand up to stop Nick's unspoken question. When Nick's comment about her luscious legs picked up on the mic and the audience erupted in laughter, Taylor shook his head at the sound techs wanting them to turn his mic off. The audience loved the interplay between Nick and Barb.

Mike jogged up to the platform when Barb sat down. Taylor introduced the famous author, Mike Green. "When Nick realized we were coming tonight," Mike began, "he told us to skip the trip and send the money." Waiting until the laughter died, he added: "As if I could miss this big night with my friend. I promised him I'd double the fares my wife and I paid to fly from New York in donations, and I challenge you tonight to at least match any money you spent to come to this event. Tonight, we've flowed in from San Antonio, Houston, New York, West Virginia, Minneapolis, San Diego, and more places than I know, all to support the Sister Marie Teresa Home for Boys.

"Like Barb, Ian, and Missy, I feel privileged to be a part of the amazing story of what God did with a fatherless, abused street kid from South L.A.," Mike continued. "When Nick does his usual speaking, he shows photos of his beautiful family." Mike pointed to a family portrait on large screens on both sides of the platform. The audience applauded. "His beautiful Rosa, he tells us, looks like his mother." The crowd gasped in admiration as Rosa's photo flashed on the screens. "When Michael was born, Jimmy and I asked where his size came from." A photo of their big, chubby boy filled the screen, and the audience chuckled. "Nick told me: 'Who knows how big I would've been if my mother had eaten regularly when she was pregnant, and if I had real food as a boy growing up.'

"I confess, I never thought much about the children in America who grow up hungry—the boys like Nick, who haunt the alleys and garbage cans to find food. We've enjoyed a meal tonight these kids cannot imagine. We sent food back to the kitchen because it was more than we could eat. Get out your checkbooks and think about these kids.

Even better, look at this little boy." A photo from family services files flashed up on the screens. A wide-eyed, skinny, frightened boy-Nick stared at the crowd out of sunken eyes. Barb sucked in her breath, tears flooding her eyes, and she grabbed Nick's hand. He looked down, a muscle working in his cheek. "You know that boy. You know the man he became. Write a check for that boy and for all the boys who have the potential to be the man of God he is today. I thank you, and God bless you."

Mike slipped behind Nick, patting him on the back. Leaning, he whispered in Nick's ear, "You did good, kid." Nick grabbed his hand. Mike winked at Barb and walked down the stairs to his table. Barb tried to follow his departing figure with her eyes but lost him as he disappeared into the bright lights. Nick was still clutching her hand, but he made a motion to rise. Taylor waved him back as Missy made her way to the podium. During the offering, she sang a song written for the occasion called "Suffer the Little Children." She stepped away from the microphone and hugged Nick. Signaling Taylor, Nick moved to the podium again.

"One of my spiritual fathers, Mike, who is obviously prejudiced, and Missy O'Malley, God's skylark—how could anyone resist God in those two? I got locked in a truck with her one day, and her songs shattered my hard heart. Missy's songs have brought her baby girl safely into the world and countless folks into the Kingdom." The crowd rose to its collective feet, applauding.

Nick continued, "Anything I may be today is because of their love, and their prayers. The boys who will live in this home are no different than the starving, bruised kid you saw on the screen, and God loves them. I'm not special. I'm simply chosen. I need to take a moment to tell you God has done a thorough work in that kid. Take the picture down, will you?" The screen darkened.

"Before the Bishop comes to pronounce the benediction, I want to add that I can honestly tell everyone in the sound of my voice that when

God's love flooded my heart, every trace of bitterness evaporated. I truly have forgiven every foster father, every social worker, and every teacher who ignored what was in front of them in me. They're no different than I was—in need of God. May God hear my prayers and forgive them."

Nick cleared his throat. "Let me add another P.S. My mother and the good sisters here kept me through the years. I was miraculously untouched by drugs or gangs, and I attribute that to their faithful intercession. But the day came when I had to invite God's presence into my life. On the Last Day, when we shall all behold Him, the Lamb Who was slain, we will have perfect bodies, glorious resurrection bodies, but He will bear the wounds He suffered—wounds we inflicted by our sin—for all eternity.

"When God invaded my being that day in West Virginia, He healed the invisible wounds: anger, bitterness, resentment, and inability to love. And He made me a new creation. I've heard it said that 'resentment is a poison we drink hoping it will kill someone else.' It doesn't, of course. It poisons *us*. I can stand here tonight and tell you I pray for those who hurt me, and I hold no grudge. I hold no grudge, for I am the chiefest of sinners." Nick turned to sit.

A voice broke through the darkness. Nick stepped up to the mic again as a man cried out from the back of the room. "God, I hope so, Nick! I hope to God you can forgive me!" Nick attempted to peer through the lights that blinded him, shading his eyes with one hand. He made out someone stumbling forward, tears streaming down his face. "I hope that's true," the sobbing man said as he broke out into the light and reached toward the platform. The audience watched, astonished, as he threw himself at Nick's feet, grabbing his ankles and weeping. "Have mercy on me. Forgive me," he pleaded.

Nick leaped off the stage and lifted the man to his feet. Nick drew a broken old man into his arms. The worst foster father he'd ever experienced fell to his knees again, clinging to Nick's legs. "Harry? Is that you?" Nick asked. "I'm not the one to have mercy. It is God against whom you've sinned. But I can and do forgive you, and I'll pray for you to have peace." And Nick did, lifting Harry to his feet and praying for him as the offender sobbed. Harry had read about the evening's event, purchased Nick's book, and screwed up his courage to come. And this one night changed his life for eternity.

The stunned audience members rose to their feet, craning their necks to see. Nick leaned forward, whispering in Harry's ear, and the old man nodded. Waving the Bishop down, Nick and the man of God prayed with the individual who had abused Nick as a boy, weeping with him until a tremulous smile crossed his face and he looked up. Nick hugged him, hard, and the newly born-again man shook his head. The Bishop climbed up to the podium as Nick stood, his arm tightly around the man's body.

"Tonight, we have heard of the regeneration of God, and we have witnessed the miracle of a man finding the forgiveness of God," the Bishop announced. "I don't do altar calls as often as my Protestant friends, but God is in this place tonight, and I feel compelled to offer prayer. If anyone wants to meet Nick, or I can help you with a spiritual need, please feel free to come up after I pronounce the benediction."

Hundreds of people surged forward a few moments later, and a hush lingered as the departing crowd made its way out the doors. Nick moved among the people, as did Taylor. Mike, Ian, Jimmy, Tim, and Jonah and Barb, Missy, Adelaide, Alice, Mother Joanna, and a pregnant Betsy moved among them, praying quietly and listening to weeping confessions. Barb looked up and saw Clare hovering around the edge of the crowd, and she waved her forward. With her arm around an elderly woman of obvious wealth, she told Clare she could relate to the woman.

"She didn't abuse her children physically," Barb told Clare. "But she neglected them, leaving them with nannies and sending them off to boarding schools. Talk to her, Clare. Comfort her with the comfort wherewith you have been comforted." Wide-eyed, Clare stared at Barb.

"You can do it, Clare. God will give you the words. Open your mouth wide, and He will fill it. I've never been there, but you have." Patting Clare's hand, Barb deliberately moved away, toward another crying woman.

Later, the Costases, O'Malleys, Greens, Raineses, Marshalls, and Wilsons gathered in Taylor's suite to debrief. "God did exceedingly, abundantly above all we asked or thought," Taylor exclaimed for them all. Stories buzzed around the room: salvation, forgiveness, and deliverance from abuse and bitterness.

"I helped three people choose to follow Christ!" Clare exclaimed. "That is such an incredible experience."

"And here I thought I was begging for money," Nick said.

Laughter echoed off the walls, and Missy's sweet, clear voice led them in the old hymn, "To God be the Glory, Great Things He has done . . ."

"Praise the Lord!" Missy exclaimed.

"This is the coolest night I've ever seen!" Alan exclaimed. Nick glanced over at him and saw Rachel clinging to his hand. Nick's eyes sought Jonah's, who winked.

Angela made her way over to Nick. "Thanks for bringing me, Brother Nick. I've had an amazing time. Wow!"

"Thank Mr. Wilson, honey. It was his plane you came on."

"But you invited me, personally, and made me welcome. I never would've been able to come."

"You look lovely, Angela. I'm proud to have you represent the Mountain State," Nick assured her. She grinned up at him, and he pushed her toward her date, a smiling Robbie.

Finally, the mood subdued, and families made their way back to their respective suites, promising to gather in the morning to travel together to the convent for breakfast with the sisters. Kids, being kids, crashed. But every husband collected on their wives' promises, because, tired as they all were, they were too excited to sleep until (as

Missy often said) they all slept well after.

CHAPTER 14

The Speeches

NICK'S SPEECH AT THE FUNDRAISER had been transcribed, as follows:

"Look at all these tuxes. I've never seen so many penguins in one place and under one roof in my life! That reminds me, Madre, we must take the boys in the Home to the zoo. I never went to a zoo until I became a father. I was thirty-seven years old the first time we took our kids to the zoo. Tonight, I'm going to tell you how a street punk from South L.A. came to be duded up in a get-up like this. In fact, I went from being a South L.A. street kid to a hillbilly from the mountains of West Virginia. Neither culture is known for being dressed like we are tonight. My son's girl saw him walking toward her in Houston and told her mother, 'You didn't tell me he was cute. I thought he was from West Virginia.' [Laughter]

"I'll try to make this brief and painless. I told Taylor that with all the money he charged for these tickets we could afford a real speaker, but he said I came cheaper, and then he goes and gives everybody here a free book. [Laughter] All profits from book sales support the Home, so we have more copies on sale for your sons, fathers, brothers, and friends on the table in the back. I'm not a speaker. Heck, I'm not a writer of books either. You can take it out on Taylor later. But we overcome by our testimony. What is that Scripture, honey? [Mrs.

Costas: 'We overcome by the word of our testimony and the Blood of the Lamb.'] See, she's my walking Bible. I've checked up, and she's never wrong.

"The last time I saw my mother as a child, I was five years old. Her boyfriend had thrown me against the wall and broken my arm. My neighbor called the cops. When they arrived, they allowed her to kiss me goodbye. One of them, a Hispanic guy, knelt and spoke in Spanish to comfort me, lured me with food, and took me to the hospital. Since I wouldn't let go of his neck, he rode in the ambulance with me, and during the months of surgery afterward, he visited me several times a week. Prophetically, his name was Jesús. He was the first Jesus to rescue me, and I owe him, big time. He played games with me in the hospital and taught me to laugh. I spent my first five years begging for food, scrounging from garbage cans like an alley rat. I would have walked on water for him, and after I left the hospital, I never saw him again. God knows, I'd love to find him.

"My mother was incarcerated as an accessory to child endangerment and for abuse and neglect. The state of California saw fit to place me in the foster care system. I don't remember the details of a parade of foster fathers I had, but they ranged from bad to worse, and I continued a life of survival, scrounging for food, ducking blows, and running away. I was the poster child for the most troublesome kid in the system.

"The first telephone number I remember was child welfare. I reported the abuse. It was investigated, covered up, and I either remained with my tormenter, or I was moved to another one. I spent as much time away from my so-called homes as possible. I joined every club and program the schools offered and excelled in academics, so I could go to math fairs, social studies fairs, and science fairs. And now I know I escaped drugs and violence because the prayers of my mother and these sisters kept me. Because of my size, I couldn't excel in sports, although I did spend a season in wrestling—most of the time my body was too bruised and broken to manage wrestling anyway.

"I didn't take to abuse, but fighting it ended up earning me more. Several times I was sent to rehabilitation centers for readjustment, to adapt to foster care. My best foster father was a plumber, who was a special man—a boy-whisperer, who took wounded boys and taught them to trust so they could be transitioned into a regular foster home. After eight months with this kind man, I was sent to the worst foster father I ever had and lived with daily beatings, constant verbal abuse, and endless cover-ups. I tried to defend myself, but he was such a big dude that it was a losing proposition.

"If any teacher called with suspicions about the Home, I suffered the worst beating, with the wrong end of a belt—took a chunk out of my back with the buckle. No one took me to the hospital for stitches, because he didn't want to lose the income. Untreated, it got infected. I remember pus oozing down my back. One of the other kids finally got some sort of antibiotic cream and put band-aids on it.

"We had four boys in that house, but I was by far the most rebellious. My only pleasure was getting back at my foster father, which was a self-defeating game. I lost count of how many times I called social services or ran away during my childhood. At seventeen, I ran away with my girlfriend, and we got married. My foster father found me and had the underage marriage annulled because he had a few more months of money to collect, and even more if I went to college, so he wanted me under his roof. Of course, my girlfriend's parents kept her under lock and key after that.

"I had nothing in life, so I got my transcripts—including my military test scores from school—called social services to report Nick Costas was no longer living in that home, and took off. I disappeared for good, living under bridges, in abandoned buildings, and out in the open. When I turned eighteen, I went down to the county courthouse, got my birth certificate, and enlisted in the Marines. I had managed to get my GED without being caught and walked into the recruitment station on my birthday. Basically, that's the history of a fatherless boy from South L.A. That is the type of boy we want to rescue at Marie Teresa Home for Boys.

"How did I get here tonight? God, Who, promising to return sevenfold what the enemy stole, has given me fathers. Tonight, I am going to introduce you to the men in my life who made a man of me, and the amazing woman who gave me her heart and made a father of me. The first father-figure who went out on a limb for me is my employer, Ian O'Malley. You've heard of him—he's the guy who wrote a little song called 'Brown Indian Girl.' [Applause] Stand up, Ian, where are you? [Lights on Ian O'Malley, more applause]

"Now, along with a free book, you also get a free CD with another of Ian's hits, the song 'In Your Arms.' That song changed my life as much as 'Brown Indian Girl' changed his. Ian, a committed follower of his Master, the Lord Jesus Christ, prayed long and hard about asking this heathen street punk to be the producer for O'Malley productions, but because he did, I'm here today. He said he saw some talent.

"I need to add something that's not in my written remarks. The very first man to give me a break was a tough old sergeant. That Goliath of a man took this cocky street kid with an attitude under his wing. He taught me to run a soundboard and produce USO shows. My first experience began badly—I overslept. He stormed into the barracks and pulled me onto the floor, screaming: 'Get your a . . .' I can't say that, Madre—'butt out of that bed and make it inspection-ready, then get to the mess hall, Costas! You pull this stunt again, and you won't eat for the rest of the day.' It was 5:30 a.m. The bus left at six. Did you know there is a 5:30 in the morning? [Laughter] He grabbed me by the earlobe. Any of you have a father lead you by the earlobe? It hurts! He was so big he almost had to lean down to get a good hold.

"I can't omit that crusty war veteran I loved to hate. God knows I owe him—he gave me my trade. Because he did, I ended up in Hollywood, where I first met Ian O'Malley. Back then he was a charming drunk with a heart of gold. I watched him walk the straight and narrow after he found Christ, and then I followed him to Nashville. He wrote 'Brown Indian Girl' and realized he had to contact the family he abandoned many years before. The welcome they gave their prodigal father astounded me. When Ian couldn't be separated from his loved ones, he brought me to Almost Heaven, West Virginia with him and continued to live his life before my bewildered eyes.

"Ian's daughter, Missy O'Malley Raines. [Applause as Nick waves his hand for Missy to rise] She prays all the time, about everything—no kidding. When you talk to her, she starts talking to God, right in the middle of a sentence. It's confusing sometimes, but you get used to it. Her crazy brother, Jimmy O'Malley—go ahead, stand up, Jimmy. [Applause as Jimmy stands] He is as insane as she is and as committed to excellence in performance as his father is.

"God was getting my attention through the lives of this incredible family: a wife who welcomed her prodigal husband home after twenty years of abandonment, a son who forgave an abusive dad, and a daughter who paid a horrific price for living in a fatherless home. I saw love and laughter instead of hatred and bitterness, and it was confusing, to say the least. Locked into a truck with an angel, hearing her touch heaven with her siren song, I first felt God squeeze my heart.

"Then, Missy and her husband dumped me into the home of another fanatic. Mike Green was a recent follower of Christ, and as contagious as only new converts can be. He sat up with me long into many nights, patiently answering my questions and knocking down my arguments until finally praying me home. My second father, best-selling author, Mike Green. Stand up, Mike. [Applause as Mike stands] Now, if Taylor wanted a book written, this is the guy he should have gotten to write it!

"During those months, an attractive widow began invading my space, though I tried manfully to keep her out. The first time I noticed Barb was at church. She was wearing Camo, and her hair was all tight behind her head. She had clunky boots on—looked like she might swing the other way, if you know what I mean. Can I say that, Madre? [Laughter] She was rude to me that day. But later, I found out she was feeling bad about leaving her kids for two weeks of Guard camp. To give you an idea of what she's made of, she was eligible for a sole surviving parent discharge from the military because her husband had been killed several years before. She was 'praying about it' because she didn't want to 'abandon her post.'

"The next time I ran into Barb, she was in the pouring rain, trying to change a tire, with a screaming baby in her car. What red-blooded American male can drive past a damsel in distress, right? So, I pull over and change the tire. She insisted we go to eat. She was wearing a pink dress, her soft blonde hair curled around her face, and she definitely swung my way. [Laughter] But she was an uptight church-lady—nice, but naïve and innocent—not my type!

"From there, I kept running into Barb. We live in a small town, and she went to my church. The next time I ran into her, she was near tears. What red-blooded American male can resist a [Nick cocks his head, urging the crowd with a wave, and the audience responds: 'damsel in distress.']. She's all forlorn-looking, sitting in Subway, trying to find a job to support her three kids.

"As we eat, Barb confronts me with the claims of Christ. Have you ever noticed when God sets His sights on you, every time you turn around, one of His kids is in your face? I told her He didn't want a loser like me, and she said God loves losers—He chooses losers. Look at Sampson, she said (had never heard of him), or Gideon (who is he?) . . . How about David, the baby of the family? I had been reading some of the Psalms, so I knew about him, but she told me he was a murdering adulterer! Who woulda thought? She placed her hand on mine to urge me to consider God, because He wanted me, and lightning struck. I never responded to a woman like that. But she was much too good for me—again, not my type.

"Jimmy O'Malley had sold his garage to work with his dad, Ian, and the buyer was looking for a business manager, so I took Barb to apply. After she got the job, she asked me if I could help her fix a faucet. By the end of the evening, her faucet was fixed, and her kids had stolen my heart, even though I knew she was too good for me and way out of my reach. By the way, I went home and looked those dudes up—the coward, Gideon, ended up some okay, but I could relate to that Sampson. I sure knew my share of Delilahs, which is why I kept running.

"Even after Father God had captured my heart and brought me into His Kingdom, I ran from Barb, because she knew the Bible backward and forward while I could hardly find the Gospels, and because I had led a life she could not imagine—an R-rated movie she would never even go see. My life was a series of bad relationships as I sought the love and meaning only God can give.

"I argued with God—I told Him He wasn't fair or even nice to give me an attraction to a woman beyond my reach. Yet, somehow, I kept getting distinct vibes that she had feelings for me. I even went to a doctor to find out the diseases I had that I might give her if we got together, to turn me away from her, but all my tests came back clean. On Alice's birthday, Ian sang 'In Your Arms' in church, and Mike and I both proposed to our now wives that afternoon. My adventures with God stepped up as God plunged me into fatherhood. The demands of being a decent father and a tolerable husband drove me to my knees, where I will stay, for I am a debtor.

"Taylor Wilson, here on the dais, came into our lives when our Rosa was on the way and we were looking for a larger house. Without knowing us, his generosity enabled us to have a home we never could have afforded. Not content to 'merely' provide an entire house for a war widow, about a year and a half later, he came personally to bring a message from God to this struggling father—now of five! Michael was about a month old then, right? [Mrs. Costas nods] He and my wife conspired to find my long-lost mother.

"That brought me to the Convent of the Angels to share my mother's last few hours on this earth, and into the formidable presence of Mother Joanna and her indomitable sisters. I owe Taylor, big time. He blessed me as a father, and he later saved my life, which is a long story—is Doc Marshall here? [Waves to Dr. Jonah Marshall] And he won't leave me alone—he makes me write a book, drags me to a men's summit, and the next thing I know I'm talking to people. Imagine . . . me—a fatherless street punk who has nothing to say but what God has done, and what He can do with anyone who puts their trust in Him.

"Now Taylor is throwing this fancy shindig to raise money for the Sister Teresa Home for Boys, and he tells me I have to wear this penguin suit. I tell him a nice suit will do fine. I've never worn one of these straitjackets before. 'If I must be tried by a jury of my peers, I say, why do I have to wear this?' He has no mercy. He says I need new peers, and the peers who can help me build a home for boys wear these clothes. So, that's why I'm in a tux tonight, for these boys. I couldn't find the buttons on this shirt, so my wife had to put these thingies in. What do you call these, honey? ['Cufflinks,' Mrs. Costas supplies. More crowd laughter]

"I'll do anything God asks me to do for these boys, because I have been there, alone and scared, and God has brought me into a large place—a place of family, a place of love and acceptance. Why do I do this? Because I'm a debtor—a debtor to God, of course. But I also owe those who put skin on Him: Ian, a man who loves His Master; Missy, a woman who brings us into His presence; Mike, who refused to give up on this sinner; and my beautiful wife, Barb, who chose to love me, to believe for me, and to survive the culture shock I brought to her well-ordered world. They make me into a man God can use, and so too does Taylor, who keeps pushing me into perfection.

"I'm no different than any of the abandoned, abused boys God will bring to this sacred place we are building. With love and patience, God can make them men after His own heart, and you can make this dream come true. You can be God with skin on for the street kids of South

L.A. I ask you, I beg you, to do unto these little ones as you would the Son of God Himself. Thank you."

Barb's speech at the fundraiser had also been transcribed, as follows:

"I, too, am here because of Taylor, and I know Nick. I'm here to give you 'the other side of the story.' To hear Nick, you'd think I'm some saint—some virtuous woman without fault who did everything for him. [Audience laughter as Nick nods vigorously] But at the time when Hurricane Nick hit my life, I was a mess. I was depressed and worried about how to support three kids, and my sons were worse.

"My son Robbie, almost thirteen, was angry and bitter—angry with a father who left him, and angry with God for taking him away. Nick poured himself into my children. Nick absorbed Robbie's hostility and simply loved him. When I questioned how Nick did what he did, or even why he did it—loving my son time after time and returning good every time Robbie shut him out—he would say, 'I was a troubled kid once, too. I treat him the way I wanted to be treated.' You see, I had memorized 'Do unto others as you would they should do unto you,' but Nick lived it.

"As for my son Alan, he hardly spoke. He was drawn into himself, quiet and timid. Nick laughed with him, loved him, and didn't require him to say a lot. He waited for and loved and played with Alan. He laughed with him, taught him to play baseball, and kept loving him until Alan became a little boy. [Pause. Taylor hands Barb a handkerchief. She blots her eyes.] And the first time Nick came to the house—the day he fixed the faucet—he played with all my kids in the hose. [Nick: 'She had on shorts. She's got the most luscious legs.' Laughter. Taylor: 'Your mic's on, buddy.' Barb blushes, fiddling with her papers.]

"I'm no speaker. Nick talks all the time—nonstop—and he'll say anything, as you can tell. Um, let's see . . . oh, yes. My daughter Ella was born after my prior husband's, Bob's, death, and she'd never known a father. She was terrified of men and refused to go near them.

When Nick came to our house, she squirmed out of her car seat and ran over to him, holding up her arms and saying, "Uppie, Unca Nick." She'd heard Missy's kids, and Jimmy's, call him that in our church nursery, and she called him that until we married. Almost immediately after we married, she started to call him 'Daddy.' She adored him. She still does. We all do, but my kids chose Nick before I did.

"To explain to Robbie how lucky he was to have had a father like Bob, Nick told him about his foster home experiences. Robbie had accidentally seen the scars on Nick's back—scars he kept hidden. And he told me later that night that God wanted our family to teach Nick the love of a family—a love he'd never known. I had never thought to marry again, but Nick's influence on my sons, the way my kids loved him and responded to him, made me realize I couldn't raise them by myself. When I prayed, God dropped this overwhelming love in my heart for His beloved son, Nick Jo Costas.

"I wish every one of you could know my husband—a man who loves God with the passion of one who has been forgiven much. He's absolutely right—I was a naïve church-lady when I met him. I was raised in church. I was the winner of every sword drill first-place ribbon and every Bible Memory award. I watched the way he changed after he surrendered to God—the explosion of God's Life in him and the way he fed upon the Word. He absorbed it like a sponge. It was his textbook—his instruction book. He researched it, and he *lived* it.

"I will tell you one more story, about my mother-in-law. Bob's mother had a hard time with Nick. He's the only Hispanic in our county, and we are not a diverse culture, to say the least. Even Missy's mother, Alice O'Malley, had a hard time as a Native American, and they were in West Virginia long before us white people. But Nick's worst flaw in my mother-in-law's, Pat's, eyes was that he isn't Bob. Robbie said his grandmother made an idol of Bob and worshipped at his shrine. Pat saw Nick as a predator—an illegal, after the benefits the children received— and she reported us to Children's Protective Services.

"Pat continued being hostile, degrading, and insulting toward Nick until the day he took Robbie to her house to cut the grass, when they found her on the floor, blue and gasping. She'd had a heart attack. Nick saved her life by giving her CPR, and when they evacuated her to Charleston by helicopter, Nick and Robbie drove my father-in-law across the state to be with her. That night, my father-in-law began his journey to God, and now he and Pat are both are active in church. Robbie called to tell me how Nick was with his grandfather, and how he had been with his grandmother that afternoon. Robbie said, 'Mom, I've heard WWJD all my life, but I've never seen anybody live it like Nick does. He turns the other cheek, returning evil with good, and forgives as a habit.' When they got home I told Nick what Robbie had said, and he asked me, 'What does that mean—WWJD?'

"All my life I had a head-knowledge of Scripture. I loved Jesus, but when Hurricane Nick blew into my life by the wind of God's Spirit, I encountered a more profound kind of knowledge—a man who loves God with all his heart and allows God to live in him, speak through him, and love through him. This home for boys is his dream. It's not just a place to live or a government handout but instead a place where boys will experience a life-changing encounter with the love of Christ. I pray these boys will come to live out Christ the way Nick does, and all South L.A will see the Living God."

CHAPTER 15

Barbara Rose

BETSY HAD FELT uncomfortable all evening, but she was glad she hadn't said anything to Jonah because he was called out about ten o'clock. He kissed her and asked her if she was okay, and she told him she was fine. He ran down the stairs. Betsy always wondered how anyone that tall could be as light on his feet.

Sighing, she rolled over and tried to make herself comfortable. By two in the morning, she gave up and wandered downstairs. She fixed a cup of tea and sat at the counter in the kitchen. She stood, stretching backward, her hands behind the small of her back, and her water broke. She grabbed a towel, threw it on the floor, and slowly climbed the stairs. She knocked on Rachel's door and pushed it open. "Honey, you're going to have to drive me to the hospital. Daddy isn't here, and my water broke."

Rachel sat up in bed. She hopped up, turned on the light, and looked at her mother with wide eyes. "What do I do? Can I help you?"

Betsy was pale, and her hands were behind her, resting on the small of her back. "First, help me change and get me a pad. Then you need to dress and take me to the hospital. I—" She gasped.

"Jesus, I need you now," Rachel said. She took her mother by the arm and helped her down the hall to her bathroom. Rachel sat Betsy on the toilet, fetched a pad, and helped her clean up. "Are you okay here while I get dressed?" Betsy nodded. "Do you want me to help you to bed?"

"Just go, Rach." Rachel gave one look at her mother's face and took off down the hall, hollering for Jacob and returning in no time. Betsy chuckled, despite her discomfort. She'd never seen her teenage daughter as thrown-together. She stood and gasped again.

"Are we going to make it, Mom?" Rachel asked.

Betsy tried to laugh, but it came out a half-sob. "We've got plenty of time, honey. My suitcase is packed." She pointed beside the door.

Jacob was dressed and ready to go. He picked up the suitcase and helped Rachel get their mother down the stairs.

"Can you go in my little car, Mom?" Rachel asked. "I'm scared to drive the van."

Betsy nodded. "Maybe you'd better get some towels for your seat, though," she suggested. Rachel ran back into the house, returning with a stack of towels, which she placed on her mother's seat.

"Have you called Dad? We don't want him coming home when we're on the way to the hospital," Jake asked as he lowered his mother down on the front passenger seat and climbed in back.

"Good idea, Jake," Rachel said as she tossed him her cell phone and backed the car out of the garage. "Maria *would* be out of town," she grumbled. "I thought you weren't due for another week." Rachel glanced over at her mother and saw her biting her lip. She sped up. "I'm running every red light. Maybe a cop will give us an escort." But no cop appeared as they raced down the dark streets of Houston.

"Dad said to come around to Emergency, Rach. He'll meet us there," Jacob reported.

When they pulled in, Jonah was waiting in his green scrubs. Opening the door, he helped Betsy out and scooped her into his arms. "Park the car and meet us on the OB floor, Rachel. You did a good job." Jonah moved toward the hospital entrance with his wife's head buried in his neck. "You had to have been feeling poorly before I left, Betts.

128

Why didn't you tell me?" She moaned. "Breathe, honey." Jonah pushed open the doors, bellowing for a wheelchair. "I told the nurses to call Sam," he said. "How often? Have you timed them?"

"Uh, pretty fast," Barb answered.

Jonah pushed the nurse aside, grabbed hold of the wheelchair, and moved it rapidly toward the elevator. When they got up to the OB floor, he followed a beckoning nurse, lifted his wife out of the chair, and lowered her onto the birthing chair. The nurse began to examine her, and Jonah moved to the sink to scrub up. "Dr. Brown is on his way, Dr. Marshall," another nurse said when she came in.

When Jonah came over to stand beside the first nurse, she looked up and said, "This baby's coming fast."

"You're telling me," Betsy said, as she grabbed Jonah's hand.

Racing footsteps came down the hall. "Where's my mom?" Rachel cried. "Mrs. Marshall—where is she?"

Rachel pushed open the door, and Jacob was right behind her. "We can come in, right?" he asked. "Are you okay, Mom?"

Betsy smiled and reached her hand out to her daughter. "We told you, it's up to you whether you want to stay. Do you want to stay?" Rachel came over to take her hand, and Jacob followed.

"Just stay out of the way, kids. We have to make room for Dr. Brown," Jonah told his children. "Hand me a warm washcloth, Jake, and both of you wash your hands." Eager to have something to do, Jacob washed like he was going into surgery, warmed a cloth, wrung it out, and carried it to his father. Jonah rolled Betsy onto her side and rubbed her back. "Put it on her forehead," he directed his son. With a tenderness unbeknownst to teenage boys, Jacob softly placed the cloth.

"Thanks, Jacob," Betsy whispered.

Dr. Sam Brown entered, hurrying over to the sink. "I was hoping for a police escort when the nurse told me what was going on. How long have you labored at home, Betsy?"

She waited until she could speak. "I guess since about . . . I don't know, shortly after dinner." Jonah stared at her, opened his mouth, and closed it as she squeezed his hand, hard.

Sam examined her. "Feel like pushing?" he asked.

"Sit me up some, Jonah. Hold me." Jonah sat behind her and wrapped his arms around her. With the next contraction, she pushed.

Rachel's eyes widened when she saw the top of the baby's head appear. She looked at Jacob and reached for him. Taking her hand, he whispered, "This is awesome."

Sweat dripped down Betsy's face as she pushed and pushed. She grunted with each effort. Jacob returned with another warm cloth. Jonah took it, looking at him gratefully, and wiped her face. The teens prayed quietly, watching their mother. Before too long, their baby sister entered the world with a squall. Rachel cried and smiled. "Oh, wow. Oh, thank you, God."

Jonah gently lowered Betsy and reached for the scissors. "She's beautiful, Mommy," he said. As soon as the nurse clamped it off, he cut the cord and placed their new daughter on Betsy's tummy. Her hands surrounded his as she reached for the baby.

Betsy looked up at her husband. "She is beautiful, Jonah."

"How could she not be, with a mother like she's got? Thank you, Betts."

"You did fine, Betsy. Just a few stitches, probably not even necessary," Sam said. He turned to the teens. "You guys did fine. Pretty neat, isn't it, to watch a new life come into the world? It's the best part of my job."

"Yes, sir," Jacob said. "I felt like God was right here with us."

"Me, too," Rachel said. "Wow."

Sam grinned. "I'll check on you later, Betsy."

"Thanks, Sam," Jonah said.

"You almost had to catch your own baby, Jonah." Sam chuckled, gave a wave, and left.

"Why don't you two let us get your mother cleaned up?" one of the nurses suggested. "Go make some calls. She'll be in 217 in a few minutes."

Rachel tiptoed to the bedside and dropped kisses on her mother and her baby sister. "She is gorgeous, Mom. Look, Jake." Barbara Rose stretched and shuddered.

Jacob grinned. "You didn't even scream, Mom."

Jonah chuckled. "She never did. She's a trooper, your mom." He looked at her proudly. When the nurse wanted to take the baby, he said, "I'll hold her." Usually, the staff carried the babies, but the whole hospital revered Dr. Jonah Marshall, and no one would argue with him.

"Call Barb and Missy," Betsy called after her teenagers.

"We will, Mom," Rachel said, as she and Jacob moved off into the waiting area. "Wanna go eat, Jacob?" The teenagers went down to the cafeteria. They called Barb, who told them she'd call Missy, and then Rachel talked to Alan for a long time.

* * *

The next time Nick and Barb saw the Marshalls, they'd flown in to Houston for the christening of Barbara Rose Marshall. Of course, Jacob, Rachel, and Alan stood beside them in a circle surrounding the fair-skinned, blue-eyed beautiful baby in her flowing, white eyelet christening gown. Jonah held her in the curve of his long arm, with his other arm firmly clasping his wife to his side.

Rachel slipped her hand in Alan's and whispered, "Isn't she beautiful?"

He smiled. "And you love her more than you could have imagined, right?" he whispered back.

Barbara Rose gave a most unladylike scream when the cold water splashed on her forehead. Rachel's eyes were full, and she reached out her hand to touch her baby sister as the priest pronounced a blessing upon her. And later, Nick, Barb, and Alan joined the Marshalls at their home for dinner.

"I can't tell you how flattered I am that you chose that name," Barb said.

"Nick and you renewed our marriage," Jonah said. "I always loved Betsy and the kids, but I had my priorities all mixed up. I spent my life at the hospital. The kids were growing up without me, and my wife was sleeping in the guest bedroom."

"Only when you weren't home, Jonah," Betsy corrected him.

"Which was too often," Jonah said. "I watched you two in the hospital. Remember when Nick woke up and said—"

"Jonah Marshall, don't you repeat that!" Barb said.

Almost everyone laughed, because he didn't need to repeat it. Alan leaned over to Rachel and whispered, "I'll tell you later."

"It was your example that helped me to understand what a blessing my sister would be, Barb," Rachel said. "I called Alan all angry and upset that my mother was pregnant, and he reminded me about Rosa and Michael. I realized how precious they are, and I felt ashamed for not making our baby welcome."

"If she'd been a boy, we would have had to name him Alan Michael," Jonah pointed out.

"I think you should try for a boy, Dr. Marshall," Alan said. "Poor Barbie will be all alone when Jacob and Rachel go off to college, and you could balance out the boys and girls in the family. Jake, don't you want a brother?"

"I wouldn't mind. But I'll still be around for a while, Alan," Jacob said.

Dr. Marshall laughed. "You can't put in an order, Alan. Who's to say we wouldn't have a third daughter? Then I'd have to pay for three weddings! Besides, I think that's Betsy's decision." He took his wife's hand, noting she looked thoughtful. After dinner, Jonah offered to let Alan take one of the cars so that he and Rachel could take a drive. "If that's okay with you, Nick?"

Nick looked at Barb, who nodded, and he gave his consent. As they sat around after dinner, they discussed the teenagers. "Robbie told me last summer, when we were here, that he thought Rachel might be 'The One,' for Alan, and he certainly seems fond of her," Nick said.

"They've kept their computers and cell phones humming," Barb added.

"Rachel has never had a boyfriend before. Honestly, I've been worried about her because she's so intelligent. I thought it would be hard to find someone suitable," Jonah said.

Nick grinned. "Are you saying a West Virginia hillbilly might be a good match for her?"

"It's too soon to tell. They both are college bound," Jonah said.

"Alan's lifelong goal has been the Air Force Academy. He's determined that's where he's going," Barb said.

"He will, too," Nick said. "When Alan sets his sights, he's like a laser. And that's one of the reasons our families might be joined in time—because he also has his sights set on Rachel."

"It's a long haul for them. Rachel is equally as determined to spend some years studying languages abroad," Betsy said.

Maria entered the living room with a fussing baby in her arms. "She want her mama, Señora."

Betsy rose to take the baby upstairs to nurse her, returning later to rejoin the group. "Have you gotten the kids married yet?" she asked.

Jonah rolled his eyes. "God forbid. Let's give them a few years."

Barb regaled them with the tale of 'The Talk' when they were in Houston, when Alan was first smitten with the beautiful Rachel. Jonah expressed his appreciation, asking Nick about when he should do the same with his son.

"Probably now," Nick said.

"And I need to give Rach a Purity Ring before this relationship gets any more serious," Jonah added. Nick asked about that concept for his up-and-coming young ladies, and the parents discussed how much more difficult it was for today's teenagers, in an age that bombarded them with sexual content.

The teens arrived home for a light supper, and the families sat around for a few hours before Nick excused them to return to their hotel. "The dedication of the Home should be sometime this fall. Construction's coming along," he said.

"Send us an invitation," Betsy requested. "We'll try to make it. I sure would like to replicate it right here in Houston. We'll be watching closely to see how it goes."

CHAPTER 16

The Scholars

IN THE FALL, Angela and Robbie started college. Angela was enrolled in a nursing program, and Robbie signed up for theater arts. He wasn't happy in his program, arguing with Nick that he could teach him all he needed to know about sound technology. But Nick felt the degree would lend Robbie credibility. "You might not always want to work for me, Robbie," Nick said.

"But Da needs me. You are on the road a lot now," Robbie insisted.

"That's true, and we're glad to have you, but I still think—"

"It's a waste of money, Nick. I'd rather be working."

"You know fallen warriors will pay for your college. Give it a couple of semesters, and we'll see," Nick said, and they settled on that compromise. As for Alan, he approached Nick eagerly, wanting to take a night class at the college. He had made 32 on his ACT as a high school freshman. "Why are you in such an all-fired hurry, Al? You're already in advanced placement classes. Don't mess up your average by taking too much. You won't have any fun at all in high school."

"I'll serve seven years for the fair Rachel. I read about Jacob in Genesis the other day. I know I'm young, but I love her, Nick. I really do. And I figure the sooner I get through the Academy, the sooner we can get married."

Nick looked at his stepson—the brilliant kid who'd always hit the mark on every target when he took aim. "Here's the deal: go ahead, but if the load is crushing and your grades suffer, drop the course, okay?"

Alan all but danced. "Thanks, Nick." He turned to go, probably to email "fair Rachel," but stopped and turned back to look at Nick. "I was six when my father died. I don't remember him as well as Robbie does, but you've always been here for me, Nick. You're the dad I remember. You've been a good father to all of us, and we love you. I love you."

Nick pulled him into his arms, and as they were holding on to one another, Barb came into the family room. She backed out quickly, after seeing her son in an embrace with the man he called Dad. Alan would never be the big man his brother was, but he already stood two or three inches over his stepfather. Barb swiped her eyes, thanking God as she had countless times for the gift this man was to her sons.

Rosa came storming into the room. "Papa, Papa, look at this!" She waved a blue ribbon. Jumping up and down, she tugged on his arm.

Nick picked her up. "What's this for?"

Ella came behind her. "She was the first one in her class to finish ten readers, Papa."

"That's mighty fine, Rosita. Were they in Spanish or English?"

Rosa giggled. "In English, Papa. Would you put them in Spanish for me? I'll read them in Spanish." She squirmed her way down, asking where Michael was, and ran off to talk to him in rapid-fire Spanish.

Barb crossed the room. "Now you've done it. You'll have to translate every textbook she's got." She gave Nick a kiss and asked her son what their heavy discussion had been about. Nick told her his request about Alan's courses, and she shared his concern but agreed to their compromise. "Why don't you choose an easy class, say Spanish, to get the credits?"

"I thought I'd take trig to knock off a high school credit. But if they have Spanish, I could do that, too."

"*Solamente uno*, Alan. Choose one," Nick said.

"Yes, sir. Trig it will be."

136

"You're a glutton for punishment. You know that, right?"

Alan grinned. "But I have a goal, and a sweet reward."

Nick patted him on the shoulder. "That you do." He took Ella's hand. "Tell me about your day," he said, walking toward the kitchen. As they chopped veggies for the stir-fry, she told him about her 100 in math and the new kid in school. Barb trailed after them and set the table. Michael and Rosa sat cross-legged on the floor in the adjoining family room, playing fish. Generally, Barb could follow their Spanish conversations, but when they were talking this fast, she got lost.

"Michael! Do not call your sister names," Nick said.

"But I did not cheat, Papa!" Rosa protested.

Nick came and sat on his haunches, scooping up the cards. "If you can't play nicely, you can't play at all. Go help Mama set the table." Michael rubbed his sleeve against his nose and stood, looking as if he would stick his tongue out at Rosa. But one glance at his father, and he marched into the kitchen.

"I didn't cheat, Papa. He was making a pair with a queen and a jack," Rosa said.

"He got a little excited. You forgive him, right?"

"Yes, Papa. Where is Ella?"

"She is helping me in the kitchen. Come on." He gave Rosa a hand, and she scampered up. Michael was carefully folding the napkins and placing them under the forks. "Good job, Mikey," Nick said.

Looking up at Nick, he said, "Sorry, Papa."

"Can you see the difference between the jack and the queen?"

Michael nodded his head. The overhead light danced on his black hair, and he looked up with his father's chocolate eyes. Rosa's eyes were black, like her grandmother, but Michael had his father's eyes. Nick sat on a chair and held his arms out. Michael climbed onto his lap.

"We all like to win, but it's a game. Always win the right way, son," Nick continued.

"Yes, sir. I'm sorry," Michael said, resting his head against his father's chest.

Nick held him for a few minutes, then patted him and set him down. "It's Rosa you must apologize to." Michael went into the kitchen and begged his sister's forgiveness. They hugged. Nick caught Barb's eye. "You have done this all day, every day, for years. You are a saint! You must be glad Rosa's in school."

Barb chuckled, continuing to put the chicken strips into the hot oil. "Next year, Michael will be gone all day, and then what will I do?" She turned to the children. "The rice will be ready in a few minutes. Are we going for Mexican or Chinese?" They chorused they wanted Mexican, so she reached for the correct spices.

Barb smiled as Rosa smoothly transitioned to her father's language and chattered away. Nick laughed at something she said. Barb understood a lot of it now, but she still couldn't come up with the words. Michael giggled. Nick looked over at him and asked him in Spanish if he understood. "*Si* Papa," Michael said. "*Ti amo*, Papa."

Nick grinned and asked Michael a few questions, and Michael responded appropriately. Nick looked at Barb. "He doesn't lisp in Spanish, honey." He raised his palm up, and Michael slapped it.

"He said, 'high five,' Mama," Ella translated.

"I heard. It's because you read him all those storybooks in Spanish, Nick."

"Yeah, but that is the first time I've heard him chatter away like that. Good job, Mikey!"

"*Gracias*, Papa."

"He talks in Spanish all the time, Papa," Rosa said.

Alan entered the room, his head wet from his shower. "Did I hear Michael babbling away in Spanish?" They told him he had. "*Bueno*, Michael. *Esta bien*. It smells terrific in here. When do we eat?"

"We're about ready," Barb informed him.

Nick went to the refrigerator and got out jalapeño peppers, which he diced for those who would want to add them, knowing that the gringo part of his family would prefer them on the side.

* * *

The school semester settled into a comfortable routine. Barb worked on her book in the mornings while Nick was at work and the children were all in school. Sally had left the family and remarried, and the girls were in her small wedding. The phone rang, and Barb glanced at the caller ID. It was the studio. "Have you looked out the window?" Nick asked Barb from the other end of the phone. "They're letting school out. The winter storm watch has changed into an advisory."

Barb could hear excited voices and Missy shouting and laughing in the background. "What's going on?"

"I have some fantastic news," Nick said. He put a finger in one ear but still couldn't hear. "Wait a sec. Let me go out on the deck." He stepped out of the room into the cold air. "Madre called. The slumlord who owns the property across the street from the convent is donating it. That means we can build the school there."

"That's terrific! The other property we looked at was such a long bus ride for the boys. You mean where that nasty playground is?"

"And the run-down apartments. It is freezing out here! Cold as a witch's—"

"Nick!" Barb cautioned. "I'm working on a Christian book here." She heard a door open and close and Missy apologizing on the other end of the line, and then her own door opened and slammed as Ella and Rosa ran in pink-cheeked and excited, holding Michael's hand.

"Did you see, Mommy? Look! It's a great storm. Let's go over to the hill behind Missy's house."

Nick chuckled on the other end of the phone. "Tell them we need a couple of inches before they can sled. Maybe tomorrow. Missy said the radio just announced the college is canceling night classes. Tell Alan. Must be a bad one. I'll be home soon. Ian is telling me to get out of here while I can."

Alan came in the garage door, shaking snow off his head. One look from his mother and he stepped back into the garage, hanging his coat out there and knocking the snow off his boots. When he came back, Barb told him night classes were canceled. "Maybe Robbie will be home at a decent hour tonight," she said. Sure enough, she heard the roar of her oldest son's truck pulling into the drive, and she heard stomping in the garage. Robbie came in, grabbed each girl, and swung them in the air, and then he threw Michael so high Barb gasped.

"I wish you wouldn't do that, Robbie!" Michael giggled and demanded that he do it again. She shook her head.

Robbie sniffed. "What's that delicious smell?"

"Potato soup. Papa's on his way home. I'll fix some grilled cheeses. How fun to have everyone home in the middle of the day." She pulled open the floor-to-ceiling drapes and looked out. "It's dark out there!"

"This is going to be a big one," Robbie said. "I need to change. I got soaked walking to the parking lot." He headed upstairs while the girls stood beside their mother, peering into the swirling flakes. Mikey ran after his brother, who scooped him up into his arms and took the stairs two at a time.

"Please don't take the steps like that with him in your arms, Robbie," Barb called.

Robbie flashed a smile, reduced his steps to one at a time, and chucked Michael under the chin. "You are getting a bit hefty there, big guy." Their voices drifted off as they went down the upstairs hall.

"Mommy, could we make popcorn balls?" Ella asked.

"After lunch, I'll see if I have corn syrup. You girls set the table."

Ella carefully counted out enough utensils for everyone to have a place while Alan flipped the grilled cheeses and stacked them on a platter. "I need to take some pictures for Rachel. I wish she could see this," he said.

Nick came in, snow glistening like diamonds on his dark hair. He pulled Barb into his arms and put his cold nose on her neck. She tried to push him away as his freezing hands inched under her sweater. "Quit that, Nick!"

He laughed, gave her a gentle swat on her bottom, squatted down, and stretched out his arms for his girls. They bowled him over with their hugs, and he landed on the floor in a heap of giggles. "Where's Mikey?" he asked.

"Me, too, Papa, me, too," Michael cried, running down the stairs. He flung himself onto the pile, and Nick rolled around on the floor with the younger children. He sat up, hair mussed and clothes askew.

Barb and Alan carried food to the table. Robbie lifted the tureen of soup and took it to the table. "This smells scrumptious, Mom."

"Better see if we have any diced peppers in the refrig," she said.

Alan returned to the kitchen area, then he came back to set the platter of sandwiches on the table. He helped Michael to the table while the girls scurried to their chairs. The electricity of the storm seemed to invigorate the entire family.

Barb looked around her table, realizing she wouldn't have everyone together much longer. She felt bittersweet and let out a soft sigh, her eyes full. She saw Nick watching her. He nodded quietly and reached out his hands. The family bowed in prayer. "Tell the children your news, Nick," Barb said, and he did.

"You mean that ugly old playground across the street will be gone?" Rosa asked.

"Yep," Nick said.

"So, he gets a big tax write-off, and the boys get an academic center. That works for me," Robbie said, reaching for another sandwich. "And I make extra money while y'all travel to raise the funds. It's a win-win for me. What are you going to do with the girls now that Sally's gone? Alan, do you think we can manage, between the two of us?"

Barb looked up, alarmed. "What is this, Nick?"

He set his spoon down. "We have a few speaking opportunities.

Jonah has his Houston conference worked out, and we have a big church in Pensacola that's extended an invitation, plus a few more along the way."

"I can't possibly go during the school year," she said.

"And I can't possibly do this without you, Barb. We'll take the little ones. Maybe they can take their schoolwork with them. We'll pray about it. God will work something out."

The family played games that afternoon, made popcorn balls, and fell into quiet activities that evening. Early the next morning, Nick heard Robbie quietly tiptoeing down the stairs. Nick stepped out of his and Barb's bedroom door and looked up as the young man held a finger to his lips and came down, boots in his hand. "Shh. I've got snow removal contracts, Nick. I bought a plow for my truck, and I'm off to make some dough."

Nick nodded. "Good plan. We'll have breakfast ready for you when you get back." He heard Robbie's truck rumble down the driveway, plowing their road on his way. He slipped back into the bedroom, went to the bathroom, and crawled under the warm covers with his wife. Propped up on his elbow, he looked at her and couldn't resist curling one of her golden curls around his brown finger.

At the gentle tug, she opened her eyes. "Did I hear someone go out?"

Nick pulled her into his arms, explaining where Robbie had gone. "I see you thinking that our boys are pulling away."

Her eyes filled. "They are, Nick. They'll be gone from us soon. They're eager to be on their own."

"That's what we raise them for—to grow up and follow after God," he replied. "And you've done a good job. They are fine, strong men."

"But Alan is still in high school," she mourned.

"When he was nine, he was nine going on twenty-nine, sweetie."

"He was, wasn't he?"

"But I'll never grow up and leave you," he teased, trailing his fingers down her neck. "We'll get old together, and I will always love you, my gringo girl." He chuckled as he drew her into his arms.

"What?"

"I never dated gringos. I thought they had no passion," he explained. "But here you give me two children in less than two years. I got passion, baby!" Barb giggled and pulled his face down for a torrid kiss.

Later, she heard Nick up, quickly turning the lock of their door. He disappeared into the bathroom with his clothes. "I hear the kids," he said.

Barb squinted in the sunlight streaming through their windows and moaned. "Why are they up this early?" she asked as she heard knocks on the door.

"Get up, Mommy. We want to sled! Let's go to Jeri's," her girls chorused.

Barb hurriedly pulled on sweatpants and a sweatshirt. "We aren't going anywhere at eight o'clock in the morning, girls," she said through the door.

Nick went out to the hall. "But we can fix Mommy's breakfast."

When the phone rang, Barb answered it. "Get your butts over here," Missy said. "These kids are dying to go sledding. I've got cinnamon rolls in the oven, and Tim wants to know how many eggs."

"We're on our way," Nick said from the kitchen phone.

"I'll bring a dozen. We need ten—twelve if Alan comes," Barb said from the bedroom phone. She could hear squealing from her kitchen and from Missy's. Hanging up, she walked into the kitchen and pointed to the stairs. "We're eating at Jeri's. Go get your ski pants on."

Nick's white teeth flashed on his brown face. "We still got a few more years, Mommy. I'll get Michael." And he chased the girls up the stairs.

His hair standing straight up, Alan met them at the top. "What's going on?"

"We're headed to the Raines's to go sledding. Want to come?"

Nick asked.

"Nope, thanks. I'll take the day to study—especially if you take the noisy rabble away."

"Aw, come on, Alan," Ella begged.

He ran his fingers through her curls. "No thanks, squirt. I've got a paper to write."

For the duration of the storm, Barb gathered her chicks under her wings and felt cozy in her nest, knowing they would start flying away too soon. Even as she laughed with Missy and Julie and watched their antics from the back window, she felt the tug at her heartstrings. She told her friends about her mixed emotions, and they echoed her feelings. Jamie was off at Julliard, and Maryanne joined the winter fun reluctantly. Willow and Sean, Julie's caboose baby, were the only ones still eager to play in her family. Meanwhile, lanky Todd Raines watched over his petite sister, Jeri.

Missy let the window curtain slip through her fingers. "You guys are making me sad. Cut it out. New every morning is His love. God will have new adventures for us."

"Speaking of that, Miss," Barb said, "Nick told me we have to travel, and we need to pray about the little ones. I can't leave them, because they have school. He wants to see if we can take their lessons with us, but I work hard at these conferences, too, and I can't teach them."

"I heard the Andersons' daughter is in town applying for a job with the school system. They've been missionaries in Argentina. She grew up there, but when they went to Springfield to take the job as head of the missions department at the university, she wanted to come here. What's her name, Julie?" Missy asked.

"Gee . . . Ellen or Edith—something like that," Julie said. "I can get her number from the church office. She's been here about a week now, I think. She's staying with her aunt."

The three women prayed together. Barb said, "Don't say anything to Nick yet. He'd be thrilled to have a Spanish-speaking tutor for his kids."

Soon, it was settled. Barb and Nick left their two older scholars at home and took the three little students off on the bus with them and a thrilled Spanish-speaking teacher, Edith, who felt like she was still in ministry and surrounded by the beautiful rhythms of the language of her childhood. The children adored her. She got textbooks in both languages, set up desks in the bus, and prepared her school-on-the-road. Edith thought God answered prayer exceedingly abundantly, above all she could ask or think, and her little students thought so, too.

CHAPTER 17

On the Road

NICK HAD INCORPORATED HIS MINISTRY, torn between naming it "Abounding Love Ministries" or "Abounding Grace Ministries." He settled on "Abounding Love," using the tagline, "Where love abounds, grace abounds" for his website. When the hired driver drove, he worked on his posts, and Barb plodded away with her book. Hearing her sigh, Nick looked up. "You work too hard. Let Taylor's editors do the cleanup."

She pushed her hair back. "Missy always says excellence brings glory to God. I want to do it right, so He gets the glory. But I'm no writer. I can't do this."

"You can do all things through Christ who strengthens you," Nick replied.

She shot him a glare. "Don't you quote Scripture to me."

He bent over where she sat cross-legged on the bed and dropped a kiss on her head. "May I ask who's talking?" He chuckled. "I'll go get you a cup of tea and see where we are." He returned with her tea. "About a couple of hours from Pensacola. The church has rented us two hotel rooms, so you can soak in a hot tub tonight."

"Praise God from whom all blessings flow," Barb said, reaching up for the tea and leaning back against the pillows. "How are the girls doing?"

"Edith has Ella writing, Rosa reciting, and Michael asleep."

"That girl is worth her weight in gold." Barb straightened her legs. Nick moved her laptop and took her feet in his hands, rubbing them softly. She leaned into the pillows, letting her breath out in a long, contented sigh. "Are you ready for tonight?"

"It's a new group. I'll give the standard pitch." Nick moved up beside her against the pillows on his side of the bed and took her hand. He began to pray, and Barb joined him. They stopped again in Mobile, Alabama and in New Orleans, Louisiana. Taylor's secretary emailed them their changing itineraries as she arranged new places. And they pulled into Houston the day before the conference there. Betsy met them at the hotel, explaining that Jonah would be over later.

"How can anyone look so graceful pregnant, Betsy?" Barb wanted to know.

"*You* were beautiful when you carried *our* babies, *mi amor*," Nick said.

Barb rolled her eyes and herded the kids into the double doors.

Nick peeled the driver's wages off a roll of bills and gave him the next three days off, although he was welcome to attend the conference, if he wished. Since he had relatives in Houston, he'd be staying with them. Nick then followed the women into the lobby. Betsy held Ella's hand, and Rosa clung to her mother. Edith had Michael, but when he saw his father, he rubbed his eyes and reached for him. Nick swung him into his arms as they headed to the elevator.

"We already have your keys, Nick," Betsy said, directing the bell-man to their rooms. "Taylor says to turn in a receipt for your driver." She told Ella which floor to push. "Alan gets in at seven, and Jonah is swinging by the airport to pick him up. How's Robbie?"

The ladies chatted, the girls plopped down in front of the TV, and Edith disappeared into her room. The girls would sleep on the other double bed in there, and Michael would be in Alan's room next door. Nick sat on the couch, leaned his head back, and closed his eyes. He heard nothing else until Jonah arrived with Alan. Standing, he stretched out his hand and shook Jonah's. "You ready for this, Jonah?"

Alan looked around. "Where's Rachel?" he asked.

Jonah grinned. "She's on her way with Barbie and Jacob. They'll be here soon." His phone chirped. "In fact, they're waiting downstairs. Anybody hungry?"

The kids clamored up and ran to wash their hands. Edith came out of her room, looking refreshed after her nap, and introductions were made. At breakfast, Alan and Rachel sat with the families, knowing they'd have the next day alone while the events of the weekend were finalized. The Wilsons had arrived late, after the others had gone to bed. But Taylor still rose early to meet with Nick at breakfast. He assured him he was quite rested, having flown in on his private jet.

Leaving the children having breakfast in the room with Edith, Barb joined the men downstairs. Nick's eyebrows rose in question as she made her way to the table. He rose, held her chair, and signaled their waiter.

"How was the trip?" Taylor asked.

"Good. The bus is quite comfortable, and most of the churches pro-vided hotel stops," Barb informed him. "Did Nick tell you about our Edith? She's wonderful with the children, and they're learning well. Every place we stop, she has historical sites to visit." Barb looked up at the waiter and thanked him for the coffee. She scooted her chair toward Taylor's and laid her hand on his. "Nick has done a fine job every-where, but he isn't using the photo from social services."

"I hate that thing!" Nick exclaimed. He shuddered.

Taylor looked at him, his eyes full of understanding. "I guess it hurts."

Nick shrugged. "It's embarrassing."

Taylor was quiet. Barb knew the look on his face. He was praying. She placed her breakfast order and reached for Nick's hand. But he wouldn't look at her. Silence was thick around the table. Taylor looked at Nick. "It's hard," he said. Nick nodded. "Who are we doing this for?" Taylor asked.

Nick blew his breath out slowly. "God, I guess."

"If you aren't, let's stop now," Taylor said.

Barb squeezed Nick's hand. "God and the kids, Taylor. You know that."

"Let's just ask Him what's best for them then, Nick," Taylor said, looking at Nick with such compassion that Barb thought she was looking into the eyes of Jesus, and she guessed she was.

The waiter set their plates in front of them. Nick blinked his eyes and picked up his fork, only to put it down again. "Will you bless the food, Taylor?"

They ate quietly, discussing their plans for the conference. When they finished, Barb went back to their room, and Nick walked with Taylor. The conference opened at 7:00 p.m. Nothing more was said about the photo, but it appeared in the slideshow. Barb reached under the table and took her husband's hand. He leaned toward her and whispered, "Snitch," but his eyes were gentle and filled with love.

"I love you," she whispered.

"I know," he replied, squeezing her hand.

* * *

The next morning, the Wilsons knocked at the door. When Barb opened it, Taylor and Adelaide opened their arms wide, and the girls ran to them. Michael began to cry hysterically and clung to Nick's neck. "What's wrong with him, Barb?" Nick asked as the boy screamed in Spanish and kept his father in a chokehold.

"I don't know. He's talking in Spanish. You tell me."

Taylor came closer and patted Michael soothingly on the back. But Michael ratcheted it up even more. "He's saying don't leave me, Papa," Rosa translated for her mother and the Wilsons.

"Come over here, Taylor. He associates us with Nick being in the hospital," Adelaide explained. She held out her hands to the girls. "Come with us, girls. Let's wash up for breakfast."

The girls skipped happily away, and Michael relaxed his hold, but he still wouldn't get down. Nick held him, assuring him he wasn't going anywhere—Papa would be right here with him, and they would stay in the fancy hotel. Michael sniffed and burrowed his head in Nick's neck.

"I wouldn't think he'd remember that. It was over a year ago," Barb said. "And he loved them. He sat on Taylor's lap for stories and played on the floor with Grammy Adelaide."

While the Wilsons sat in the bedroom and chatted with the girls, Nick reminded Michael of the fun they had with Grandpa Taylor and Grammy Adelaide in California. The toddler relaxed his hold and craned his neck. When they returned to the living area, he wouldn't get out of his daddy's lap, but he smiled shyly at them. Taylor was crushed and tried to coax Michael to come to him. Michael shook his head but grinned.

"Ignore him, Taylor," Adelaide instructed him. "It's a game now." She began pulling toys out of a big tote bag for the girls. She took out a Thomas the Tank Engine toy, saying, "I wonder who this is for?" Taylor, getting into the spirit, asked the girls if they liked to play with Thomas.

"No, Grandpa Taylor," Ella said. "That must be for Michael."

"Yeah." Rosa's dark curls bobbed as she nodded solemnly. "Michael likes Thomas."

Michael slid off Nick's lap and tentatively approached Taylor. "You want this, buddy?" the older man asked.

The boy said, "*Si, Señor*," and he reached for it. He darted back to his father, babbling away in Spanish and clutching his new toy.

"Does he speak any English?" Adelaide asked.

"He does, but he's more fluent in Spanish. He lisps a lot in English," Barb said. "I understand almost all of what they say, but I can't think of the words to talk back."

Rosa walked over, eager to show off, and talked to Michael. They giggled.

"Rosa started really learning after we went to California together, but I've raised Michael with it," Nick said.

Barb chuckled. "Do you remember when you got home, and Rosa asked me why she didn't speak 'Spanic,' because her Daddy was 'Spanic' and her *abuela* was 'Spanic?'"

"*Hispanic*, Mama. Daddy, Michael, and I are *Hispanic*."

"That's how you said it when you were little, Rosita," Nick explained. "But you speak Spanish very well now."

"Better than Robbie or Alan. Right, Papa?"

"Right," Nick confirmed, and then he asked if they were ready to eat. The three little ones enthusiastically responded, and Edith rose to get ready, but the Wilsons looked from one to the other, waiting for the interpretation. Rosa took her father's hand to walk to breakfast, asking why Edith's Spanish was so funny. Nick told her Edith grew up in Argentina, and they spoke a different dialect. Edith joined the conversation, explaining to the girls what a dialect was and adding that her Spanish teacher in college in the United States said she couldn't speak Spanish!

As they walked down the hall, Nick had the girls giggling as he repeated the same thing: "She can't speak Spanish," sounding Texan, southern, and Appalachian in exaggerated dialects.

Taylor shook his head, offering Barb his arm as they walked behind them. "He's a regular Pied Piper."

She agreed. "He's such a good daddy."

"That's why you're here at this conference, my dear," he said. "And you are a very important part of this. Nick tells me you had some reservations about speaking, but you have much to offer."

Barb shrugged. "I'm not a talker. We have role reversal in our family: Nick talks ninety miles an hour, nonstop, and I'm the quiet one."

"Dan Murphy was talking to Jonah about the conference. He was teasing him about Betsy's second pregnancy, and Jonah told him about you two. Dan wants you to prepare a sexuality workshop."

Barb stopped and stared at him. "I could never do that!"

"Have you discussed it with the Father, Barb? You can do all things through Christ who strengthens you. This is a desperate need in the church, and you and Nick certainly set off sparks."

"Dear God, help me. Taylor, you know how he is. He'll say anything and embarrass me to death."

"We are crucified with Christ, my dear." Taylor smiled.

"Would you and Nick stop spouting Scripture at me?" Barb said.

Taylor chuckled then. "Look who's talking." He shook his head. "How's the book coming?"

"Slow. I'm no writer."

"I've heard you talk to these women who are struggling with their broken husbands, Barb. Pretend they're sitting in a chair in front of you and talk to them."

Barb's eyes brightened. "I'd love to talk to them and share what God has done."

"Do it."

"I can do that, but I don't know about the other stuff," she said.

"We'll see. I'll get the others to pray about it," Taylor assured her.

Barb groaned. "You're ganging up on me. Please, God, give me a break."

* * *

Alan stayed in his room working on his lessons most of the day Friday while Rachel was in school, and on the weekend, they went to the Marshalls', returning to the hotel for the general session that night. The time flew by for them, and their parents watched them grow even closer and more committed. Nick told Jonah about what Alan said when he asked to double up on his classes.

Missy flew in on Saturday afternoon to sing for the dinner, and she and Alan flew home on Sunday. After spending the day with the Marshalls, Nick and his family boarded the bus in the evening, blowing kisses and waving as they pulled off. Nick told the driver he'd take over after his shift. "What did you think of it, Edith?" Barb asked her while the children watched a movie.

"I'm blessed to be a part of this incredible ministry. Nick gives me hope for the street children in Argentina."

"He was a diamond in the rough when I met him, but God gave me a vision for him. He has always had an incredible thirst for more of God."

"And you love him," Edith said.

"And I love him," Barb confirmed. "I'm blessed to be his wife."

Edith sighed. "I hope someday someone loves me like he loves you." She stood. "If you'll excuse me, I'll go read."

Barb nodded and scooted up between the girls. Michael climbed up into her lap and put his head back. "Where's Papa?"

"He's in the bedroom, reading his Bible," she told him.

"Okay," he murmured. Before long, he nodded off, and she slipped him into his bunk. She watched the rest of the movie with the girls, supervised their brushing of teeth, pulled out the double bed above the bunk, and fastened the safety harness tightly. She gave them kisses and prayed with them, turning the lights low.

When she went into the bedroom, Nick was asleep, with his Bible on his chest. She quietly pulled it out of his hands, changed, and got into bed. When she woke in the middle of the night, he was gone. She knew it was his turn to drive.

The bus pulled into a truck stop, and Barb woke up and dressed. The girls stuck sleepy heads over the side when she came up front. "Where are we?" Ella asked.

"I don't know, sweetie, but I think we're stopping for breakfast." At that, the girls tumbled down and rushed to wash up.

Nick walked back and picked Michael up. "You ready for break-fast, buddy?" Michael nodded sleepily and promptly fell back asleep on his father's chest. While the driver got diesel, the family went into the truck stop for breakfast. Michael raised his head and looked around, then asked Nick to take him to go potty.

They drove straight through, all the way home. Barb got out sweaters and warm pants as they moved north. Edith directed the children's studies, and the girls thrived under her teaching. She had prepared a big map, with cutout states, and each time they crossed a border, she helped them put the next state down where it belonged. Geography had never been this fun.

Leaving their driver in Charleston, Nick drove the last leg of their journey. It was late afternoon when they pulled into O'Malley Productions. Alice had dinner waiting. Robbie and Angela joined them for the meal and took them home. Alan was at his night class, and Edith had left her car at the O'Malleys', so she drove herself home.

No one complained about going to bed that night. They were all glad to be home. The girls still shared a room, and Michael slept in the room on the other side of the bathroom that they shared. Nick leaned to kiss his son goodnight and watched Michael's long, dark lashes flutter over his chocolate eyes. *My son. My very own beautiful boy. How did You surrender Your beloved Son, God?* "Goodnight, girls," Nick whispered as he tiptoed through their room, giving their beds one last tuck.

"'Night, Papa," they chorused.

CHAPTER 18

The Dedication

W HEN THE BOYS' HOME and academic center were finished a few months later, the Marshalls flew out to Los Angeles to join Nick and his family for the dedication. They arrived on a Friday night, and the next morning, the families hung out while Nick and Taylor had their heads together, planning for the next night's dinner.

"How are you doing with all the traveling, Barb?" Jonah asked.

"Thanks to Edith, we do fine. Sally was wonderful when the children were babies, but now we need a teacher. The children are doing quite well educationally. It's like being homeschooled, and Edith has them in a program that missionaries use in the field. Her parents were missionaries in Argentina. We bring Missy's children and ours on the bus when she's with us. Nick insists we remain a family. Robbie works in the studio when Nick is gone."

"I was hoping to see Robbie. I like that young man. What a strength he was to you in Houston," Jonah said.

"He and Angela are coming in tomorrow morning with the O'Malleys," she told him. "This is a much smaller event, but I'm excited. I'm always amazed at how the Holy Spirit moves whenever Nick speaks." Barb went on to tell them about several of the conferences he had led after the one in Houston.

"We need to organize another one in Houston," Jonah said. "Remind me to talk to Taylor about that tomorrow, Betts." He put his arm around the back of her chair. "You okay, honey? Want to go lie down?"

"I will. If you'll excuse me, I'll take Barbie back to the room, and we'll both take a nap." She reached out her arms, and Jonah extricated his tie from his daughter's fist.

"You want me to carry her upstairs?" Jonah offered.

"No, I'll be fine."

"When's Nick's next book coming out?" Jonah asked Barb. "What's it called?"

"Tentatively, *Little Boy Nick*," Barb said. She smiled. "How's she doing?"

Jonah grinned. "This one is planned. She's almost seven months now."

They were sitting on the patio under an umbrella. "Excited about a boy?" she asked, waving to the waiter. "Could I have lemonade, please?"

Jonah lifted his glass, indicating his drink request. "We didn't care, really. Alan got us to thinking about Barbie being alone."

Barb's face lit up with the smile Jonah knew was reserved for Nick. He turned in his chair and then stood to greet him.

"Sit. Sit, doc," Nick shook his hand. "What time did you get here last night?"

"Late. About midnight. When we got to the hotel, it was one in the morning. Barbie had slept, and she was raring to go. She has the sweetest disposition—like her mother—so we didn't mind too much."

Barb chuckled. "Having children later in life is different, isn't it?"

"Yeah, but it keeps you young," Jonah replied.

"Where are Betsy and the kids?" Nick asked.

"Alan, Rachel, and Jacob are off somewhere. Betsy and Barbie are taking a nap."

"She's doing okay?"

"Yep." Jonah looked up when the waiter set down their drinks.

"You want something, Nick?"

"Whatcha got?" Nick ordered lemonade. "You and God saving any more lives, doc?"

"Sometimes I have the privilege of God using these feeble hands," he said. "I hear He's using you in a big way, Nick. He needed you around for a while. I'm grateful to have had a part in making that happen."

"A big part, man. And I'm the one that's grateful. I don't know. I guess. I open my stupid mouth, and God reaches down and touches people. I had no idea how many abused men are out there. You should see the crowds. If broken people keep coming, I'll keep on talking." Seeing the waiter, Nick stood to reach for his wallet, but Jonah took the tab and signed his room number.

"I was telling Barb I'd like to think about planning another men's conference in Houston," Jonah informed him.

"You might want to think about a family conference. Barb is much in demand. Taylor's got the schedule. He's got this thing down to a science." The men talked about the possibility until Nick rose and held his hand out to Barb. "The kids' lessons should be over. You want to go find them?" They arranged to meet for dinner in the hotel dining room, and Jonah sent Nick and Barb upstairs while he went to make reservations.

* * *

Robbie and Angela arrived with Missy and Jamie the next morning. Jamie was home for spring break. His violin and fiddle playing had matured to new levels, and he was an excellent musician. Missy visited before going upstairs. "If you don't want me to fall asleep before I sing," Missy said, "I'd better get a nap."

That evening, they gathered in the same downtown hotel in Los Angeles where the fundraiser had been held, but in a smaller room this time. Sitting at the head table, Nick looked at the crowd. He noticed lights flashing off metal and looked closely. "Well, I'll be. Be right back, honey."

Leaving Barb confused, Nick ran nimbly down the stairs and jogged across the room to a table where a group of military men sat. He pumped hands vigorously. Back slapping, laughter, and military grunts flew. "Gunny, you old son of a gun, how did you find me?" Nick turned. "And if it isn't the LT! Excuse me . . . *Colonel*. And Sarge. What a surprise." Nick pulled up a chair, trying to catch up on twenty years.

"Will Nick Costas please return to the head table?" a voice said overhead.

Pointing to them, Nick said, "Don't you dare leave until we talk more," and he ran up to the front of the room. Sitting, he excitedly whispered to Barb, explaining who those men were. "You've got to meet them," he implored.

Taylor looked at him with amusement. "Are we ready now, Nick? May we begin?"

Nick started to nod his head but stood instead. He came to the microphone. "Those of you who have heard me speak before know those gentlemen back there." He pointed and directed the lights to the table he had just returned from. He introduced each man, explaining their influences in his life. "I wouldn't be here tonight without those fine Marines. Let's give these men a hand. The colonel has served two tours in Iraq and three in Afghanistan, and I'm sure Sergeant Major Johnson has made repeated trips. Let's give our heroes a round of applause." The crowd stood and applauded.

Nick took his seat. This night he spoke briefly. Mother Joanna stood and described the backgrounds of the boys who would be the first enrolled in the Home, which would now include an academic center. Missy sang "Suffer the Little Children," to the soaring accompaniment of Jamie's lovely violin. When the Bishop stood to close the evening, he invited anyone forward who needed prayer.

"I swear, he's a Pentecostal Catholic, Barb," Nick whispered.

When the formalities ended, Missy told Nick to go visit his friends. "Jamie and I will work the book table, Nick. Go on." They walked back to the table to sell books and DVDs while Nick and Barb went up to the bar to visit with Nick's Marines. All of them had read his book. They exchanged current addresses and phone numbers. The colonel was at the Pentagon, so they planned to work out a visit between their families. Gunny was currently stationed at Miramar in San Diego and heard about the event, so he'd gathered all the men together.

Robbie and Angela went back to the hotel. When Nick and Barb returned, Angela was asleep on Robbie's lap, and his fingers were tangled in her hair. "That was cool for you, Nick, to see those guys again," Robbie said.

"It was. They each did a lot for me. Gunny and the LT went out on a limb for me when I was a kid."

Angela sat, rubbing her eyes. "What does LT mean, Nick?" she said through a yawn.

"It stands for lieutenant, but he's a colonel now. He's going to bring his family to the mountains. We'll meet at the O'Malleys' place one weekend. I'll tell you more about him on the plane tomorrow. Thanks for coming, Robbie. I'll have to have some meetings tomorrow, but you guys can have fun. Do you have the key to Edith's room, Angela?"

"Yes, sir. See you in the morning."

* * *

Nick was surprised to see Robbie already in the hotel exercise room early the next morning. Sweat dripped off Robbie's face, and the treadmill was set to a dead run. Nick watched him and raised his eyebrows, waiting for him to slow his pace. Robbie ticked it down and wiped his brow. "Didn't sleep too well, Robbie?"

"Following your advice, Nick. Trying to work it off."

"It's hard, isn't it?" Nick asked. Robbie agreed. "You think you and

Angela can make it? Have you been obedient so far?"

"Yes, sir, but keep praying for us!"

"Come on. Let's go get some coffee." They walked into the dining room together. "I'm proud of you, son. You two have done well." They sat, and the waiter brought coffee to them right away, but they explained they'd be back later for breakfast with the family.

"I remember the first cup we shared. How many creamers and sugars did you put in that day?" Robbie reached over and took one of each.

Nick chuckled and sipped his black coffee. "Three. You were almost my height then—what, seven years ago? We've walked a long road since then. You were such strength to your mother when I had the heart surgery. Thank you for that."

"Thanks for being open and straightforward with me and Alan. I know I wouldn't have made it without you, especially with Angela. Youth pastors can teach it, but you have to see it at home."

"You've maintained your grades and your scholarships, as well as your relationship. With both of you going to D and E, you see each other every day. It has to be hard."

Robbie kept his head down. When he looked up, his eyes were glistening. "I never dreamed it'd be this hard. I love her, Nick. I really do."

Nick remained silent. Robbie knew he was praying and waited without comment. Finally, Nick covered the young man's hand with his own. "Maybe we can figure something out."

Robbie snorted. "Yeah, right. We've talked about eloping, but we can't afford to get married, and we want our folks with us when we do, so that let's that out. I figure we couldn't keep it a secret anyway, and if she got pregnant . . . You know it could happen."

"You're right about that. Look at your mother and me."

Robbie grinned. "Two in less than two years. If you get any bright ideas, let me know. Meantime, I'll carry on. Thanks for always being there for me, Nick."

Nick asked for more coffee, making no effort to stand. "If some way you two could get married, do you think you could work as hard as it takes to make a young love into an old one? God hates divorce, and failures hurt."

"The O'Malleys were young when they got married."

"Yeah, but Ian was gone for twenty years."

"I meant Jimmy and Julie. They were teenagers, too."

"They were, weren't they?" Nick remained thoughtful. "Tonight, after dinner, I want you and Angela to sit down with your mother and me. I'll think on this today and try to talk to her before then."

"It's hopeless. We both need to finish college. I don't want her to lose her dream of being a nurse. I could probably learn all the sound technology I need from you."

"That degree is worth a lot. I told you, you may not want to work with me forever."

"None better in the business, Da O'Malley says."

"Julie got her nursing degree after they were married. All things are possible," Nick said and rose to carry the check to the counter. "Guess I missed my workout. Mom's going to need help with the kids."

"Here comes your next problem, Nick." Robbie indicated Alan coming in to breakfast with Rachel and her family.

"She's a good girl, too. We're fortunate you boys chose well."

"Thanks." Robbie put his hand on Nick's shoulder. "I'm beyond grateful that God sent you to us."

"You had as much to do with my fathering as I did, and your mom even more."

"But to God be the glory, right?" Robbie flashed Nick a smile.

They exchanged greetings with the Marshalls but politely refused an invitation to join them and headed upstairs to help Barb with the little ones.

* * *

That afternoon, when the older children were out and about, and Edith had the girls out viewing historical sites, Nick and Barb put Michael down for a nap. "Home tomorrow. It's been an exciting and blessed time, but I'm looking forward to being home," Barb said as she stretched and asked Nick if he wanted to watch a movie.

"We need to talk."

She laughed. "That's role reversal." But Nick didn't join her laughter. "What? Is something wrong?"

"Not yet, but we've come to a dangerous spot." Barb waited. "I went down to the gym this morning and found Robbie working himself into a lather. He told me he was taking my advice." She gave him a puzzled look. "One of the things we men do to control our overactive libidos is to exercise hard."

"Oh," she said quietly. "You think he and Angela are in trouble?"

"Not yet, but it's getting tough."

"Bob and I were married when we were their ages. I didn't realize. What can we do?"

"I was thinking they could do the same thing you two did."

"Get married? But they need to finish college."

"They need to be holy even more, and who says they can't finish school after they marry?"

"Oh, man, I don't think Angela's dad's gonna like this." Barb frowned. "Have you said anything to Robbie about what you're thinking?"

"I asked him if he and Angela would talk to us tonight, after I'd talked to you. But I didn't say much about what or how it could be done. What do you think?"

"I remember Bob said it was a good thing we got married. We didn't have Robbie for six years. Bob joined the Guard right after high school, and when we had Robbie, I joined."

"We'd have to make sure they have all the medical advice they needed to prevent pregnancy. But if we maintained Robbie's support, and Angela's folks agreed to maintain hers, and they kept their scholarships, they could finish school. I did tell him it takes a lot of work to make a young marriage work, and he told me Julie and Jimmy did it. Good role models."

After they talked longer, they prayed for Angela's family, the Hicks, knowing both sets of parents would have to be on board and work together. "Thank God, Angela's family's in church now. Let's ask the Holy Spirit to show us all what to do and keep us in agreement." Barb took Nick's hand, and they bowed their heads again.

After casting their cares on the Lord, Nick read aloud Paul's admonitions to couples in First Corinthians 7: "If you've found your soul mate, you can serve the Lord together." Then Nick said, "God knows I couldn't have kept away from you very long. We married two weeks after I declared I was hopelessly in love with you."

"We weren't kids, Nick." When Nick's eyes danced, she slapped his shoulder, "And don't you say it, either."

Nick knew she was sensitive about being six years older than him, so he contented himself with a growl as he grabbed her and kissed her. "I love my cougar, baby."

"You remain incorrigible!" They sat quietly, her head leaning on his shoulder, until Michael woke up.

When Rosa and Ella returned, they wanted to find their brothers, so they called the boys' cells and joined them, wandering around the grounds and shopping for souvenirs to take back.

* * *

Later that night, Nick and Barb had a heart-to-heart conversation with Robbie and Angela. The young couple was relieved to get everything on the table. Angela was amazed how understanding Nick and Barb were, and she asked Robbie later if he thought it was because they were relative newlyweds themselves.

"No. I've always been able to talk to Nick about anything," Robbie explained.

"I'm afraid my folks will freak out if we suggest this to them."

"Nick's got the best idea. We'll let him talk to them first."

"God help him."

Robbie chuckled. "I've never known a more Spirit-led man. He'll pray first, and we'll pray, too. We can't do anything about it right now, but I'm getting you a ring. Do you want to help me pick it out?" Robbie tucked her under his arm, and they wandered over to the fountain to throw pennies and make wishes.

* * *

A few days after arriving home, Nick called Angela's father, Linden Hicks, and invited him to lunch. They sat at a booth in a sandwich shop, and Linden thanked Nick for taking Angela to L.A. twice. "She had a really good time. With four kids, I don't make enough at the Department of Highways to travel with the family too far. You gave her the thrill of a lifetime."

"It didn't put us out. Taylor Wilson was generous to send his plane for us, and we had plenty of room."

"Angela said the dinners were successful—not just financially, but lots of people got saved. I'm glad. That's a neat thing you're doing."

"God's been good to us. I want to pay it forward, you know? But I asked you to meet with me so that we can pray for the kids. They've loved each other a long time."

"You think they're too serious? Ruth and I have worried about that, but they're both such good Christian kids. We couldn't be happier with Robbie as her boyfriend."

"They are serious, all right. Robbie wants to get her a ring."

"I'm not surprised, but it'll be a long time before they finish college."

"Maybe too long. You're a man. Think about it." Linden flushed and shifted uncomfortably in his seat. "I've been studying Paul's advice to young men. Are you familiar with it?" Nick asked him. "I jotted down the references for you to look over." He handed Angela's father a piece of paper. "Why don't' you reread these, pray about it, talk to Ruth, and we can meet again in a few days?"

Linden agreed. "I'll tell Ruth to expect the ring, but you'd better have Robbie talk to us first. She's been worried about the kids, but I trust him. They seem to have level heads and keep in groups." The two men finished up their lunch and shook hands before they parted.

Robbie and Angela prayed constantly and even fasted, seeking God for their own answers. Angela worked as a nurse's aide to save money for the next semester, and Robbie worked at the studio, freeing Nick to develop the foundation and prepare for some speaking engagements. Ian mentioned that Robbie was doing a fine job and that God was providing for the studio to free Nick for greater ministry.

When Nick met with Linden again, Angela's father straight-up asked him what he thought they should do. Nick took a breath and looked in Linden's eyes. "I can imagine what it's like for you. I dread this day coming with Ella and Rosa, but I sincerely think we can't put too much on them, and if they want to get married, we ought to do everything in our power to help them make it." They discussed getting Robbie and Angela through school, the possibility of pregnancy, and the pros and cons facing them.

"Ruth tends to think that way, too. She says God doesn't put on us more than we can bear. I said maybe that's why He chose us to be their parents, because we'd understand and support them in this. She's willing to get Angela started on birth control so they can get married by the end of the summer. She seems awfully young, but Ruth was only a year older when we were married."

"Barb said she and Bob were married at their age, too."

"Yeah, and I bet Robbie was born the next year!"

"No. They were married six years before they had Robbie. Jimmy and Julie were teenagers when they married, and they didn't have Jamie for six years. Robbie pointed to their example. They've done well. Julie finished up nursing school after they were married."

"I guess that's right." Linden scratched his head thoughtfully and took a deep breath. "Jimmy's song . . .?"

"You mean 'Always, Only You?' That's a beautiful song, isn't it?" Nick said.

"Yeah, it's a tender song. I like it. I've done a lot of praying about this, and you're right. God doesn't put on us more than we can bear. Tell Robbie to come talk to me, and we'll start planning."

* * *

At the end of the summer, Robbie and Angela were married in a lovely ceremony and set up housekeeping in a cute little apartment near their college. Jonah allowed Rachel to fly up and be in the wedding but threatened Nick with physical violence if Alan got ideas. Nick laughed. "Alan's always been goal-directed, Jonah, and he's set his sights on the Air Force Academy."

"Rachel's planning to study linguistics overseas," Jonah replied. At least they won't be thrown together. If they last the separations, it will be the real thing. Meantime, they're good for each other."

CHAPTER 19

Young Love

ROBBIE REACHED FOR HIS BRIDE and came up empty. Angela was gone. *What did I do wrong? I must have hurt her or hurt her feelings. Nick cautioned me to cuddle. Women like to be held. I did that. I remember pulling her into my arms. She snuggled up to me and sighed. I thought things were good. It was good for me. Maybe I did hurt her, or her feelings—something.*

Robbie stood up so quickly his head spun. He fumbled around for his pajama bottoms, groping the floor. He pulled them on and noticed a light in the living room of the little condo he and Angela had rented for their honeymoon. Some honeymoon—he'd blown it on their first night.

Going into the other room, Robbie saw Angela sitting on the couch, her knees pulled up, her arms clasped around them, and her head resting on them. Her long brown hair hung like silk down her back, luring him to run his fingers through it. Her white robe pooled around her. "Angela, are you okay?"

"Yeah. Did I wake you? I'm sorry."

"Did I hurt you?"

"Oh, no. Maybe a little, but not for long."

Robbie crossed the room, sitting behind her. He tentatively touched her glistening hair, shimmering auburn in the lamplight. "You're beautiful," he whispered. She turned her head sideways on her knees, and he saw a smile curve on her face as she looked up at him through her lashes. "Look, it's gonna get better. Nick said it's like any physical skill—you improve with practice. I'll do better."

She turned to face him then and leaned forward so that her forehead rested on his chest. "It was . . . It *was* good, Robbie. I didn't realize that women would enjoy it as much."

Robbie's features relaxed, and a smile creased his own face. "You *enjoyed* it?"

Angela sighed. "Yeah." Her arms surrounded his neck. "I know that men can't . . . perform for a while . . . after. I wondered when . . . you know . . . we could do it again."

Robbie softly removed one of her hands, moving it low on his body so that she could tell he was indeed ready. Angela giggled. "You wanna go practice some more?" he whispered. Feeling her nod against his chest, he picked her up to carry her into the bedroom. Her robe fell open, revealing she had nothing on under it. "Where's your gown?"

"I couldn't find it in the dark."

He lowered her back on the couch and stretched out over her. This time, her soft cries assured him that she was as excited as he, and when they rested in a soft languor of satisfaction later, she slept peacefully. Robbie, however, couldn't get comfortable on the narrow couch, so he roused her and guided her back to bed. He wrapped his arms around her and held her close.

After a moment, she asked, "Are you awake?"

Robbie pulled himself out of a slide into oblivion and affirmed that he was. Nick told him women liked to talk—that listening meant love to a woman.

"Is it supposed to be this good for women?" Angela asked.

"Did you think women didn't enjoy making love?" he asked.

"I didn't think it would be . . . like this."

Robbie propped himself on his elbow. "You really liked that, didn't you?"

"Yes," she whispered. "Will it always be this good?"

"I will make it my mission in life to ensure it," he said, pulling her to him. She sighed and ran her hand across his chest. At this rate, he thought, he wouldn't get any sleep tonight. Not that he was complaining.

* * *

After five days of bliss, Robbie and Angela returned to Elkins and their little apartment next to the college. They hung curtains and made love. They shopped for dishes and hurried home to make love again. They ran up the stairs on the side of the brick apartment house, tumbling into the kitchen. Robbie swept Angela into his arms and carried her to the bedroom. They went back to his truck later and carried their dishes into the house. Robbie broke open the boxes, and Angela washed the pots and pans. Robbie cooked dinner, and after they ate, he carried the plates to the sink. They cleaned the kitchen, and he asked his bride what they should do that evening.

She grinned. "Do you have to ask?"

He laughed. "You're something else, girl!"

"But you like it, right?"

"You betcha I do." Robbie took her in his arms and kissed her until they were both breathless.

"I've been reading that book you gave me," Angela said. "We could try something new."

"Feeling adventurous, are we?" Robbie raised his eyebrows at her.

She pulled the book out from under the side table and pointed to a line drawing. "You think we could try that?"

Robbie shook his head and stood, offering her his hand. He led her to the bedroom. "We could try, if you don't mind the practice."

"Oh, I like the practice!" She giggled and pulled him down on their rumpled sheets.

"You want dessert?" Robbie asked later, as she lay in his arms.

"I've had dessert," she said. "But that's definitely going to take more practice."

They laughed. He pulled her tighter. "I love you, Ange."

"I know. Isn't it great?" She stretched. "We have some ice cream, and we've definitely burned the calories."

Robbie took her by the hand and pulled her out of bed. "I'm glad we came home early. No one knows we're here."

"I can't believe Nick talked my dad into this," she said. "I've always loved Nick. I couldn't understand all the fuss when they first got married."

"They are a different couple."

"Oh, pooh. So he's Hispanic—what's wrong with that?" Angela walked ahead of him into their tiny kitchen. She reached down and grabbed two dishes while he got the ice cream out of the freezer compartment of the refrigerator.

"Nothing, unless you've never been anywhere, seen other cultures. And the Westfalls haven't been out of the county, let alone out of the state."

"*I'd* never been anywhere until Nick took me to Los Angeles," Angela reminded him.

Robbie scooped ice cream into the bowls. Holding the spoon in his hand, he looked at her. "He's lots younger than Mom, you know."

"Nuh-uh," Angela said, carrying the dishes to the small table. "I look in his eyes sometimes, especially when he's talking about the kids in the Home, and he looks ancient as the hills."

"That's what Missy said. She told Mom he was way older than his years because he's seen so much, lived through so much."

"She's right."

"God gave him to us. That's what I told Mom. She almost didn't marry him when she found out how young he was."

"But they are perfect! They're such a cute couple."

Robbie smiled. "I can't imagine her without him now. He loves her like crazy. I remember one day I walked in on them . . ." Robbie told her about the day he and Alan came in and Nick had his music up loud. They went to put their new school clothes away, and when they came back, Nick had his hand on Barb's bottom, and he'd held her up tight against him as they danced. "I pulled Alan back down the hall so fast I all but tripped him!" He laughed.

"I've never seen my folks like that. No wonder you make it so good."

Robbie raised his eyebrows. "I make what so good?"

Angela blushed. "You know."

"Making love? Do I make making love good for you, Angela?"

"You know you do, Robbie, now quit that."

"They were good role models for us," Robbie said. "And Nick always talked to us guys straight."

"You never came onto me, Robbie. I always felt respected."

He stood and held out his hand for her dish. "I love you, Angela. I honor you—but I did want you!" He carried the dishes to the sink.

"I was scared, you know?" she admitted, softly.

"I know. That first night I thought I'd blown it. I woke up, and you weren't there. I was afraid you'd left me."

She giggled. "I was already addicted to you. To the way you made me feel."

He went back to the table and pulled her into his arms. "That's a good thing, because I need you so much. But not just for that, Angela. I need you in my life. I need your goodness, your friendship, and the way you make me laugh. I've loved you for years."

"I wish we didn't have to start school," she said.

"This is a lot better than last year."

She grinned impishly at him. "Yeah, study breaks will be a lot more fun this year."

"You sure aren't scared *now*, sassy woman." Robbie looked down at her and kissed the top of her head.

"Nope. I'll never be afraid of you, Robbie."

The young lovers scarcely left the apartment. Robbie painted, and Angela made curtains, and before the end of the weekend, they had the place looking cozy. Angela stood up from the sewing machine. Robbie pulled her into his arms for a kiss, and she giggled. "You've got paint on your nose," she said.

"I'll get it on you," he threatened, rubbing his nose on her neck. Since it was dry, he failed, and she got a wet cloth and scrubbed it off. "Come see." Robbie pulled her into the bedroom, now a soft green. She pulled the curtains out of the machine and handed him the café rods. He climbed up a step ladder and hung them. "Wow, you matched this color perfectly!"

"Missy helped me pick it out," Angela informed him. "We took a swatch of the material to the paint store. She picked out the kitchen colors, too, and she paid for it all. Said it was her wedding gift." Angela rolled her shoulders. "But I've got to quit now. I'm stiff. The rest will wait until next weekend."

"How about a hot shower? I could rub your shoulders." Robbie set the water in the shower, and while they waited for it to warm, he stripped her shirt over her head. "Oh, wow," he whispered. "Do you know how beautiful you are?"

"I am not," she said.

"Oh, yes, you are." Robbie reached around her back and unsnapped her bra. It fell to the floor. He kissed down her body, hooking his thumbs in her sweatpants. She stepped out of them. He led her to the shower and hurriedly took off his own clothes. Angela had never had such fun talking a shower. For that matter, neither had Robbie.

CHAPTER 20

Contagious Love

R OBBIE CAME INTO THE STUDIO about nine on Monday morning. Nick was alone in the sound room, singing to himself. Robbie smiled as he looked at him, his heart full of love for this man who had been his father for almost a decade now. Nick felt his presence and turned around. "Hey, I thought classes start tomorrow. What are you doing here?"

"Angela's started today. She left at 7:30. I wanted to see if you need me to do anything. No, mostly I came to tell you thanks." Robbie brushed away the tears that sprung to his eyes.

Nick grinned and crossed the small space to stand in front of him. "I don't need to ask. It was good, wasn't it?"

Robbie nodded wordlessly and finally said, "Yeah, thanks to you."

Nick pulled him into his arms. "Ah, you did what comes naturally. You made her happy."

Ian entered the studio. Seeing Robbie, he smiled. "The conquering hero has returned to us. Your feet on the ground yet, laddie?"

Robbie stepped back, swiping his eyes with his sleeve. "Yeah, I guess so."

"Had a good time, did ya then? As if I had to ask."

"We did. I'm still amazed. Angela is quiet—you know, shy? And I was afraid. I mean, we've waited so long, and I was a bit . . . ready. I was worried I'd . . . be too much."

Both men chuckled. "Now me Alice says, 'watch out for the quiet ones.' She's quiet, but she's full of passion, me lad."

"I'm glad it was good for you both, Robbie," Nick said.

"It was better than 'good.' I expected it to be good, but it was . . ." Robbie searched for a word. "It was magical."

"Ah, yes indeed. 'Magical' is the word," Ian confirmed. "Now, didn't God make an excellent thing when He made a maid to love a man? Sure, and we are fearfully and wonderfully made." Robbie thought again how, whenever Ian was brimming with emotion, his brogue got thicker and thicker—like when Nick ran out of words and lapsed into his native Spanish. Nothing like the mother tongue, he guessed. "The shy lassie came out of her shell and gave you herself, did she? That's a good laddie. You loved her well, and you'll never regret it."

"Thanks to Nick," Robbie said.

"I steered you to some excellent books."

"And gave me some excellent advice."

"It's always worth the time you take with a woman, laddie, and don't you ever forget it. We men, we can get right down to it. But if you wait for the lassie, if you pleasure her. Ah, well, it's worth the wait now, isn't it? When you hear her little cries and feel her body reach out to you. Sure, and it's heaven on the earth."

Robbie grinned like a lovesick puppy. "The first night I woke up, and she was gone. I thought it was good—that I'd done everything right—but when she was gone, I thought I'd blown it for sure. I found her in the other room and asked her, you know, if I'd hurt her. I promised I'd do better, and you won't believe what she asked me. She asked me if it was supposed to be this good for women and when could we do it again."

Ian's head went back, and he roared with laughter. He slapped Robbie on the back. "She asked that of a young man on his honeymoon, did she? Now, I'd say that was an instant up for ya."

Robbie blushed. "Yeah, well . . ."

Nick took pity on him. "You did fine, son. And, like Ian said, it was a lifetime investment and a lifetime lesson. If you want the work, I can take off and spend some time with your mother preparing for the workshop we're slated to do in Denver next week. Edith has taken the kids off on a field trip with the other homeschooled children."

Ian shook his head, laughing. "No kids at home? I'd say after all this honeymoon talk, you're ready to practice one of those lifetime lessons yourself, Nickie boy." He walked to the door. "I'll be in there." He pointed to the studio. "Go to work, young lover. We need to get the sound set up for this group coming in a few minutes. I need to write meself a new love song for me Alice." He stood in the studio, guitar in hand, and strummed a few chords. Robbie quickly donned the headphones and began twisting dials.

"I think it's The Mountain Men coming in," Nick said, and he called out to Ian to confirm that. "You need to turn down the bass for them. Their percussionist is a bit heavy." And he stepped out with a song in his heart and joy in his step. He was going home to a house empty of everything but the love of his life, his Barb. *Maybe we will have a little of those life lessons. Nothing like loving in the full light of day. I'll take it slow, make her sweat and cry out. Thank You, God, for that woman.*

* * *

Nick slipped quietly in the door and watched Barb at the computer. She was frowning. Hearing him, she turned. "I didn't expect you home."

"Robbie is back. He came in to work. Angela's classes started today."

"Was he okay?"

"I'd say he was glorious, glowing, and delirious." Nick grinned and went to stand behind her, rubbing her tense shoulders. "Nothing like young love—unless it's old love, experienced love. I know your body, Barb, and I can make it sing." A tremor went through her, and he smiled, lifting her up against him and reaching under her shirt to touch her. His arms went around her back, and he unsnapped her bra so that he could tease her body. She moaned, and her head fell back. He began to devour her neck, moving up and then down. Soon her clothes were off, and she was tugging at his belt buckle. "Not so fast, my love. I intend to take my time and pleasure you thoroughly. We have all day."

"Nick—"

"Shh," he whispered into her hair before he plunged into her lips.

When they broke apart, she was breathless. "Dear God," she whispered as his hands traveled over her body. He led her to their bedroom, but he took his own sweet time until she was begging, and then they traveled together to paradise.

When they were spent, and Barb was tucked up next to Nick in the crook of his arm, he said, "You were frowning when I came in. What's up?"

"Hmm? Oh, I was working on that stupid workshop. I'm frustrated!"

"Still?" His hands began to rove over her body again.

She slapped at them. "Not that way, you goof. I'm thoroughly satisfied with you. But I can't talk like you can, Nick. You open your mouth and stuff pours out. I can't come up with a thing to say. And let me warn you, if you start pouring out our personal stuff, I'm walking out of there! Do you hear me?"

He tried to suppress his laughter, but it slipped out as he pulled her closer. "I love you."

She snuggled next to him. "I love you, too, but you embarrass me to tears."

"But it's the personal glimpses that make it come alive, sweetie." He nuzzled her hair. "*Mi amor,* how could I love you this much?" She started to get up, but he pulled her back into his arms. "We'll use your greatest strength, Barb. Use Scripture. Teach the Word. God has lots to say about love."

"He gets embarrassing, too, sometimes," she said.

"Did you hear that, God? My beloved accuses You of embarrassing her." He shook his head and patted her naked bottom. "Make a list of those embarrassing Scriptures, and we'll go over them." He released her then and swung his legs off the bed. "I guess we'd better get dressed and get to work since I took the day off to do this."

Turning, standing in her naked glory, Barb swept her hand over the rumpled bed. "This?" she asked.

Nick's white teeth flashed against his dark face. "That, too." The phone rang, and he answered it, standing in his nakedness while Barb hustled to the bathroom.

"Hey, Nick. Hope I'm not interrupting anything. You guys done?"

"What do you want, Robbie? You scamp."

"I can't get this switch to work."

Nick identified the stubborn switch. "I meant to call the company about that. Toggle it left and then push it up. That work?"

"Yeah, thanks, but we need to get it fixed. Where's the number?"

"On my phone, I'll get it." Nick started to walk into the living room where he'd left it. "Ouch," he called out, beginning to hop on one foot.

"What happened?" Robbie asked.

"I stubbed my toe on this stupid footstool."

"Didn't have your shoes on, huh? Got anything else on, Nick?"

Nick laughed. "Do you want this number or not?" he scrolled down his contact list.

"I'd kinda like to picture you now, wandering around the house naked as a jaybird." Nick hung up. The house phone rang in Nick's hand. It was Robbie again. "I'll shut up. What's the number?"

Nick gave him the number. "Thanks, Robbie. I'm sorry I forgot to do that yesterday. Jimmy went up to Pittsburgh with the Macs. He can pick up the part while he's there. Give him a call."

"Getting any work done on that workshop?" Robbie chuckled.
"Okay, I'll shut up for real this time." Robbie disconnected.

Barb came in, steamy from the shower, in a green shirt that set off her hazel eyes and shorts that drew his eyes to her long, slender legs. He groaned. "Now how am I supposed to work with you looking all gorgeous?" He paused and looked closely at her. "You lost all that baby fat when I was sick, didn't you?"

"Not the best way to lose it," Barb said. "But yeah. You just noticed?"

"You always look perfect to me, Barb."

She put her arms around him. "You'd better get some clothes on, or I won't be able to work."

"Is that a threat, or a promise?" His dark brown eyes twinkled at her.

She slapped his firm, naked bottom. "Go, you lecher."

"Lecher, am I? Who's the one that was begging for it?" He backed her up.

"Quit, Nick. We've got to get to work on this stuff."

"Keep your hands off my body then."

"I will—for a while. Go get dressed."

Nick dressed quickly, pulling on his black jeans and a snug black tee. He came back into the room, and Barb scanned his muscular body. She sighed. He leaned over her and saw she had a long list of references already written. He smelled wonderful. She sighed again and rolled her eyes.

Nick picked up the sheet of paper and sat, resting his left ankle over his right knee. "I should've known you'd have a dozen passages in ten minutes. You never cease to amaze me, Barb." She shrugged. "Okay, tell me what these are." And she began to describe each passage. He watched her face light up as she quoted and explained each verse. "That's your part, honey," he instructed her. "You convince these people that the Creator invented marriage and said, 'It is good.' That'll set His people free."

178

Barb leaned back in her chair. "I can do that."

"Sure, you can, baby. You know the Scripture better than any seminary professor I know."

"How many seminary professors do you know?"

Nick laughed. "Why don't you print out those verses with the references, and we'll use them as a handout. I bet half the people don't even know those are in the Bible. All the men will have Proverbs 5:19 memorized before the workshop is over." His eyes traveled significantly to her breasts.

Barb crossed her arms. "We need to teach these first and then hand them out at the end—since men, *obviously*, are such visual creatures."

Nick laughed again. "I agree. But you need to teach them, Barb. You are an anointed giver of the Word, and you have them all memorized already. I'd be thumbing through my Bible looking for them."

She shrugged. "Okay, that's easy enough."

He shook his head. "You don't realize how gifted you are, do you?"

"What do you mean? Because memorizing is easy for me? Even parrots can memorize."

Nick looked at her. "More like how singing flows naturally out of Missy. When it's God's gift, it isn't hard, is it? I'd better figure out my gift."

"You have the gift of gab."

Nick laughed. "I'm not so sure that's God's gift."

Barb's eyes softened when she looked at him. "That wasn't fair. I'm sorry. You live it, Nick, and you have a way of speaking that makes each individual in a room full of people feel like they are the only person in the world, and you're their best friend. That's God's gift, Nick." She stood and went to stand in front of him. "I feel privileged to be your wife. Every time I hear you speak, I see God move and people's lives changed."

"Before you loved me I was a rude, crude street kid. I don't know how you stood me back then—and I'll always be a street kid."

"You're *God's* street kid. He saw the man you'd become, and He put His love for you in my heart. I never thought I'd want to remarry, and one day I thought: *I'll never be able to live without this man.*" She drew his head against her and kissed the dark curls. She felt her shirt get wet and looked down to see his tears running down.

"Thank You, God," he whispered against her softness. "How can you do this to me, *amada*—reduce me to tears? You make me weep all the time. I never cried until I knew you." He looked at her, brought his hand up, and caressed the curve of her face. "How do I teach this—that a man must cry? A man must be broken before God can get a hold on his heart."

Barb leaned her face into his hand. "We'll do our best and pray for the Holy Spirit to bring the revelation. This is going to be a good workshop, sweetheart!"

"Not frustrated anymore?" he asked.

"Not in any way," she said.

"I'll make another handout listing the good books on the marital relationship: the Penners' book, Lehmen's books, and . . . what's that one on the *Song of Solomon*?" Barb told him it was with the other books, on the high shelf in their bedroom, where the kids couldn't reach. Nick returned with the books stacked on top of his laptop. He sat on the couch and began to type.

"You know you do your best without a prepared script, don't you?" Barb asked.

"Yeah, but I write a lot to get my thoughts straight before I do that. I read it over and over, and the Holy Spirit always brings more stuff to my mind."

They worked in companionable silence, side by side, until late afternoon, when their children burst through the door. The girls threw themselves up against Nick, talking nonstop, and Michael ran to Barb. "Was he too much, Edith?" she asked.

"He loved the game farm. And the picnic lunch was terrific! Thanks for fixing it for us. Can you tell your mother thank you, kids?"

"Thanks, Mom!" they chorused.

Edith nodded toward Michael. "He had a long nap in the van. He should be good for you." She leaned down and kissed the top of his head. "You were a good boy, Michael. I can take you with me next time."

He grinned at her. "Me haff fun, Eeiff."

"And you learned a lot, too, didn't you? Tell your mommy your favorite animal."

Michael looked up, his eyes big. "Da woof. He haff eyes. Eyes like you, Mommy."

Barb narrowed her eyes and leaned toward him. "Like this?"

He shook his head.

"I bet he means the color," Nick said. "Hazel eyes, right, buddy?"

Michael grinned. "Yeah. Hazel eyes. Ha-zel, ha-zel," he sang.

"Mommy has beautiful hazel eyes, doesn't she, Mikey?" Nick prodded.

Michael leaned against her. "Yeah. Mommy's eyes."

Edith rubbed his curls. "A new word for today, Michael: hazel. Okay, since you're home, I'm out of here. We'll take you to Mrs. Brugger for math tomorrow, girls. Ten o'clock in the morning."

"Bye, Eeddie," Ella and Rosa chorused.

"You girls ready for Papa to fix you supper?" Nick lifted them off his lap, and they skipped beside him to the kitchen.

Michael slipped off Barb's lap and ran after them. "Me, too, Papa." Nick lifted him up in his arms and set him on a barstool at the counter.

"Where's Alan?" asked Ella.

"He's at baseball practice," Nick said, reaching for the chicken marinating in the refrigerator. Mommy made us scalloped potatoes. Don't they smell good?" He opened the oven door and peeked at them.

"How do they look?" Barb asked, coming into the kitchen behind them.

"Beginning to brown. The chicken will take twenty minutes. They are thin breasts," he glanced significantly at her.

She stepped behind Michael and stopped before sticking her tongue out at him. "Should be timed right then, and ready when Alan gets home."

"Robbie got home today, Girls," Nick said.

"Is he coming to dinner with Angela?" Ella asked.

"No, I don't reckon they'll be visiting us for a few days."

"I miss Robbie," Rosa pouted.

"He'll be around," Barb assured her.

The side door slammed. Alan was home. "Hi, guys. How was your day at the game farm, kids?" He came into the kitchen, smelling of sweat and dirt. "Hi, Mom."

"We saw da woof, Awen," Michael said.

Alan tousled his black curls. "You saw the wolf? Did he growl at you?"

Michael giggled. "No, he had eyes like Mommy. Ha-zel."

"I bet I can make Mommy growl." Alan grabbed her and pulled her into a bear hug.

"Get your stinky self out of here and go take a shower, young man," Barb fussed, but her eyes were sparkling and tender as she looked up at her son. Laughing, Alan left the room. "When did he get so tall, Nick?"

"I swear he's grown four inches this year. We'll need to get all new jeans before school starts. You got a vegetable planned? I've got some squash I can pan-broil with onions."

"I was planning on some beans from Alice's garden, but that sounds good."

"Can we have both, Mommy?" Ella asked.

"Let's do that," Nick said, reaching for two pans under the counter.

"I hung-y, Papa," Michael announced.

"Me too, Mikey," said Ella. "Let's go wash our hands and get ready for supper."

"I'll set the table, Mommy," Rosa said as she went to the drawers and began to carry things to the table.

Barb frowned. "Do you think Michael's speech is slow, Nick?"

"I asked Edith that. She said boys are slower than girls, and we're used to little girls. She seems to think he's right on track and has a lot of words for his age. He's only three."

"He's almost four, and the girls were much clearer."

Nick scoffed. "You women always talk more, better, and clearer. It's a male thing. Besides, he's a native Spanish speaker. English is his second language."

"I guess."

"Missy said the other day that Todd lisped until one day he started talking like a twenty-year-old." Nick took some hot pads out of the drawer. "Here, Rosa, put these on the table for the hot dishes."

"*Gracias*, Papa."

"Thank you, *bonita Rosita*." You set the table very nicely."

CHAPTER 21

More Contagious Love

IAN LOOKED UP when the back door closed. Alice threw her keys on the counter, put her hands on her back, and leaned, stretching. She rolled her head. "I hope you're cooking. I'm so tired I could collapse," she reported. "We had three babies born today and almost had to do a C-section on one. They were all . . . no, two of them were like Julie used to be with her first two." Alice shook her head impatiently. "As if God didn't create women to have babies. Honestly, they make it such a big deal these days, like it's a sickness!" She scooped up her keys and put them in her pocketbook, which she carefully stashed on a shelf.

"Are ye tired now, lass?"

"Beat! I hope you didn't have any big plans for tonight."

Ian raised his eyebrows and grinned at her. "Now, what would ya be havin' in mind, me girl?"

She rolled her eyes. "What's gotten into you?"

"Ah, the young lovers are home from their honeymoon, and Robbie came into the studio today. Sure, and they had a wonderful time in their love nest."

Alice's eyes softened as she looked at him. "We were younger than they are when you first loved me."

"Aye. Robbie said it was 'magical,' he did. And 'tis magical still, after all these years."

"Why did you wait those many years to come home to me?"

"I wandered around a hopeless old drunk for many of them. And then I thought you would never want me back." He turned to the skillet, pushing chicken pieces and garden veggies around. He wouldn't look at her.

Alice came around the bar and slipped her arms around him. "Now I've gone and made you sad. You're here now, and God is restoring what the locusts ate."

"Robbie told us he was nervous because Angela is quiet and shy. I told him ya always say 'watch out for the quiet ones,' and he discovered what I know. The quiet ones are full of passion—like our Tim. He does love Missy well. She has the glow of a satisfied woman now, wouldna ya say?"

"I would, and so does Julie. All the women in our family, I'd say."

"Including you, me love?" Ian put the spatula down and circled her tiny body with his arms.

"Especially me, Ian." Alice lifted her lips for his kisses.

"Ah, brown Indian girl, me forever love. Sure, and I'd best get you fed and full of energy. I've drawn ya a nice bath in the Jacuzzi, with some lovely scent." He ran his hands down her body. "And I will wash you meself." He described where he would put his hands and what he would do.

She sighed and whispered, "Maybe I'm not so tired after all."

He chuckled and reached for the plates, serving up the food and leading her to the counter. They sat on the barstools and bowed their heads as Ian blessed the food and thanked God for the love He'd given them. Throughout the meal, he told Alice how beautiful she was and ran his fingers down her arm until she could scarcely swallow.

"Ian . . ."

He raised innocent eyes at her, but a smile teased his lips. "Aye?"

She slipped off the barstool and took the plates to the sink. "Let's soak these. We can do them later."

"Ah, me love, I intend to make sure we willna do them tonight. We have many pleasures before us this night." He led her to the bedroom, where he had turned down clean linens on the bed and soft candles flickered in the evening light. He took off her clothes, piece by piece, caressing her body each place he made bare. She trembled at his touch. "Ah, you're beautiful beyond words. I look on your loveliness, and I canna believe you are mine."

"Always, only you, my love." She stood quietly but proudly before him as his eyes roamed up and down her body and his hands followed. He led her to the tub full of scented water, and he added hot water because he had drawn it an hour before. He took her by the hand, and she stepped in. It was still warm. She smiled at him. "Will ya be joinin' me now?" she whispered.

"Are ya making fun? Ya know I canna talk when ya undo me like ya do."

"Come, get in here with me." She sank slowly into the water, lifting her arms.

"I thought ye'd niver ask," he said, dropping his clothes on the floor. He reached for her, touching her in all the places she loved to be touched until she was whimpering in his arms. "Are ya too tired now, me love?"

"Love me, Ian. Love me right now."

When the water cooled, they got out together and tumbled into the bed. Ian held Alice for a while and slowly began to awaken her again. Later, they would clean up the water that splashed over the top of the tub.

"Goodness, what's happened to you tonight?" Alice wondered.

"Young love is contagious, but old love is experienced," he replied, kissing her in the places only he had ever been. And when they slept, they slept soundly, her head lying on his chest.

* * *

Like Missy, Alice always woke up early. She smiled at Ian. His curly dark hair was a bit too long. He had white strands in it now, but it only made him more handsome. She slipped on some running pants and a T-shirt and quickly wiped up the tile with the towels they had abandoned. She carried them to the washer with a smile on her face.

I wish I had his poetry and his songs. I wish I could tell him how I love him. He and Jimmy and Missy, they can put things into words. I can only give my heart. Alice reached up and caught her salty tears, pushing them off her cheeks, roughly. *I can only love him in my silence. I can give him all of me when he makes my body cry out, but I am trapped in this silence. Oh, God, tell him I love him.*

Alice walked over to the couch and sat down with her Bible, and Ian found her there. He crossed the room and leaned down for her kiss. "I woke up and me arms were empty, and me love was gone, but I know ya were here and I came ta find ya. You were always here."

"I was. I am. I always will be," she said.

Ian's sea-green eyes searched her face. It was open, without guile, and full of tenderness. He touched her cheek. "I can lose meself in your dark eyes. Alice, me poor words canna tell my love."

"Oh, Ian, you are the poet, my beloved troubadour. And I am dumb."

"I must go to the piano. I asked God for a song—a song just for me only love."

Alice cleaned the kitchen cheerfully, listening to a haunting new melody, as Ian sang:

Your silence speaks to me.
Through the years it sang to me, calling me home.
Your silence followed me, wherever I did roam.
Your love, your love.
Your silence speaks better than my words.

Poor words you cannot see.

But your love calls to me.

Your love, your love.

You give your all to me, crying silently.

You give me all your heart.

And I come apart.

Your love, your love.

I will always be waiting here for you, I heard your silence cry.

And though I said goodbye, I always heard your sigh.

Across the miles, your tender smiles followed me.

And I could always see love so strong and true, calling to me anew.

Your love, your love."

Alice stood in the doorway, the dishcloth hanging from her hands. Her mouth formed an "O" and tears streamed down her face. Ian rose quickly and pulled her to himself. "Did ya think I dinna know?"

She could hardly gulp out the words. "I prayed. I asked God to tell you. I'm no poet, Ian. I can cook and clean, I can garden and sew, but I cannot sing. I prayed, 'Tell him how much I love him, God.'" She sobbed and clung to him.

"Shh, me love. I know, I know. Your silence speaks to me, and you were always here for me. Your love drew me home. Your love, your love," he continued singing. And then he kissed Alice tenderly, nibbling on her mouth, sucking on her lips. "I know."

Her arms went around his neck. "I'm glad. I can't tell you how much I love you."

"Alice, ya tell me every moment of every day. Your heart beats for me and for this family. We all draw strength from your love. Do ya like me poor feeble song then?"

"Oh, yes, Ian. It is one of your greatest gifts to me, and you have given me many."

"Will ya write the words now, while I play the little tune?"

"It's a beautiful melody, Ian. One of your finest." Alice sat beside him on the piano stool, taking up his pencil and writing as he sang and re-sang, correcting, changing, honing it to fall into the melody.

"Now we will have Missy and Jimmy have at it, shall we?" Ian suggested.

"The three of you always make each other better, but this is good as it is, Ian. Thank you."

"You go in at three today?"

"I'm off today. I'm off tomorrow. But I have to work the weekend."

Ian stood up when he heard the back door open.

"Where is everybody?" Jimmy called.

"We are in here, at the piano," his mother called back.

"Are you singing love songs to Ma?"

"Oh, Jimmy, listen to this. Play it, Ian."

"Ya gotta help me, laddie. It has ta be perfect for ya mither."

Jimmy smiled. "This will be good. When you go into the brogue, you're full of emotion."

Ian played his song, and Alice looked at him with adoration.

"Da, that is perfect. Don't change a note. That's a God-inspired song. Oh, Ma, it captures you, doesn't it?" Jimmy slipped his arm around his mother and pulled her close. "My sweet, silent mother, whose silence speaks louder than all our noise and clamor. You are our stable rock, our sure foundation. Isn't she, Da? You captured it. Anything else would be nothing." Jimmy turned to his father and hugged him. "God knows we're glad you're home, Da. You want to record that today?"

"No, it needs to sit a bit. I will wait on the Lord."

The back door opened again, and Nick came in. Jimmy told him he had to hear the new song, and Alice sat beside Ian as he ran through it one more time. When he finished, he looked down at her and smiled. She laid her head on his arm. Nick's chocolate eyes danced. "Robbie was contagious, wasn't he? I hope you two had as fine a time as Barb and I did!" He limped a bit when he walked.

"What happened to you, Nick?" Jimmy asked.

Ian chuckled. "Robbie says it's what you get when you walk around the house naked."

"That boy talks too much," Nick grumbled.

"Gets it from you," Jimmy said. "The honeymooners are home, huh? I bet he's one happy guy."

"Sounds like she's one happy gal," Nick replied.

"You gotta watch out for the quiet ones," Jimmy said, glancing at his mom and winking. "Right, Ma?" He laughed out loud as her face turned dark tan. "Oh, yeah."

"Have some respect for ya mither, Jimmy," Ian said.

Jimmy raised his eyebrows. "Okay, Da. I love you, Mom."

"I love you, too, Son."

Jimmy offered Nick his arm. "Can I help you to the studio, crip?"

Nick ignored him and limped along. "Did you pick up my switch while you were in Pittsburgh?"

"I did, and I got all the Macs cleaned up and updated. We got a lot done."

"We? What's this 'we,' white man? Who went with you? Don't tell me you took Julie on a business trip?"

"Agnes offered to stay with the kids. Who could refuse an offer like that from a mother-in-law?" Jimmy said.

Nick put his hands on his hips. "Ian, don't tell me you are going to stand for the company paying for him to feather his little love nest?" Though his voice sounded stern, the merriment in Nick's eyes gave him away. They all laughed.

"Love is contagious, but it looks like he did fine without any contagion," Ian said. "We canna talk about love nests around here, Nickie boy. We let you go home to a childless house, and Robbie told me you stubbed your toe running around 'naked as a jaybird.' Are ya casting any stones?"

Nick held his hands up, laughing. "I have nothing to say."

"Did you get any work done on the workshop?" Ian asked.

Nick chuckled. "After a bit of hands-on inspiration, we got a lot done."

Ian threw his arm around Nick's shoulders, and they walked together into the studio, laughing. Alice smiled her quiet smile and watched them as they went to work.

CHAPTER 22

The Trip to Denver

NICK GOT TO THE STUDIO early on Monday, knowing he had to get ahead on his work because he and Barb would leave Thursday for another conference, this time in Denver. He found Ian drinking coffee at the kitchen counter. Alice had already left for work. He walked over to the coffee pot, poured himself a cup, and dropped down beside Ian. "I worked on those tracks some after you left to take Alice to dinner Friday night. Did you have a nice time?"

"We drove up to the Cheat River Inn and enjoyed Missy's favorite, pecan crusted trout," Ian said. "Can we put that CD together today?"

"Is Missy coming in? If she is, we need to redo that duet with Jimmy on track four. I think I can wrap it up after that."

"Will ya be wanting the tour bus to go to Denver? If so, we need to have it ready to go."

"Nah. They're paying our way for the three of us to fly out. Edith is staying with the kids, and Tim isn't going with Missy."

"Think about it," Ian urged him.

"I wouldn't be able to do workshops after driving all that way. Thanks, though."

"The price they'll pay for three round-trip tickets would pay a driver and mileage, I figure. But, you're right. When we drove to Nashville, Jimmy and I traded off, and it was a chore, and that was a relatively short trip. You would need ta hire a driver like ya did when ya went to Houston. Pray about it and let me know." Ian set his cup in the sink, and Nick refilled his.

When Nick called his house that day, he mentioned the possibility of driving to Barb. He kind of wanted to have the time to themselves, but she was thrilled that she wouldn't have to leave the kids for five days if they drove. She said she'd talk to Edith and call him back. "Don't get all excited until I check on prices, baby. And I'll need to run this by Taylor."

Later, Barb called back. "Edith says she can make more fantastic geography lessons out of this trip, but we didn't say anything to the kids. Have you talked to Taylor?"

"Waiting for a call back now. It's about six to one, half dozen to another, if I do some of the driving."

By the end of the day, a driver was hired, and Barb was frantically washing and packing for five. Alan was staying home with Jamie because he had baseball games and were on the same team. Nick, Barb, and their youngest children pulled off on Tuesday, with much horn tooting and many shouts, waving and blowing kisses. Nick drove to Charleston to pick up the same driver they had used before, and they were on their way west. They built more than the twenty-plus hours driving time into the trip, because Edith had planned stops along the way to look at historical sites. She had lesson plans, including map-drawing, historical research, and even botany and indigenous wildlife.

Nick cuddled Michael in his lap and leaned back in his chair beside Barb, one arm around her shoulder. She leaned on his chest, with her hand curled around Michael. Nick shook his head in amazement and thanksgiving for his family and his boss and this next adventure with God. "What, Nick?" Barb asked.

"I'm thinking about a street punk married to a saint—father of five fantastic kids and speaking at a Christian conference. How did that happen?"

"Couldn't you have done it without dragging me into it?" Barb asked.

He dropped a kiss on her hair. "Nope. This is all about you. I would be nowhere near here without you, Barb." He pulled her closer and whispered, "We're the only couple on this trip again. We've got the big bedroom. Do you wanna make love at 65 miles an hour?"

"Only you would think of that!"

"In this family? With Ian, for goodness sake? And Tim, and Jimmy? I don't think so. We have a lot of love in this family." Nick and Barb and their children all thought of the O'Malleys as family: Da, Gram, Aunts Julie and Missy, and Uncles Tim and Jimmy. For a kid with no parents, Nick was surrounded with family now, including the Wilsons. The girls chattered excitedly about seeing Grandpa Taylor and Grammy Adelaide. Nick sighed. God was good.

St. Louis and Kansas City, Kansas were among the stops along the way. The family spent time exploring the big cities, including the famous arch, while their driver slept. Nick said, since they were going right through Kansas City, he wanted to stop by the International House of Prayer. They arrived in the middle of the night, but the girls danced in the roped-off area with other worshippers, including children, and Nick, Barb, and Edith participated in the prayer vigil that went on 24/7. Walking out hand in hand as the sun was rising in Kansas City, the adults rejoiced at the move of God this place represented.

They made Denver that evening, with Nick spelling the driver for a nap and breaks. The Wilsons were waiting for them when they pulled in. The girls hopped up and down, and Michael held up his arms to Taylor. "Ah, that's more like it, my boy," Taylor greeted him. "How are you, Mikey? Now, you must talk to Grandpa Taylor in English, remember?"

Michael told him about their trip and the stops, the arch in St. Louis, and crossing the wide, wide "Sippy" river. Taylor carried him up to their rooms, while the girls held Adelaide's hands and danced happily alongside her. She showed them into their room, and Michael slipped out of Taylor's arms to follow them.

"Are you ready, Barb?" Taylor asked.

"I'm terrified, but I know God will help me," she said.

"And, if you open your mouth wide . . ." Taylor paused, waiting for her to complete the verse.

Barb smiled and finished, "God will fill it. Thanks, Taylor."

When Edith arrived a few minutes behind them, she insisted Michael's daybed would go in her room, and the girls would be on the other double bed. "You two have to prepare. You need to work. I'll keep the kids in here." Nick tucked the girls in and knelt beside their bed. Barb held Michael on her lap while they prayed. They kissed each of the children, thanked Edith, and went to their room.

"You want to work, Barb?" Nick asked. "Don't roll your sleeves up, take your shirt off." She shook her head. "Here, I'll help you." He unbuttoned her blouse.

"Nick . . ."

"Hmm?"

"What's in that box?" She pointed.

He tore his eyes away from her and looked. "Oh, that's something for the workshop. It's a surprise."

"You won't tell me?"

"Nope." He began to distract her with his kisses until she entirely forgot about the box.

CHAPTER 23

The Workshop

NICK AND BARB SLIPPED OUT of the room early, leaving the kids with Edith. After they ate, they went to worship and then to the workshop they were leading. Nick took Barb's hand. He could tell she was nervous, so he whispered to her that she'd do well. He waved off the formal introduction and broke the ice, introducing himself as a street punk who married a church lady. When he had everybody laughing, he waved Barb up. "Come on up here, beautiful, and do your thing."

Barb nervously arranged her notes and cleared her throat. Nick was praying for her. She began to go through the Scriptures on marriage, even the embarrassing ones. The more she shared, the more confident she became, making the meaning behind each of the passages clear by using different translations and examples. When she finished, she got an enthusiastic round of applause.

Nick stood, clapping. "I have to follow *that*?" He shook his head. "Boy, are you going to be disappointed." Nick went on, "It may come as no surprise to you that women and men are different. We like the physical differences, guys, don't we?" He looked around. The men were grinning. "After all, they have places we don't have, and places we want to explore, over and over. They are an endless source of pleasure in that way. But emotionally, we'll never comprehend them. You never know what a woman is thinking, or what she wants. Sometimes she'll tell you, and other times even she doesn't know.

"When you go home, this is a little homework assignment. Watch one of my favorite movies, *Shenandoah*. Jimmy Stewart gives his future son-in-law some excellent advice that every married man needs to hear. Basically, he says don't try to understand women—just love them."

Nick went on to talk about a woman's need for touch and words and regaled them with tales of his failures in those regards. Walking over to the box Barb had asked him about earlier, he pulled on a string and took out a top hat. He set it jauntily on his head and sang the "Hymn to Him" from *My Fair Lady*: "Why can't a woman, be more like a man?" His gestures, the expressions on his face, the tone of his words had everyone laughing hysterically.

Nick took off the hat, threw it in a corner, and asked the group, "Now, do we really want that? Women are unique and special creatures that we must learn to appreciate and treasure, listen to and respect. You heard Barb talk about a woman submitting to her husband, and she gave the whole truth—that we are to love our wives as Christ loved the Church, giving Himself for her. Much as I'd hate to submit to a lunk-head like me, I like even less going to the Cross for her. But here's a revelation: sometimes we are required to submit to our wives. Ever heard that before?" And Nick turned them to Genesis, reading how the Lord told Abraham to submit to Sarah and about putting away Ishmael because Isaac was the child of promise. He told the group about the times he'd failed so miserably to love his wife as Christ loved the Church.

He continued, teaching about the woman's "weakness" as her greatest strength. "The very sensitivity that makes them emotional fine-tunes them to hear the still small voice of the Spirit. While we are slaving to provide, flexing our muscles in feats of strength, they are growing life in their bellies, cooperating with God to give us our sons and daughters. The most magical thing in my life—after sex—is watching Barb nurse our babies. Hour after hour women sit and let these little mewling creatures suck the life out of them. This is after they have carried them around inside their bodies for nine months and pushed with the force of an eighteen-wheeler to birth them. And we call *them* the weaker sex? Come on, men, get real!"

Nick was full of practical advice, self-deprecating humor, and wisdom, openly sharing his many mistakes and God's unfailing mercy and correction. As he closed, he opened it up for questions. A man stood. "I read your book, and you refer to Barb as a church-lady. I'm married to one of those, and I confess, it's really irritating. She's not here at this conference. I came for help because . . . well, I can't stand it. She purses her mouth and corrects me constantly, and I honestly want to smack her. What did you do? Barb's obviously not like that now."

"You want to answer that, honey?" Nick turned to Barb.

"Number one, he loved me," Barb began. She shrugged. "Looking back, I don't know how he stood me. I was self-righteous and narrow-minded, always correcting his language—which *was* rather abominable. But he lived a life in front of me. He walked out the Scriptures I'd memorized. He did unto others, including my sons and my mother-in-law." She told the stories of Robbie's anger, Alan's withdrawal, and Pat Westfall's betrayal, with Nick's return of love, forgiveness, and service. "I was ashamed. I learned to go the second mile by watching him. And he was always reading the Word and praying. He loved me, and my frozen Christianity melted into God's grace." She looked at him, her eyes brimming with tears.

Nick shook his head. "That's a bit heavy, babe. Why don't you tell them when you pursed those little lips, I kissed the thunder out of them until they got soft and pliable, like this." He took her in his arms and kissed her thoroughly. She felt his hand slipping down her side, reaching for her bottom. She reached around behind her back, grabbed his hand, and tugged it up to her waist. She heard the crowd laugh and broke away, blushing furiously. He turned to the crowd and winked. "Good sex. It works every time."

"Nick, I warned you . . ."

He looked at her with innocent eyes, fell on his knees, and said, "Just forgive me. Can you forgive me, Barb?"

By this point, the entire crowd was laughing, including Barb. But she sobered up to tell them about the horrible afternoon when she found his switchblade and accused him of not being careful to protect "her" children.

"To prove my point, do you want to know what she did?" Nick asked the crowd. Barb's hands flew to her flushed cheeks. "I'm standing in the bathroom, minding my own business, washing my hands, and something hits me on the neck. I turn around and see her shorts on the floor at my feet. I look at her, and she's stepping out of her pan . . . clothes." He nods and raises his eyebrows. "Make-up sex after a fight can really be great!" He looked at her imploringly.

"I walked into that one, Nick," she said, laughing. "I have to admit . . ." She trailed off, fanning her face with her notes. "I cannot believe this!"

Nick put his arm around her and pulled her close. "You have survived the ordeal, sweetheart. Time's up. Our books are available on the book tables, and feel free to come up to us, but please, not when we have our kids with us, okay?" The crowd applauded thunderously.

* * *

That night, Barb felt Nick awake beside her. He was on his back and very still, one hand under his head. Was he praying? Maybe. She didn't want to disturb him if he was, but finally, she whispered, "Honey?"

"Did I wake you?"

"Not really, I felt you awake."

His arm slipped down and pulled her close. "How do you know me this well to feel my thinking?"

"I love you, Nick. What are you thinking?"

He gave a soft sound—half snort, half chuckle. "I am thinking I bother you too much."

"Bother me?"

"Yes. I want you too much. I ask of you too much."

"You mean, we make love too much?"

"Yeah. Am I a bother to you, Barb? Too demanding?"

She chuckled then and rolled over to slide her hand under his T-shirt. "You take me to paradise every time, Nick. You have taken me places I've never been before. Never stop loving me."

He groaned. "I could never stop loving you any more than I could stop breathing." He smiled in the dark and toyed with her hair. "You think I'm a good lover, hmm?"

"Oh, yes, Nick. I never imagined loving could be like this."

Nick still lay on his back. He fell silent. "What about Bob?" he eventually asked. "Was he good to you?"

She was quiet a minute and then said, "He was. It was good. I always liked to make love, and had he lived, I'd have been satisfied the rest of my life, fulfilled, and faithful. But you have taken me to heights I never dreamed were there, made me feel things I've never felt before. I was frightened at first, the way you take me out of myself, and I splinter into a million pieces. But they always come together again. And you do that over and over when you love me. I didn't know I could do that." She propped up on one elbow and looked down at him. A small smile played across his lips, and she gently leaned to brush hers against them. Then she cuddled up next to his side. "Never hesitate to love me."

"It's because I need you, you know. I've been lying here thinking. I need constant reassurance of your love. I feel unworthy. And, I don't know . . . I need to belong. I've never belonged to anyone before. Just saying 'I love you' doesn't cut it. I don't know how to tell you, so I try to show you, but I got to thinking I might be a pest."

Barb put her hand on his cheek and felt moisture. "Oh, no, never. Have I made you feel like that?"

"No, you always respond to me—in fact, rather enthusiastically."

"I can't not, Nick. You touch me and my body sings. You reach into me, and I can't breathe. I fly away. How do you do that?"

"You mean this?" He sent her over the edge.

She cried out. "Yes, that," she gasped.

Nick put his arm around her and pulled her close. I missed your body like crazy after Michael was born, Barb. But it was good for me to hold myself in check. I learned that what we had was sacred, and it was all I ever wanted"

"Do I please you, Nick?"

"Oh, baby, you don't know the half of it." Nick growled and rolled on top of her. Their lips melted together, and her hands roved all over his body as softly as his traveled over hers. When they were spent, he said, "If every husband had a woman like you, they would never stray."

"Good," she whispered dreamily. "I don't want you going anywhere." She said, and she drifted off.

"Thank you, God," Nick whispered before he slipped into sleep himself.

Later, Taylor told Nick and Barb that theirs was the highest ranked workshop of the entire conference, and the one universally requested to be repeated at the next conference.

CHAPTER 24

Why Do Things Change?

AFTER ONE LAST BREAKFAST with Grandpa Taylor and Grammy A, the Costas family boarded the bus for home. Michael sat on Taylor's lap all through the meal and cried when he carried him to the bus and told him goodbye. Nick extricated him from Taylor's arms, promising to read him stories on the bus. But Michael still screamed, "No-ooo."

Adelaide linked her arm through her husband's and told him he had certainly made a conquest on this trip, and he said he guessed he'd have to learn Spanish to communicate with this little grandson. They waved as the bus pulled off, and Taylor fumbled in his pocket for a handkerchief. He blew his nose thoroughly, took a deep breath, and asked if the limo was ready to take them to the airport.

The bus made no stops on the way home to West Virginia, except when its occupants wanted to eat. Nick spelled the driver, and they drove straight through. He was keen to get home because Madre had told him the packet of photos and case histories of "his boys," who would soon be residents of the Home in Los Angeles, were awaiting him there. Once again dropping the driver in Charleston, Nick drove the last few hours to Elkins.

When they pulled in the driveway about nine that night, Ella saw Robbie's truck. "Robbie's home!" she cried. She and Rosa joined hands and jumped around in a circle in the aisle of the bus. The bus door slammed shut, and Nick heard the squeals and laughter stop cold. Silence.

Then, from Angela: "Robbie, you said they wouldn't be home until tomorrow. What are we going to do? Oh, this is awful . . ."

Nick chuckled and grabbed the girls' hands. "Go inside now, girls."

"But, Papa, we want to see Robbie," Ella pleaded.

He tightened his grip. "Not now. Mind your papa, Ella. If you are good girls and go straight upstairs and put on your pajamas, I'll have Robbie come tuck you in." When they protested, he stopped and looked at them. "Mind your papa, girls. Do you hear me?"

"Yes, sir," they mumbled. With drooping heads, they whispered, "It's not fair," and they slowly climbed the stairs.

Nick walked through the sunroom off the master bedroom, noting hastily strewn clothing—exactly what he expected. He opened the door, loudly saying, "Perfect night for a moonlight swim, isn't it?"

Angela groaned, and Robbie responded, "Yeah, Nick, it is."

Nick set two robes on a nearby chair. "I'll leave these robes for you and close our bedroom door, so you can dress in there. I promised the girls you'd come say goodnight, Robbie."

Robbie was laughing, and Nick heard Angela smack him and hiss: "This is not funny."

Smiling, Nick went back into the house. Barb had carried Michael up to bed and came down the stairs with a knowing smile. "We caught them in their altogether?" she asked.

Laughter bubbled out of him. "Angela's fit to be tied."

"If only she knew how many times we've done that."

"I expect Robbie's telling her."

Barb stopped cold. "Do you think he knows?"

"I expect there's not much that young man doesn't know, Mom. Have you found the packet?"

"No, but Sally probably put it on the counter." Although their former nanny had married, she still came twice a week to clean for them. Sure enough, they found it there, and Nick carefully sliced it open with his knife. First, he looked at each photo, studying it as if to memorize each boy's features. Then, he began to read each history, putting it beside that boy's photo.

Robbie came in and went directly to the stairs. They could hear the girls' squeals and demands for hugs and kisses. Barb went to find Angela, who had carefully folded the robes, laid them on the bed, and was closing the door of the sunroom to slip out.

Barb called, "Angela?" Angela turned, her face red. "Don't be embarrassed. Nick and I have done the same thing on beautiful nights many times. I'm sorry we got in earlier than we expected." She crossed the space quickly and put her arms around her daughter-in-law. "We've prayed for you two to have the joys we do. I'm happy you're a good wife to my son. You will have a fine life if you love him well. We did a workshop on that in Denver."

"I do love Robbie, Barb," Angela whispered.

"That's good. And is he gentle and kind? Does he give you time? Is he good to you?"

"Oh, yes, ma'am . . . very."

Barb patted her and stepped back. "Good. You let me know if he gives you any trouble. And remember, your loving will get you through the tough times. They are bound to come, you know."

Angela's eyes glistened. "You guys are great. My mom was always . . . shy, I guess. But you and Nick make married stuff . . . just . . . natural."

"It is. It's wonderful. When God had made the world and everything in it, He said, 'It is good,' and that includes the sexual beings He created. We are fearfully and wonderfully made, right?"

Angela smiled. "It's magic."

Barb chuckled. "You got that right, girl! You want to come in for hot chocolate?"

Robbie came into the room and asked Angela if she was okay. She said she was fine but added they'd better not stay because she had an early class the next day. "But thanks to your mom, I'm not embarrassed anymore."

"You certainly shouldn't be. You're a married woman, for Pete's sake!" Barb assured her.

Robbie leaned down and kissed his mother's cheek. "Thanks, Mom."

"You've got a good woman there, Robbie. You treat her right, you hear?"

"Yes, ma'am, I intend to. I figure you or Nick will take me to the woodshed if I don't!"

Barb patted him and pushed him out the door, and then she returned to her bedroom to get ready for bed. She smiled as she heard Robbie's truck roar off, knowing he and Angela would go home to finish what they had begun in the pool. When she came out of the bathroom, she heard voices coming down the stairs. It was Ella and Nick. Ella was crying, and Nick made soothing sounds, telling her they mustn't wake Rosa. Barb cracked open the door and peeked at them. Nick settled into the big chair across the hall in the living room, and Ella snuggled in his lap.

Thinking her little girl might be sick, Barb went into the bathroom to get a thermometer. When she turned around and looked through the crack in the door, Nick was calmly moving the chair back and forth, still holding Ella. In the still, small voice she was accustomed to, she heard in her mind the words, "Listen—listen and learn." She did. And Ella sniffled.

"What's wrong with Papa's girl? Can you tell Papa?"

"I don't know," she cried.

Nick continued the gentle movements, back and forth, back and forth, holding the child to his chest.

"Why does everything have to change?" she whispered.

205

Nick leaned closer to hear her, asking, "Why do things have to change?"

She sniffed. "Why can't Robbie live here?"

Nick softly sang their song: "'I know something the prince never knew. One day the clock will strike midnight, and she'll be gone.' One day you'll leave Daddy, too, Cinderella. You see, God made us to have someone in our lives who becomes the other half of us. Daddy was lost and alone until Mommy loved him. It's like magnets or puzzle pieces that come together."

"I'm glad you're my daddy."

"Me, too, sweetheart. And the greatest gift of all was that you *chose* me to be your daddy. And now God has given Angela to Robbie, to be the other half of him."

"Why couldn't I go see them in the pool?"

"Well, baby, they didn't have any clothes on, and I knew Angela would be embarrassed."

"Why didn't they have their suits on, Papa?"

Nick gave a short little sigh. "Married people share their bodies in a special way, Ella Marie. They share secrets no one else does. God made our bodies to fit together. But it's a private thing we don't talk about to anyone but Mommy and Daddy, okay?"

"Sometimes you touch Mommy in her private places—like her boob."

"Oops. I shouldn't let you see our secrets."

Ella giggled. "Mommy likes it. She smiles. Does Robbie do that to Angela?"

"I'm sure he does, but we shouldn't talk about their secrets, okay?"

"Then it's a good thing he moved, so they can have their secrets," Ella said.

"Yeah, but it's hard sometimes when things change."

"I miss him."

"I know. Mommy and I miss him, too, but we are happy for them."

"I like Angela, Papa."

"She's kind of like a big sister to you now. She's part of our family."

Barb watched silence cover them like a soft blanket. Ella's golden curls spread across Nick's chest, and he idly ran his fingers through her hair. Barb thought maybe her daughter had fallen asleep, but she saw her rouse a little.

"Papa?"

"Hmm, Ella?"

"Would you dance with me, Papa?"

"It would be my pleasure, princess." Nick stood, gave a courtly bow, and extended his arms to his Cinderella. She stepped gracefully into them. "'I'll dance with Cinderella,'" he sang as they spun around.

Barb felt her shirt was wet and realized soft tears had been raining down on it. "Oh, God, thank You for giving this man to us. Thank You that he lived to be a father, and to be here for those children, and for me, Lord. Thank you," she whispered.

She stepped back into the room when she saw Nick and Ella hand in hand walking toward the steps. She pulled her wet shirt over her head and fumbled through her drawer to find another. She crawled into bed and waited for her husband, who joined her a few moments later. He went quietly into the bathroom and slipped into bed, thinking he wouldn't wake Barb, but she reached for him. Oh, how she loved this man, and how she wanted to show him.

"What was that all about?" he asked her later. "I thought we were tired."

"I saw you and Ella." Barb ran her hand over the dark curls on his chest. "It was precious. You have words for things like no one I ever knew. God gives you words."

Nick drew her closer. "Sometimes my words embarrass you. I'm sorry for that. They get ahead of me sometimes."

"If you keep trying, you'll make a real woman out of this uptight church lady," she said.

"Oh, you're a real woman, baby! You always have been."

"I blossomed under your love—your magical touch—and now Robbie is doing that for Angela, too."

"I hope he's good to her."

"I'm sure he is. I asked her, and she said he is 'very' good."

Nick chuckled. "She amazed him—she responded somewhat more enthusiastically than he dared hope."

"You've been a good father to my sons, and to all my children."

"You gave me good kids, *amada*. You gave me a family. Have I ever thanked you for that?"

"Only about a million times. I think you wrote a book about it. I love you, Nick. I knew you were tired, and I shouldn't have asked you to make love to me tonight, but I needed to show you."

"And you loved me so sweetly, Mrs. Costas. Thank you for that gift."

"Angela is right; it's magic."

"She said that?"

"Yep."

"Then I've done my job."

Barb rolled over on her side, and Nick pulled her to him. He loved to feel her long legs against him. He put his arm around her, and his hand cupped her breast gently. She sighed, he smiled, and they drifted off to sleep.

CHAPTER 25

Christmas

B ARB AND NICK TRAVELED to a conference every month or so: Orlando, Atlanta, Pittsburgh, Columbus, and more. They finally called a halt before Thanksgiving. Sometimes they took the bus, and twice while they took a short trip, Angela and Robbie stayed with the kids. Barb busied herself decorating the house and shopping for Christmas. One night, Nick came in, thumbing through the mail he'd gotten out of the box at the end of their lane.

"But, Mom, *please*?" Alan begged.

"Alan, it's Christmas. I want everybody to be home for Christmas. This is Robbie and Angela's first Christmas together. The girls miss their brother, and now you want to go away? They've had too many changes. They've left their school and traveled many places. No, Alan. I know Rachel will be there, but you can go see her another time."

"What about what I want, Mother? Have you thought of that? A ski trip to Vail! This is not fair."

Barb sighed. Nick entered the kitchen where they were arguing. "Actually, we can all go," he announced. "Taylor said he'd send his plane for all of us, and Jonah and Betsy will be there with their family."

"Oh, Nick, we've traveled too much. I want to be home. I want to have a big fire in the fireplace, a hot mug of cider, and my family," Barb said.

Alan gave her a look of disgust. "You'll have your family, and snow. I bet Angela would be thrilled to go to Colorado."

Nick said softly, "We will all pray, and God will show us what He wants, and we'll be obedient to that, won't we Alan?"

"Yes, sir," Alan muttered.

Nick put his arm around Alan's shoulders. "God gives us the desire of our hearts. He puts those desires there. If you aren't supposed to go, He'll change your heart. If you are, He'll change your mother's, and we will obey, right?"

Alan gathered up his books off the counter and headed for the door. "Right," he said.

"You will pray, Barb, and ask God with an open heart?" Nick asked, turning to her.

Taking a deep breath, she agreed.

"Good. Let's see about supper."

"Couldn't we send him to Houston over the MLK weekend instead?" Barb asked.

Nick hesitated, frowned, and said, "We can't afford it, Barb. We could go to Colorado if Taylor sends his plane, but we've been living on savings."

She stared at him, open-mouthed. "We've been living on savings?" she repeated incredulously.

"Yep."

"What's happened?"

"We travel a lot, and I lose time in the studio. Ian has to pay Robbie, so I can't ask him to pay me when I'm not working."

"That's true. I guess I could go to work."

"Barb, you can't have a job when you have to be traveling every month. Besides, I want you to be with the children."

"Can we pray about this, too?" she asked.

"Of course. I have been, but I haven't heard anything."

"You should call Taylor and talk to him."

"I'm not going to beg, Barb. He's generous enough with us as it is."

"But he's a businessman—a *successful* businessman. He can give you advice," she said.

"I'll think about it. What's for supper?"

Barb lifted the lid of the crockpot. "Stew." She gave it a quick stir. "I thought it'd be nice on this cold night." Nick pulled open the drawer and began to gather knives and forks.

Dinner was a quiet affair, each family member thinking their own thoughts, until Ella finally asked, "What's up?"

"Nothing, sweetie," Barb responded. "We are thinking about Christmas. Wouldn't you like to have a big tree?"

Alan glanced at his mother and took another bite. "Good stew, Mom." He stood. "I'll get the dishes."

"I'll help, Alan," Ella said, and she and Rosa carried the plates to the sink where he rinsed them and put them in the dishwasher.

Nick carried a drooping Michael up to the tub. The girls came up and played in the tub while he rocked Michael in his adjoining room. After they finished, they asked him if they could read a while. Nick agreed, kneeling and praying with them. He gave each girl a kiss and stopped by Alan's room to ask if he was all right. "We'll pray, Alan, your mother and I. And we'll listen for an answer, I promise."

"I know, Nick, thanks," Alan answered with a shrug.

Nick went downstairs and found Barb reading her Bible. "Got any answers yet?" he asked. She looked over the top of her reading glasses—he thought she looked cute with those glasses—and she shook her head. Picking up the packet, Nick once again drew out the boys' photos and histories. Keeping his hand over the identifying information, he tried to recall each name from memory. He missed a few and went through them again. Barb heard him softly pray for each boy. She looked over at him and smiled.

"*Mommy*," Rosa cried. "Come pray!"

Barb set her Bible down and went up the broad stairs. "Ready to go to sleep, girls?"

"What's Papa doing?" Ella asked.

"He is praying for the boys at the Home and memorizing their names."

"Mama?" Rosa studied her mother's face. "What do those boys do for Christmas? If they don't have a mama and a papa, what do they do?"

"I imagine the nuns will do something for them."

"Sister Brigit told me she goes home for Christmas, to see her brothers and sisters and her mama and papa," Rosa said.

"Do you think the boys ever even had a Christmas, Mommy?" Ella asked.

Tears sprung to Barb's eyes. "Do you know Robbie and Alan and I gave your Papa his first birthday party? He was thirty-five years old, and he'd never had a birthday party."

"That's sad, Mama," Rosa said.

"Let's pray," Barb said, and she led her girls in prayer. She went through the bathroom and glanced in at Michael. Walking over to his bed, she put her hand on his head. "Your papa looked like this once, and he never had a party. And he never had a Christmas." Suddenly, she knew what they had to do, and she turned and fairly skipped down the stairs. "Nick, I've got it."

He looked at her and smiled. "You're sure about this, are you?"

"Absolutely. We have to go—"

And he spoke the words at the same time as her, "To Los Angeles!"

"We'll borrow the money if we have to," Barb said firmly.

"The foundation could send a big tree," Nick said excitedly. The phone rang, and Nick checked the caller ID. "Taylor," he told Barb, and he answered. Barb left to give them privacy, going into the bathroom and drawing a hot tub in the Jacuzzi. Humming softly, she sprinkled lavender salts and went to the room for her night clothes.

When Nick came into the bathroom, Barb was lying in the tub with her eyes closed. He sat on the edge of the tub, and she opened them lazily. "Hey," she said.

"Hey, you."

"How's Taylor?" She arched her eyebrows, watching him shed his clothes. With her big toe, she flipped the faucet on and added hot water. Nick climbed in, and they didn't talk anymore for a long time.

* * *

The next morning, Barb was in the kitchen scrambling eggs when Nick came up behind her and pulled up her hair, kissing her softly on her neck. She shuddered. "I had a wonderful time with you last night," he whispered. She turned into his embrace and kissed him.

Hearing the girls clattering down the stairs, they stepped back. Ella immediately went to the drawer and began setting the table. Barb scooped the eggs onto a platter, arranging sausage around the edge. Nick pulled biscuits out of the oven and put them in a basket. Alan rushed into the room and sat at the table. Nick prayed and then told Alan that God had given them the answer. Alan was going to Vail, but without them.

"What are you guys going to do?" Alan wondered.

"I betcha I know," Ella said. "We're going to Sister Teresa's, aren't we?"

"What makes you think that, Ella?" Nick asked.

She looked at him with smug satisfaction. "I know 'cause me and Rosa dreamed exactly the same dream. Didn't we Rosa?" Rosa's head bobbed. "We are, aren't we, Papa?"

"Do you girls want to do that?" he asked.

Rosa's eyes spilled over. "I do, Papa. Mama told us you never had a birthday, and we thought maybe those boys never had a Christmas. Oh, Papa, please, please, can we give them Christmas?"

"If we do that, we won't have much Christmas left for you," he said.

"Oh, that's okay. It will be more fun to give them Christmas. It would be like giving Jesus Christmas, wouldn't it, Papa?"

Barb froze by the stove, the breakfast platter in her hands. "What good girls we have, Papa. Yes, girls, it would be the best Christmas present we could give Jesus." She set the food down on the table. "Now, we'd better eat before the eggs get cold and Edith gets here for school."

Alan hurried out, and Edith came and took the girls upstairs to the schoolroom she had made in Robbie's room. Nick made no move to leave for work. He poured himself another cup of coffee, held the pot up with a question in his eyes, and poured one for Barb. "Going in late?" Barb asked.

"I wanted to tell you what Taylor said to me last night. First, he said our travel to California is a legitimate expenditure for the foundation. When I told him I was strapped for cash, he asked if I hadn't received the honorariums for speaking. I told him those were for the foundation—I had said our revenues for the books and speaking would fund the Home." Barb covered his hand with her own and squeezed it.

Nick continued, "He asked me about my salary, and I explained that Ian had to pay Robbie, but Taylor wanted to know what my wages had been before I started traveling. When I told him, he said, 'That's what God gave you, Nick, and you shouldn't make less than what He had provided for you. You need to withdraw enough salary from the foundation to bring you up to at least that level. You can make whatever donations you want, but that is your base salary.' I never thought of it like that, but it makes sense. I'll call the accountant today and see how to set it up."

"I told you he'd give you the answer."

"Yes, ma'am. That's one of those submitting-to-your-wife when she has a word of knowledge deals, right?"

Barb shrugged. "I don't know about that. It seemed like common sense to me."

"Missy told me once that God often disguises himself as common sense," Nick said. "But, here's the rest. Taylor asked how much I paid you for the speaking gigs, and he was upset when he found out you hadn't been paid. 'All that time she puts into this, and you haven't seen to it she gets paid? Haven't you ever heard that the laborer is worthy of his hire?' he asked me. He even said God would get him if he didn't make sure you got a fair wage!"

"This means we'll have a raise?" Barb wondered.

"Looks that way. He said he'd bring it up at the next board meeting and make it in the form of a motion, so that I'd feel better."

Barb leaned toward him and placed a kiss on his lips, tasting his coffee. He pulled her onto his lap and nuzzled her breasts. "Ella said she saw me touching your boob and that you liked it." He chuckled. "Do you like it, Barb?"

"You know I do, but I don't think she should see it."

"I know. I said, 'Oops, Papa shouldn't let you see our secrets.' She asked if Robbie did that to Angela now, and I told her probably, but that we shouldn't talk about their secrets. And I explained that we don't talk about private things between married people to anyone but Mommy and Papa."

"I heard you say that to her. Honestly, I don't know how you come up with the words to explain things as well as you do to the children." She stood. "You'd better go. You're late."

"You're right. Love you, honey."

* * *

When Nick got home that night, he explained that the accountant wanted to cut them a check for the salary differential before year's end, so they'd have plenty of money to fly Alan to Vail. In addition, he'd reimburse their Christmas travel and hotel in L.A. from foundation funds.

They put Alan on his flight, and they caught an evening flight to

California. Because they arrived around nine Pacific time, which was much later their time, they went to the hotel. Nick had rented a car, so he drove them to the school the next day. They arrived in time to share lunch with the boys in the gleaming cafeteria. Mother Joanna introduced them, and Nick stood to bless the food. Barb waved at the boys, and her girls looked at them curiously. They walked through the halls, impressed with the quiet order and the well-mannered students. Nick sat in on a couple of classes and met his family at the hotel later, for a rest.

"They aren't taking a Christmas break, Barb," Nick noted.

"Why not?"

"The faculty prayed and felt that since the boys had nowhere to go, they needed to keep them busy. They've eased up, giving them fun projects to do. Keeping their minds occupied is better than them dwelling on what they're missing."

"They're giving up on breaks, too? God bless them."

"I haven't met a staff member I don't like. They seem to have a genuine love for the boys. I'm going to head over this afternoon and kick the soccer ball around. You want to come?"

Barb was pleased that after her children got over their initial shyness, they chatted easily with the students. A few of the boys were withdrawn, and one boy seemed sullen, but most seemed to have responded to the warmth of the place. Nick had purchased gifts for each boy but realized he wanted to shop for gifts for the staff, too. The large tree they had shipped stood in the central hall of the Home, and the cheerily-wrapped gifts were stacked around the base. Several boys had obviously shaken their packages, and many of them told Nick it was the first present they'd ever had.

"Can you believe that, Nick?" Barb asked when he told her.

He looked at her. "I never had a personal Christmas gift until I started working for the O'Malleys," he pointed out.

* * *

The next morning, Nick, Barb, and their girls went shopping for gifts for each staff member, but the boys wanted them to be at school by one o'clock for their gift. The Costases were escorted to the auditorium and treated to a performance of amazing music and a hilarious skit, making fun of everyone from Mother Joanna to the janitor—and in complete costume! Nick laughed until tears rolled down his cheeks, and Rosa identified each nun when the nun appeared in the skit, loud enough for everyone to hear. The English teacher assured them over cookies and punch that she had assisted but that the writing was the boys' own.

The boys pulled them by the hand, wanting to show them their dorm, so they walked across the street. Each floor had two apartments, one on each end of the floor, so every seven boys had houseparents. Nick had insisted the houseparents be couples because he didn't want any hint of sexual impropriety, and he wanted the boys to have a family atmosphere. Several of the couples were college students.

At this point, they had twenty-eight students in the Home, but Madre said they had requests to take more. She and Nick prayed together about presenting the need for more to the board at the next meeting. Every student had his own cubby, with a locked door and a bookshelf. Downstairs, in the library, they had access to desks and computers and comfy chairs.

The next morning, Nick met with the staff. He thanked them for the love he had seen for the boys. Some were difficult to love, he supposed, but he prayed for the staff and the boys every day. He spoke a bit about what we have done to the least of those being what we have done for Christ: "Matthew 18 says the angels of children constantly behold the face of the Father in heaven, so we want children to love us and give God a good report. And," he added in a half-tease, "I promise you, if you cause one of these little ones to stumble, I will personally come out here, tie the millstone around your neck, rent a Criss-Craft, and take you out into the ocean myself and throw you in."

One of the staff members said, "I believe he'd do it, too!" adding, "But we promise you we'll love these hurting lads. We are privileged to love them."

CHAPTER 26

Nick's Boys

ON THEIR THIRD NIGHT in California, Nick asked Brother Dean to take his family back to the hotel, and he stayed for devotions with the boys. Nick met the boys in the library, and he told them how delighted he was to have had a small part in establishing the place for them. He shared a bit about his childhood, gave them his address and cell phone number, and told them to call him anytime for prayer or help. He didn't want silly whining, he said, or tattle-tales about minor personal offenses, but he promised he'd come back immediately if they reported any serious problems.

"I never want a boy to face the abuses I lived with when I was your age," Nick told the boys. "This place is a place of peace and rest—a new page in your life, providing stability and opportunity." He sat and had another cup of coffee with Mother Joanna while the boys completed their nighttime rituals, including bathing and brushing their teeth, and then he went up to the dormitory. Tonight, he would pray with the first group, and tomorrow night with the other fourteen boys.

Nick moved down the row of beds, seven on each end. He sat on the edges and called each boy by name, commenting on something individual with each one—their favorite class, their hopes and dreams, or a personal struggle. One boy asked Nick how he knew his name. Nick told them about the photos and background information he had studied, and then he patted the boy before he stood, saying he prayed for each boy every day. Another asked if it was true he had been a Marine and wasn't he too short to be a Marine.

Several boys wanted to know how Nick made a living. He told each boy who wanted to be rich by becoming a star athlete that he should develop his skills and shoot for the moon, but that he also needed to prepare for a regular day job in case he wasn't one of the very few who made that dream come true. But if they ever did, he added, he exhorted them to remember the Sister Teresa Home for Boys and all the kids who lived on the streets. He prayed for each lad, mostly in Spanish, but also in English. He listened to stories from their past, their wildest hopes for the future, and their struggles in school or in living there.

The next morning, in devotions, Nick talked about family—how the boys and staff there were their family for this time, and how he'd found family. "Sometimes in a family, we rub each other the wrong way," he said. "Can you believe I ever get mad at that sweet, beautiful woman God gave me? But we had to learn how to live together. You guys know how to survive on the street. I was a survivor of these streets. She lived in a small town, and the worst thing she faced was gossip." They all laughed, but he added, "Of course drugs are everywhere now, and one of my best friends in that small town was raped, so violence can be found anywhere. Only God can protect us," he said, and he taught them Psalm 91.

The first question Nick faced when he prayed with the older boys that night was if Nick's friend who had gotten raped was a Christian, why God didn't protect her? "Sometimes, because we live in a cursed and fallen world," he said, "bad things happen to God's children. But God kept her in her inner man. She turned a horrible experience into a joyous one, helping two of the girls in the home where she lived to pass their GED tests, and she led another girl to Christ. "She didn't become bitter, and she brought a beautiful daughter into the world. When she chose to place her daughter for adoption, she made lovely Christian parents very happy." He flipped open his worn Bible, reading from Psalm 34:19 in the God's Word Translation: "The righteous person has many troubles, but the Lord rescues him from all of them."

The boy in the next bed asked Nick how his friend knew the adoptive parents didn't hurt her baby. "Maybe they made her a slave, Brother Nick," the boy suggested.

"First, the home where her baby lived was a Christian place," Nick answered, "and the adoption agency screened all their applicants, getting a letter of reference from pastors. Then, she met with the couple personally." He patted the boy and assured him he'd met the now-grown daughter and that she even traveled with her birth mother to share their story.

"That's cool," the boy said.

"I like your Bible, Brother Nick. We all got nice Bibles, but yours reads easier," one youngster said.

Nick checked the boys' Bibles, which a charitable organization had provided. He made a mental note to challenge his church youth group at home to provide each resident with an easier translation, like the ones the boys used in their meetings. He prayed with each boy, moving down the aisle as he had downstairs the night before. But when he sat on the last bed, the boy turned his face away.

"I don't want no spic praying with me in Spanish," the boy said to Nick. "Go pray with all your spic kids. I know they're your pets." Nick didn't say a word. After a quiet moment, the boy eyed him. Nick reached into his back pocket, and the boy threw his arm over his face and shrunk back. When no blows fell, he rolled over and said, "I don't want your prayers. Can you even pray in English?"

Whether black, Hispanic, or white, this turning away is the universal sign of an abused child, Nick recognized. His heart wrenched as he realized this. "Have you ever seen pictures of my family, Hank?" he asked the boy. He showed Hank a picture of Robbie, his oldest, and Alan, his middle boy, and Ella—Hank had already seen Ella and his

221

wife, though. "Since most of my family is Anglo, I obviously love Anglo kids, too."

"But the two little ones are spic, like you." Hank's eyes narrowed. "I get it, the white ones are *her* kids—they're your stepkids. They aren't even yours. I bet they hate you."

"I need to bring them here, so you can see them, Hank, and see us as a family." Nick tucked his wallet back into his pants pocket. "I'll never make you pray with me, but I assure you I can pray in English. My first prayers were in English. My spiritual father is an Anglo, and I asked Jesus into my heart in English. My wife taught me to pray, as did my boss. They are both Anglos. God knows every language."

Nick patted the boy on the shoulder. "Let me know when you're ready to pray. But it's like Jesus said: 'Behold, I stand at the door and knock, if any man opens the door I will come in and dine with him.' I'm knocking at your heart's door, Hank." Nick made a light fist and tapped gently on Hank's chest. "But you must open the door to me, and to all the folks here at Sister Teresa's who want to love you."

"Nobody loves me. I killed a man." Hank rolled his face to the wall, literally giving Nick the shoulder.

Nick squeezed the shoulder. "God brought you here, Hank, but you have to let us in." Nick rose to leave, but he would come back early the next morning because he promised one of the younger boys he'd take him to a nursing home to see his grandmother. "See you guys at breakfast," he called softly, and he heard several whispered goodnights as he left the room. *How is it, Lord, that I can have sweet interactions with so many, but my heart remains with the one troubled and angry kid? Help me break through to him.* Nick thought of the ninety-nine safely in the fold and the shepherd leaving them to search for his lost lamb.

* * *

When Nick got back to the hotel, he sank down beside Barb in the soft pool of light around her as she sat with her Bible open in her lap. He told her about his conversation with the lost lamb, and she immediately knew it was Hank, the sullen boy she had first noticed. They prayed quietly for him. "You ready for bed? I told that little Angelo boy I'd take him to see his grandmother tomorrow morning. She lives in a nursing home. I knew I needed a car." Barb switched off the lamp and followed him into their room. "Sorry I left you with all the kids these two nights," he said.

"You did exactly what you were supposed to do," Barb reassured him. "And the kids have been golden here. Michael cried for you a bit, but I told him you'd be here when he woke up."

"You want to get them all up early to have breakfast over there?"

"They are looking forward to it—it's Christmas Eve. Madre said the boys are singing for church, and they plan to go caroling in the neighborhood. Ella and Rosa asked if they could go with them."

Nick threw his dirty clothes in the growing pile on the closet floor. "You want to have these sent out?" he asked.

"We'll leave in two days. We have enough."

"Michael spilled his chocolate milk all over himself today," Nick remembered.

Barb laughed. "I brought lots of extra clothes for him. He's at that stage."

"You are such a good mother, Barb. No wonder God wanted you to have more children. My children know the word of God because they have a godly mother."

She lay down beside him and reached up to turn off the bedside light. "They know the love of God because they have a godly father."

Nick pulled her to him, but soon, she rolled over on her side. He spooned up behind her, placing his arm around her waist. Before he knew it, Nick heard running feet and braced himself before three kids tumbled on top of him with happy shouts. He gathered them all into his arms, ruffling blonde curls and black ones, laughing, and tickling wiggling little bodies.

Ella sat back on her haunches. "Why are you crying, Daddy?"

Rosa suddenly stopped giggling and looked at him. Her little brown fingers gently wiped his tears. "It's 'cause you're happy, Papa, isn't it? Mama says sometimes when she's very happy, the tears spill over." She snuggled close to him. "We love you, Papa, and that makes you happy, right?"

Nick hugged his daughter briefly and threw the covers back. "Right you are, Rosa. I'm so happy my eyes leaked. And now I will leak somewhere else if I don't get to the bathroom!" His words were met with a chorus of giggles.

Barb said, "Up, up, kids, we're leaving soon for Sister Teresa's. Who'll be the first one dressed?" With shouts and running feet, the children scrambled into a race. Michael cried because he couldn't keep up. Through the door, Nick heard Barb say, "*Michael es un grand chico, no?* Come, Mommy will help you." Amazingly, she had all the children dressed, and they were in the car in half an hour.

"You are a wonder woman, *mi amor*—the general of my little army."

The family sang Christmas carols on the way to the Home. "Did Mama tell you we're going caroling, Papa?"

Nick caught Rosa's eye in the rear-view mirror. "She did. Won't that be fun?"

"This is the best Christmas ever, Papa!" Ella said.

Nick looked over at Barb and winked. "God had good plans for us this Christmas, no?"

The boys crowded around Nick when he walked in with his family, confirming to Barb that his time the last two nights had been well spent. "What? Are you out of your chairs? They'll never give us any break-fast, and we'll starve," Nick teased, placing his hand on his stomach and pretending to stagger. With great shouts of laughter, the boys rushed to their seats. Mother Joanna approached them with a smile and a greeting. "I thought you didn't eat until after Matins, Madre. Are you joining us this morning?"

"I heard it's something I should see," she replied, watching each of Nick's children run to a familiar face. Michael climbed on the lap of one of the bigger boys—a black boy, who ruffled Michael's dark curls and laughed at him. The boy scooted a chair up between him and another boy, and Michael reached for a breakfast muffin. The boys gently reminded him to pray first, and Nick tapped his spoon on a glass to quiet the excited group before he led them in prayer.

Barb looked around quickly and saw Rosa beside Sister Brigit and Ella on the other side of Mother Joanna. "What do you think of all this, Ella?" the nun asked.

"Papa's boys have made our family very big, *Abuela*."

"Do you know what I think, child?" Ella looked up at Sister Brigit with a question in her eyes. "I think your father has a very big heart— the biggest heart I've ever known—and I think he's given it to all of his children."

"Papa says we must strive to have the heart of Jesus," Ella replied. Mother Joanna hugged her hard.

* * *

After breakfast, Nick got Angelo, and they went to the rental car. Angelo read from a scrap of paper, and Nick entered the address into the GPS. They drove a long way across the almost empty streets of Los Angeles. "Where is everybody, Nick? No cars today."

Nick glanced down at the boy beside him and explained that on Christmas Eve folks gathered with families, and everyone was in their homes. Angelo pointed to loiterers on the corners and slouching around garishly-decorated bars. "Some people have no home, Brother Nick." He looked at Nick. "Thank you for giving us a home. Why did you do that?"

"I didn't do it alone. Lots of people gave so we could build this place. But I wanted to do it because I didn't have a home when I was a boy either." Nick told Angelo about his life as a child. "Do you know Barb and her children gave me my first birthday party? I was thirty-five years old."

"And now you are a good man," Angelo said. "How did you become a good man?"

Nick told him about his years in the military but said his goodness came when Jesus became the Lord of his life and gave him his family. "I didn't know how to love when I married Sister Barb. I was angry and selfish. I don't know how she put up with me!"

The voice on the GPS guided them through various turns. Once it said, "rerouting," and Nick realized they had missed a turn because of their intense conversation.

"You love her very well now, Brother Nick. She looks happy."

"I think so. *I* sure am happy! God has been more than good to me. Here we are, buddy." Nick pulled the car into a parking place, and they went into the gaily decorated lobby.

"I hope I recognize her. I haven't seen her in two years," Angelo confessed, but a quavering voice called out to him. He broke into a run and knelt in the skinny arms of a fragile old woman. Nick left the two of them to themselves and sat in a corner. He pulled out his cell phone and read from his downloaded Bible. After a while, he heard Angelo call for him and walked toward the boy and his grandmother.

"She wants to thank you for bringing me to her, but she's afraid you won't understand." Nick spoke in Spanish to the old lady, and she beamed. She told him he spoke the language very well, and he told her his children spoke Spanish, too.

"They do," Angelo confirmed for his grandmother, "but not like Mexico. Where are you from, Brother Nick?"

"I was born and raised right here in Los Angeles, Angelo, but my people were all from El Salvador." The grandmother said that explained it, and he told them about Edith who grew up in Argentina and about how her teachers in the United States told her she couldn't speak Spanish. Nick noticed Angelo's grandmother appeared very tired, and he squeezed the boy's shoulder. "Your grandmother needs to nap now."

Her eyes filled with tears as she agreed and gathered the boy in her arms. She thanked Nick for providing the Home for Boys where her grandson could be off the streets and learning. Nick left them to their goodbyes and walked to the nurses' station to ask about her condition. It was as he feared: she didn't have much longer, and the nurse sadly told him that Angelo would probably never see her again. "This is the brightest we've seen her in months. When she heard her grandson was coming to see her, she perked up. She's a sweet lady and says her rosaries every day. You've made her very happy. At least the boy will remember her and know he was loved by someone."

"He's a good boy. He is loved by many at the Home where he lives. And he's a fine student," Nick informed her.

"He's written her every week and sent her some of his papers and a copy of his report card. She was very worried about him. He'd gotten into a lot of trouble. I'm glad to hear he is loved by others. She can die in peace now."

Nick signaled Angelo with a wave and dropped his hand on the boy's shoulder as they went through the doors. Angelo was quiet, and tears ran unchecked down his brown face. Nick reached into his pocket and handed him a handkerchief.

They walked wordlessly to the car. They buckled up, and after they drove several blocks, Angelo sniffed. "She told me goodbye. She said she would go to heaven. I'll never see her again."

"Oh, but you will, son. You'll see her when you arrive in that wonderful place. But you have much to do here, so don't be in too much of a hurry, all right?" They talked about heaven and seeing Jesus. Nick told him about his mother. Nick told him she had been a very bad person but that God had given her new life and that he looked forward to seeing her in heaven.

Angelo sighed. "*Abuela* was always a good person. I lived with her until she fell and broke her hip. Then I had to stay with my mother, who was a drug-whore." Nick cut his eyes over to where the boy sat stone-faced. "She's in prison now. She did this to me." He ripped his shirt over his head. "She put gasoline on my shirt and set it on fire."

Nick looked at the horrific burn scars all over the boy's torso and gasped, softly crying out, "Sweet Jesus!"

"I hate her. I hope she rots in hell. I will never know love like you have with your wife. No one will love a monster."

Nick had read that Angelo had been burned, but since few scars were outwardly visible, he had assumed the boy was healed. Thankful he hadn't reached the highway yet, Nick turned at a sign that read "DANGER, CHILDREN AT PLAY" and found his way to a neighbor-hood park. He stopped the car and pulled Angelo into his arms. At his touch, Angelo melted into sobs that racked his body. He sobbed and sobbed, and Nick simply held him, touching his scars tenderly.

When the boy was spent, he pulled away and groped for the hand-kerchief. He looked embarrassed. "It's wrong to hate, but I do. They tell me to forgive, but how do you forgive this?"

Nick pushed the seat back and pulled his own shirt over his head. He turned so Angelo could see his scars. While at the hospital in Houston, Jonah had suggested plastic surgery, but he felt strongly he shouldn't do that, and now he knew why. Angelo took in a sharp breath. "Who did this to you, Nick?"

"You know him. Madre told me he's the janitor in the cathedral now."

"Old Harry? *Harry* did this to you?"

"Most of it," Nick replied.

"You have some burn scars, like cigarettes, too."

"That would be my mother's boyfriends. They liked to put them out on my back. It was a game."

"But I thought your mother was Sister Teresa?" Angelo was incredulous.

"She was. God's in the forgiving business, Angelo—the making-all-things new, redeeming business of love. She turned her heart over to God when she was in prison and came off drugs. She joined the Convent of the Angels and became Sister Teresa."

"Did you forgive her—your mother?" the boy wanted to know.

"I did." He told Angelo about getting to see her on her deathbed, adding, "And old Harry came to a speech I was giving last year, here in Los Angeles. He threw himself on the mercy of God and begged me to forgive him. He was old, as you know . . . and broken. I took him in my arms. You see, these are God's arms now, for believers like me are the Body of Christ. We prayed together, and God gave Harry a new heart. Jesus has wiped away his sins, and we must cover them with our love, too. Don't tell anyone about old Harry, okay?" Nick was quiet, and then he added, "And Jesus can do that for your mother."

Angelo sat back. He picked up his shirt and pulled it back over his head.

"And one more thing. I will tell you about the love of a woman—God's woman. When I married, I wore a T-shirt all the time, even to bed. I wouldn't let Barb see my ugly back, but she sneaked into the shower behind me. When I realized she was there, I was scared, like you. I thought she'd be repulsed by my body. But she kissed each scar, Angelo, like the woman who kissed Jesus's feet. She kissed them, and her tears dropped on them and healed them. You may still see them, but I no longer do."

Angelo was quiet. His glistening eyes looked up. "She is a good lady, Sister Barb."

"That she is," Nick agreed, and he started the car. "Are you going on this caroling deal? I'm afraid we missed mass."

"I can go at midnight. I need to go to confession first."

On the way back to the Home, they practiced the carols and talked about their favorite lines. They got louder and louder, laughing as they sped along the freeway.

CHAPTER 27

Hank Opens the Door

BARB HAD OBVIOUSLY BEEN WATCHING for Nick and Angelo. She rushed to the car, demanding that Nick pop the trunk. "The girls' dresses are in there. What took you so long? We're holding everybody up! Angelo, they're waiting for you, too. They say they can't go without your alto." She talked as she reached into the trunk and pulled out a suitcase. She rushed up the steps before Nick could take it from her, and Angelo ran ahead of her.

Nick followed them up the steps and barely caught Barb's flying skirts as she pulled the girls into the ladies' room. Mother Joanna gave him a steely glare and looked at her watch. He felt like a little boy in parochial school and dropped his head. "Forgive me for being late, Mother." He looked up at her. "It's a long story. Angelo showed me his scars."

Immediately, her eyes softened. "We let him bathe alone. No one has seen them. That is great trust, Nick."

"When I was in the hospital in Houston, Dr. Marshall said he could get my scars treated. I'll ask him about plastic surgery for Angelo. We'll pay for that, but the wounds on his soul are far greater, and we must pray for him. I told him about Mama, and he couldn't believe she became Sister Teresa. I told him all things are possible with God."

The bathroom door opened, and Barb flung some clothes at him.

"Go! Find Michael and get him changed." She disappeared again.

Chuckling, Nick went to look for his son. Not only were the boy's clothes dirty, he was covered in dust. "What have you been doing?"

One of the boys answered for him. "We have been playing soccer, Brother Nick. We have no rain, and the field is very dusty, no?"

"I'd say. Can we get him a wet washcloth?" Nick wondered. The boys led him to a bathroom and provided him with a cloth and a towel. Nick sponged Michael down as best he could and put his clean clothes on. "Oh, this is my boy!" he said, pretending to be amazed. "This little pile of dirt is actually my son."

Michael giggled and threw his arms around Nick's neck. "You knew it was me, Papa. See," he pointed, "I have your eyes. That's what Mama says."

The boys who had watched the transformation looked at Michael closely and then at Nick. One of them said, "He really does. They look exactly like yours, Brother Nick. He has his father's eyes," he announced to the assembled group.

Nick never ceased to be amazed at the goodness of God, who gave him his beautiful children, who carried his genes—Rosa, with his mother's black sparkling eyes, and Michael, with chocolate brown eyes like his own. He reached for his son's hand, and Michael's little brown fingers laced with his own. He held the child's filthy clothes between the fingers of his other hand and approached Barb, who held a bag open for him to drop them in. "Who is this calm, lovely lady? And where is the wild woman who charged my car a few minutes ago? And who are these beautiful girls, huh?" Nick asked playfully.

Barb swore his girls preened whenever their father gave them a compliment. "I'm sorry, honey, but we're holding everyone up. What took you so long? Did you get lost?"

"It's quite a story, but I'm glad we went. It's the last time he'll ever see his grandmother."

"Shh," Barb whispered as they lined up at the door behind one of the nuns. "Are you going with us?"

Rosa tugged at his hand. "You are, Papa."

"Angelo made me practice all the way home," he assured her and fell in step in the straight lines of his childhood, following the softly swaying skirts of the nuns. Not everything was bad, he remembered. This—the school and the nuns—had been his safe place. God had always been his refuge and his fortress, he realized.

The children sang sweetly, and Nick could hear Angelo's harmonies. No wonder they wanted him. At each stop, when they prepared to move on, one of Nick's daughters dropped a curtsy and extended a handwritten invitation to midnight mass at the cathedral. "Who taught them that?" Nick whispered to Barb.

"Sister Brigit. She had all the boys writing invitations while we waited for you two," Barb whispered back.

"Mother Joanna forgave me, Barb. Can you forgive me, too?" Nick's eyes twinkled at her, and he winked.

"You know I can never stay mad at you." He caressed her with his eyes, and she shuddered. "Quit!"

"Later," he said.

She closed her eyes, and he saw a slow flush mounting, traveling up her fair neck and spreading across her cheeks. He trailed a finger up her neck and watched the color deepen. He chuckled. "Nick, quit that!" she whispered furiously.

"Later," he repeated, and he joined in the singing. He felt her hand slip into his, and he held it in a firm grasp. After a light Christmas Eve supper, Nick's family returned to the hotel. He would go to mass with the boys, but when he leaned down to give Barb a light kiss on the cheek, he whispered, "Later" once more.

The boys were well-behaved in church, though Nick noticed that not every one of them went forward. He was grateful the Catholic ministry had allowed the Protestant children to remain faithful to their own preferences. After service, Nick started toward his car but felt he should go with the older boys to their dormitory. He briefly prayed with them as a group, first in Spanish and then in English. He stopped by Hank's bed. "Goodnight, Hank."

"Brother Nick, would you pray with me?" Nick sat on the edge of his bed. Noticing the boy's hand edging toward him in a slow crawl across the bed, he took it in his own. "I prayed with Mr. Redding today," Hank said. "He says Jesus is in my heart now."

"If you invited Him in, He says He surely will come and make His home in you," Nick assured the boy.

Hank asked him if he could go to a Protestant church with Mr. Redding, and Nick told him he was sure that would be allowed, but he would check and make the arrangements. "I'm a Protestant, too," Nick informed him.

Hank was surprised, saying he "thought all Sp . . . Hispanics were Catholic."

Nick chuckled. "In the country of my origin, El Salvador, the Assemblies of God have built schools all over the country, and many people are Protestant, Hank."

"My heart is open to Jesus now, and to you, Brother Nick. Will you pray with me?" And Nick did.

When Nick returned to the hotel, the light was on in his and Barb's bedroom, but Barb had given up. The lamplight spilled over her, and his heart ached with love, but he decided to let her sleep. He took a quick shower and slid quietly into bed. He was tired. It had been a full day—a wonderful one, but a long one. It felt good to lie down! He thought he would fall asleep the minute his head hit the pillow, but he felt a familiar touch. Barb's gentle fingers moved on him, and his body sprang into action. Nick heard a soft giggle. "Maybe *you* forgot your promise of 'later,' but your body sure didn't," she whispered.

Nick growled softly, low in his throat, and drew her into his arms. "I was trying to be a good boy, and you bring out the animal in me."

"I like the animal," she said, continuing her slow, maddening strokes. "Aren't you going to love me, Nick?"

"You bet your sweet bottom I am," he said and kissed her. He moved on top of her. Her responses never ceased to amaze him—his sweet gringo lover, his passionate wife.

* * *

Barb kept the children out of the bedroom where Nick slept because he had gotten in late and she had kept him up even longer. After their love-making the night before, they lay in each other's arms. Nick told her about Angelo and Hank, and they prayed for them and for all the boys.

The phone rang about 9:00 a.m., and Mother Joanna apologized as she explained that the boys didn't want to open their gifts without them there. Barb promised they would be there soon and went to wake Nick. She watched him for a minute, loving the look of him and the soft, sleepy smell of him, and he felt her. He opened his lazy eyes, and they traveled up and down her body, remembering the familiar places, the feel of her in his arms. "Merry Christmas, my favorite little elf," he finally said to her.

"The boys want us there to open presents."

Nick rolled over and looked at the clock. "You let me sleep in! We were supposed to be there." He sprang into action, pulling on his boxers. She handed him a knit shirt and a pair of slacks. He grabbed a roll off the kids' breakfast tray and hustled them to the car. Because he had driven it so much, he knew all the shortcuts, and soon they were in front of the Home. A few boys were by the tree, but as soon as the Costases came in, hollering and running steps moved toward them. Nick and Barb marveled at the excitement, and their children were infected.

"Can I give out the presents, Papa?" Ella asked.

"*I* want to!" Rosa protested.

"You can't read the names."

"Can too."

"Girls," Nick said, "Let's remember the spirit of Christmas. First, we will read, right?" He held up his Bible, and his children fell quiet and gathered at his feet, looking up. The boys followed suit, and Nick read the familiar passage from Luke and led them in a prayer of thanksgiving for Jesus, the greatest gift of all. Looking at Ella, he instructed, "Now you. Read the names and give the presents to Rosa and Michael to distribute."

Presents were distributed in an orderly fashion, and each boy found a specific gift to his own liking. A scientifically-minded boy was thrilled with a telescope. A reader delighted in a series of books. A youngster proud of his Mexican heritage was excited about artifacts from that country. And on it went. Nick had studied their case histories closely and had asked the Holy Spirit to guide him. He'd spent hours and hours searching for the last gift and found it—exactly what would please the last boy—in the airport. God was never too late. One spiritual lad looked up at him with tears in his eyes, fingering a masculine rosary and clutching a prayer book.

And then the boys came, shyly offering their gifts. There was a potholder for Barb, made on a small, plastic loom. There were hand-carved dolls for the girls, and a toy soldier for Michael. And there were other precious handmade gifts: cards, photos, and some sort of pottery dish that stood lopsided, leaning on one shorter leg. It would remain on the Costas's counter for many years. For Nick, the boys unrolled a huge banner with personal greetings and drawings from each boy, including a last-minute scrawl from Hank: "My heart is open." It would hang in the Costas's family room.

Nick stood, but when he tried to thank the boys, all he could do was weep. Barb stood beside him, wrapping an arm about his waist. "The River of Life always seems to flow out of my husband's eyes," she explained. "He tells me he didn't cry from the time his mother was taken from him at age five until Christ came into his life."

Nick sniffed, wiped his nose, and added, "And now I'm a crybaby." The boys laughed, but it wasn't a mocking laugh, it was a laughter filled with love.

"Nick's boss, Ian O'Malley, says it takes a real man to cry, boys. And Jesus wept," Barb informed them. "Don't ever forget that. We need to cry. God knows our every tear, and He will wipe them all away in heaven."

"Is that true, Sister Barb? For real?" one of the boys asked.

And, as she always did, she gave chapter and verse: "Revelation 7:17."

"He must have a big handkerchief," one of the littler boys said, "Because I sure have cried a bunch!"

Nick put his arm around the boy's shoulder. "The sisters, your dorm parents, and your teachers all have big handkerchiefs. You will never cry alone at Sister Teresa's. Now, go put your gifts away. I think we have dinner waiting." With glad shouts, the boys ran to their rooms to put their prizes in their special cubbies.

The hall was quiet. "Papa?" Ella tugged on his hand, and Nick looked down. "This *is* the best Christmas ever!"

Rosa agreed, and Michael beamed and said, "*Feliz Navidad*, Papa."

"*Feliz Navidad, hijo de mi corazón,*" Nick replied.

"What did you call him, Nick?" Barb asked.

"Son of my heart, *mi amor*."

The boys scurried downstairs one by one and in groups of two or three. Dinner beckoned from across the street in the school cafeteria. Older boys took the younger ones' hands. One of the nuns marched to the middle of the street to hold up traffic, and another one took the lead, while yet another came behind the last boy. Various parishes and churches in the community had spread a royal banquet for Nick's boys. He stood and returned thanks, and all the boys repeated, "Amen."

Nick looked around for his family and saw them scattered about the cafeteria. Michael sat on the lap of the black boy he had befriended, who was popping a buttered roll into his mouth. Michael licked the drips off his friend's fingers and laughed. Rosa bent her head over the new rosary that one boy proudly showed her. Ella ladled punch into cups, and the older boys carried them carefully to the tables.

Barb leaned her head on Nick's shoulder, and his hand found hers. "Ella was right. This was the best Christmas ever," she said.

Nick dropped a kiss on her cheek. "I'll build you a huge fire first thing when we get back to our mountain home. Robbie says we have plenty of snow."

She pulled his head close to hers and whispered in his ear. "Will you build two? One in the fireplace and one inside of me?"

He winked at her. "Sounds good to me."

Because they would be leaving the next morning, the Costas family bade their farewells that evening.

* * *

Overtired, the children fussed on the plane. Nick separated the girls, one on either side of Barb in the three seats, and he took Michael across the aisle with him. He asked them if they wanted to come back to Los Angeles and see the boys another time. When they all said they did, he told them if they couldn't be good on the plane, they couldn't make the trip again, and Papa would have to come back alone. "Without us, Papa?" Rosa asked.

He nodded solemnly. "By myself," he repeated firmly.

Her black eyes lost their sparkle. "I'll never see Sister Brigit again?"

"That's your choice, Rosa. I know it's a long, hard trip, but you must mind your mama."

"Yes, Papa," Rosa said, scooting her little bottom back against the seat.

"We'll be good, Papa. I promise," Ella agreed.

Michael's soft brown eyes were wide as he held his arms up to his father. Nick lifted him out of his seat and held him against his chest until he fell asleep. The steward helped Nick settle his son against a pillow and re-buckled him. Nick whispered his thanks.

Barb caught Nick's hand. "Thanks be to God," she said, indicating to her side with her head.

He looked around his wife and saw that Rosa had dropped off, too—her little hands folded in her lap, her fingers curved around a carved wooden doll. "Amen!" he said. Ella read quietly, and Nick praised her. Soon, Barb was easing the book out of her sleeping daughter's hand. She put a pillow under her own head and fell asleep.

CHAPTER 28

In the Mountain State

L UNCH WAS SERVED, and the children woke up from their naps. It was a fun break, but the flight home ahead was still long. Barb pulled books, puzzles, and various activities out of her bag. She and Nick played with the children and tried to keep them entertained. Whenever they got querulous, however, Nick simply looked at them, and they straightened up, promising to be good and begging him to let them go back to Sister Teresa's someday.

"Look, kids," Nick pointed to things out the window.

"Do you hear the plane?" Barb asked. "That's the landing gear coming down. We'll be on the ground soon." In a flurry of straightening up, collecting toys, and putting up tray tables, the last minutes of the flight went quickly.

"Mama, will Robbie be there?" Ella wanted to know.

"He's picking us up."

"And Angela?" Rosa asked.

"I think she's with him." Both girls clapped their hands.

Seeing the ground quickly approaching, Nick asked Michael if he was ready for a big bump. When it came, the boy's eyes opened wide, but at a nod of reassurance from his father, he asked if they were home. Nick told him they were at the airport in Pittsburgh and that they still had a drive home, but soon they would be in the Mountain State.

As soon as they got out of the secure area, the girls dropped their parents' hands and ran with outstretched arms to Robbie. He swung them up, one at a time, and they leaned to give Angela kisses. Michael pounded on his father's shoulder, clamoring to have his turn and reaching out to his big brother. With a chuckle, Robbie took him. "Long trip?" he asked.

Barb rolled her eyes, and Angela laughed. "Let's collect your bags. Robbie and I thought we'd stop at Chuck E. Cheese's and let the kids blow off some steam."

"Good idea!" Nick said, reaching for his baggage claim tickets as they walked toward the carousel. "Thanks for coming to get us. Was it an easy drive?"

"We came up yesterday," Robbie said. "Got a great rate at the William Penn. It's almost vacant because of Christmas."

He and Nick walked over to pull the bags off, and Nick leaned close. "Did you take care of your mother's gift for me?" Robbie assured him it was wrapped and under the tree. "She'll be surprised," Nick said.

"You will be, too. She's got you beat." Nick looked at Robbie with a question in his eyes, but Robbie laughed and refused to say anything else.

With both men pulling suitcases on rollers, and each girl tugging her own little suitcase—a Cinderella one and a bright yellow and green one—the family moved toward the parking lot. At the door, Angela handed out coats and helped Barb get the children suited up. "Lord have mercy. It's freezing!" Barb exclaimed.

"Ready to move to California, Mommy?" Nick asked.

His question was greeted with a chorus of no's. Everyone wanted snow. When they walked outside, they realized they had plenty of it, and Robbie told them it had been coming down hard for several days. "But it stopped yesterday afternoon," he said, "and it's supposed to be sunny the rest of the week."

Because of the time difference, the children were wide-awake, even though the winter sun was quickly dropping in Pittsburgh. They regaled Robbie and Angela with tales of their adventures, and Michael had them in stitches singing *"Feliz Navidad."*

"All right, Michael. It's excellent singing, but that's enough!" Nick said. Michael looked at him with dancing eyes and started again. Biting back laughter, Nick sternly instructed him to stop.

"Girls, don't laugh at him," Barb said. Robbie and Angela bit back their own amusement.

"Tell Robbie about Leroy, Mikey," Ella urged him. Michael got distracted from his singing by talking about his new best friend who fed him rolls and played soccer.

"How can you play soccer in the snow, Mikey?" Robbie asked. The girls were quick to instruct him about California weather, as if he didn't know. Pulling into Elkins much later, Robbie asked if it was too late for the "T-R-E-E."

"We have a tree, Robbie?" Ella screamed. "Mommy, did you hear that? We have a tree at home, Rosa!"

Angela laughed. "Spelling doesn't work anymore, Robbie," she reminded him.

Nick pretended to be thoughtful. "It's awfully late, kids. What do you think, Mommy?"

Barb put her hands over her ears. "All right, children. Pipe down. Nick, don't tease."

"Are you teasing us, Papa? Do we have any packages?"

"After that expensive trip? You told me that was what you wanted for Christmas," Nick continued teasing.

The girls fell silent. "It was, Papa," Rosa said. "And it was the best Christmas ever, wasn't it, Ella?"

"It was. Thank you, Papa," Ella agreed.

Robbie couldn't stand it. "Angela and I saw a few things under the tree. Let's go see." The family spilled out of the van, and the little ones ran for the house. Nick and Robbie rolled the big suitcases, and Barb and Angela pulled the girls' as they followed.

Ella sat on her haunches, looking at each gift. "This is for you, Michael. And this is for me," she said as she set it down beside her. "Here's yours, Rosa." She jumped up with a small one and ran to Barb. "This is for you, Mama. It's from Papa, because he loves you."

"Open yours first, Mama," Rosa said. But Barb laughed and pointed to where Michael sat, torn paper all around him and a gleaming fire truck in his hands. He began busily pushing buttons and making siren sounds.

"Who got him that?" Barb asked.

"Oh, Mama. Little boys must have their noise," Nick said. He pointed to her package. "Open it."

She carefully undid the bow and took the paper off. Nick rolled his eyes, waving his hand in a get-on-with-it motion. She looked up at him, eyes sparkling and a smile teasing him. When she opened the velvet cover, she gasped. "Oh, it's beautiful!" She lifted out an emerald heart with a diamond cross hanging in its center.

Nick took it from her hands, put his arms around her lovely neck, and fastened it. "It looks better on," he said.

She drew him into a hug and whispered, "You shouldn't have. Can we afford it?"

He chuckled, giving her a quick kiss on the lips. "We got a raise, remember?"

After all the packages were exchanged, including those to and from Angela and Robbie, Alan's were carefully placed back under the tree.

"Where are our gifts from the boys at Sister Teresa's, Papa?" Ella asked.

"We had to ship those, honey. We'll have them in a few days." The girls were disappointed not to be able to show them to their brother, but they described them, and the girls got their hand-carved dolls out of their little pocketbooks.

Nick quite forgot his gift from Barb that Robbie had hinted about, and he hustled his children up to bed. Robbie told his mother that everything was in order for the next morning, and furthermore that he and Angela would stay the night, so they'd be there when Nick's gift was unveiled.

Barb grinned. "He'll be surprised. He'll love it."

Robbie agreed and went to fetch their suitcase. "You staying over?" Nick asked as he came back down the stairs.

"Thought we'd have breakfast with you guys in the morning," Robbie said.

"It's late, but it'll work out well, getting them adjusted back to east coast time," Nick said. He gave Robbie a hug. "Thanks for all this, son."

"You're welcome, Dad. It was great to share the excitement. Sounds like the Home is doing well and is everything you prayed for."

"And more," Nick affirmed, choking back emotion as he always did when Barb's sons called him Dad.

"You guys have got to be tired," Robbie supposed. "We'll see you in the morning."

* * *

Everyone got up late the next morning, and Barb and Angela fixed an elaborate breakfast. Angela and Robbie had purchased some Christmas breads, and they cooked bacon and sausage with eggs. Barb looked at Robbie. "All set?" He nodded. Her eyes danced.

About noon, a voice called out from the living room. "Brother Nick, are you there?" Ella and Rosa stared at each other, big-eyed.

Nick said, with a confused look on his face, "That sounds like Hank."

The girls grabbed each other's hands and tore into the living room. Nick followed. They jumped up and down screaming, "Look, Papa, it *is* Hank! And Angelo, and Leroy!"

Nick stared at a huge screen and his boys from the Home laughing

243

and pointing at him. "What is this?" He turned around.

"It's hooked up to the computer, Nick. It's called Skype. See the camera?" Pointing while she smiled and waved at the boys, Barb showed him how the video call worked. And Robbie pointed to the couch, where he had the camera focused.

Nick collapsed onto the couch, and the boys laughed and shouted, "We see you!"

"Gotcha. Were you surprised, Brother Nick?" Hank asked. "This is so cool."

Jostling, various boys tried to get in front of the camera. Nick could tell they were in the library. "You aren't going to cry, are you?" one of them asked, and the others laughed.

"I'm not," Nick insisted, swiping at his eyes. "Watch your tongue, young man!"

"We miss you, Brother Nick," Angelo said. "When are you coming back?"

"We'll plan on it, boys. When did you rig up this gizmo? It wasn't in the library when I was there." The boys explained that it had been delivered and set up the day before, and the library bounced crazily as they tried to show him by moving the camera around. Nick heard Brother Dean cautioning the boys about breaking it and suggesting they leave it in place. The boys came into view again.

"Can you boys see Nick all right?" Robbie asked. As they directed, he arranged the Costas's camera to focus on the couch. "Is this good?" At their approval, he tightened the camera down. "We'll leave it right here."

"Is that your son, Nick? The oldest one—Robbie?" Hank asked. When Nick said it was, they wanted him in the picture, so Robbie sat on the arm of the couch. Then they wanted to see the girls, and Michael, and Sister Barb.

Michael kept looking around behind the computer. "*Dónde es* Leroy?" he asked. "*Te amo*, Leroy."

"In English, Michael. Leroy is Anglo. Say it in English," Nick instructed him.

"I loff you, Leroy. *Dónde está él*, Papa?"

"Where is he?" Nick prompted. "He's on a camera, Mikey. He's in California, at Sister Teresa's."

"*Dónde está él*, Papa? No here? Leroy no here?" Michael asked, struggling to understand.

Nick pulled him up on his lap. "Leroy's not here, but he can see you." Nick pointed to the camera. "See? Wave to Leroy." Michael waved and laughed, and the boys laughed and waved back.

After a nice call, Nick arranged devotions with the younger boys and the older boys for two evenings later in the week, and they signed off. "That is totally amazing," he said. "Whose idea was this?" Barb stood, smiling at him, and he looked at Robbie. "This was her present to me?"

"I told you she had you beat."

"I'd say. This is incredible! It's like we're right there with them."

"No, Papa. We can't feel them," Rosa pointed out.

Barb put her arm around the child. "You mean touch them, Rosa?"

Rosa nodded, swiping her eyes. "I want hugs, Mama."

Barb pulled her into her arms. "I know, Rosita. This is second best. But we'll go back."

Rosa sniffed, and Ella put her arms around her. "I told *Abuela* that Papa's boys made our family a lot bigger, Rosa."

"Looks like we're gonna have to go to Los Angeles to meet the rest of Papa's big family, Angela," Robbie said. Laughing, he pointed at Michael, who was looking behind the big screen, trying to figure out where the boys had gone.

After Robbie and Angela left, and the children were happily playing, Barb sat on Nick's lap. She told him she and Taylor had planned this and that Taylor had given them the big screen for Christmas. Nick kept shaking his head and saying he didn't believe it. Barb stood to answer the phone and returned to flip on the screen.

Alan's face appeared. Taylor stood behind him, his hand on his shoulder. "How was the surprise, Nick?" Taylor asked.

"Can you see me?" Nick asked.

"Sure can. You're right there on the couch next to the big chair where several years ago I told you what God thought of you."

"Thank you, Taylor. I almost convinced Barb to move to California, but she wouldn't budge. West Virginians are devoted to these mountains. Having fun in Vail, Alan?"

"Oh, yeah. Skiing here is something else."

Hearing Alan's voice, Ella and Rosa came barreling down the stairs. They crowded up beside Nick and began talking at once.

"One at a time, girls—Alan can't understand you. You first, Ella,"

"Isn't this cool, Alan? We talked to Papa's boys today."

"It is cool, Ella. Ask Papa if I can use it to talk to Rachel sometimes."

"Is she there?"

"She is," Alan said.

"Tell her hi," Ella requested.

Rosa tugged on Nick's arm, and he said, "Rosa's turn."

"When are you coming home, Alan? I want to hug you."

Alan laughed. "I'm coming home New Year's Day, Rosa. And I'll give you big hugs, okay?"

"How many days?" Rosa wanted to know. Nick whispered in her ear. "That long? No, come home now!"

"He wants to get his New Year's kiss, Rosita," Nick said.

Alan shook his head with a smile and asked the girls about their trip. They told him all about the Home, the gifts for the boys, caroling, and their big dinner. "We have a big family now, Alan," Ella told him.

"Sounds like the Home is exactly what we prayed for, Nick. Mom okay? Where is she?"

"She's putting Michael down for a nap," Ella said. "I'll get her."

She slipped off Nick's lap and ran upstairs.

Barb came down and sat on the arm of the chair. "Having fun, son?"

"I am, Mom. Thank you."

Barb blinked back tears and smiled. "Tell the Marshalls hello for us. I wish we could be two places at once, but we were right where God wanted us to be. Nick was wonderful to those boys. We have a lot to tell you."

"Dad, if you impact those boys a tiny fraction of what you did for Robbie and me, they are really blessed to have you in their lives."

Nick closed his eyes and choked, "Thanks, Al."

"I mean it! Give my love to Nonna and Gramps. I got the coolest gift for them. See ya soon."

"Bye, Alan," the girls chorused and waved.

Nick stood abruptly and walked into his and Barb's bedroom, shutting the door behind him. "Is Papa mad, Mama?" Ella asked.

"No, he's . . . emotional, I guess,"

"He's crying happy tears, Ella," Rosa said, "because Alan was nice to him. Right, Mommy?"

"Yeah, Rosa, you're right," Barb said.

"Can we go watch TV?" Ella asked. Barb gave them permission, and Ella added, "You go hug him, Mama. That'll make him feel good."

Giving her daughters quick embraces, Barb followed her husband into the bedroom.

CHAPTER 29

Back to Sister Teresa's

A T SPRING BREAK, Taylor sent the big plane to bring the Costas and O'Malley families to Los Angeles. He'd arranged a conference in Sacramento after Easter, and the O'Malleys were contracted for leading worship and a concert there. They all decided to go see the Home and make a vacation out of it. By that time, everyone had met the boys via the magic of Skype, and they were looking forward to being around them physically, as Rosa had wanted. Taylor had a bus and a driver waiting for them. They went directly to the school for lunch.

"Seems weird having two lunches," Alan said.

"Lunch on the plane wasn't enough to keep a chipmunk alive," Robbie complained. "I'm starving. How's the food, Nick? Typical institution?"

"The food is good," Ella assured her brother.

The cafeteria was a din when the group walked in, and choruses of greeting welcomed the two families. Nick's family moved among the boys, the males shaking hands and the girls distributing hugs. Nick held his hands up and quieted them for grace. He thought he'd pray, but several of the boys wanted to hear Ian instead, "Because he talks funny."

Of course, Ian could really lay the accent on when he wanted to. Nick had watched him years ago when he was entertaining folks in Irish pubs, and since he'd come home, he no longer worked hard to speak with an American accent. Ian stood, and with mocking sternness said, "Sure and ya nice boys in a godly place like Sister Teresa's won't be making fun of an old Irishman, now, would ya?" After the laughter quieted, he led a prayer, and they all said amen. "Now a treat for ya would be me daughter singing ya a little song. Would ya be likin' that now?"

When the boys hooted and hollered, Missy stood up and sang a blessing. The rowdy crowd fell under her spell, sitting in hushed reverence. Then Sister Brigit lined up the tables at the buffet line. The adults were served at a head table, but Rosa, Ella, and Michael passed through the line with the boys' tables where they sat. Leroy spooned Michael's food onto his plate and carried it on a tray.

Michael chatted easily, and Leroy told him his English had improved. Ella leaned across their table. "He's been practicing speaking with you, Leroy. He never cared about his English before, but he wanted to speak to you. You've been working hard, haven't you, Mikey?" Pulling a strip of chicken off a drumstick with his teeth, Michael nodded. Leroy pulled a bowl of potatoes toward them and spooned more on his little friend's plate.

"*Gra* . . . Thank you, Leroy," Michael said, correcting himself from Spanish to English.

"*De nada*, Michael," Leroy said. "I've been practicing, too, little buddy."

Rosa made her way to where her father sat and climbed up onto his lap. "Are you sleepy, Rosita?" He explained that the sun was still up in California but that it was going down in West Virginia and her body knew that. "You want to go to the hotel to take a little rest and come back later?"

Barb rubbed circles on her back. "We should do that, Papa. You want to come or stay here?" Since Nick had napped on the plane, he decided to stay and go to classes with the boys. Robbie and Alan stayed with him, but Angela went back to help Barb with the children. Ella protested, but her father promised her if she rested, she could spend the evening with the boys when they were out of classes, which would be more fun.

"How do you handle the jet lag that well, Barb?" Missy asked on the bus ride to the hotel. "I'm zonked," she added as she yawned.

"We start going to bed earlier and getting up earlier," Barb said. "Nick starts setting the clock a half an hour earlier each week for about three weeks. We get up with the stars and go to sleep with the sun. It's harder in the summer, when the sun is bright, but we try to change our body-clocks."

Ian carried Rosa into the hotel, and Angela lifted Michael out of his seat. Ella walked, but she rubbed her eyes and made no protest about lying down. Everyone took a nap. Barb may have trained her body, but she had worked nonstop for days, washing clothes and packing. Because they didn't fly commercially, she brought everything they could possibly use, and of course, they had to have professional attire for the conference.

Taylor and Adelaide arrived about five that evening and helped get the children ready to return to the Home. Hearing Taylor's voice, Michael ran out of the bedroom, arms outstretched. "Ganpa Taylor," he cried with a flying leap. He hugged him. "I lobe you!"

Chuckling, Taylor caught him and stepped back a bit with the impact of his sturdy little body. "Listen to you, Mikey!"

Barb looked up as she brushed Ella's hair and fastened her barrettes. "The 'v' and the 'b' sounds are close in Spanish. He hasn't gotten 'v' down well yet." She beckoned to Rosa, "Let's do yours now. Do you have your ponytails?" Rosa dropped her bows in her mother's hand and turned her back. Barb gently pulled out Rosa's tangles with a brush and expertly gathered up her hair, twisting it into two curly masses of long tails. She patted Rosa on the bottom. "Hurry now and brush your teeth so we can go."

"Mama . . ." Rosa started to protest. But at her mother's look, she shrugged and trudged to the bathroom.

"Is everyone ready?" Barb asked.

"You might want to brush the bedhead out of your own hair, Barb," Missy suggested. Laughing, Barb hastened back to her room and brushed her hair and repaired her makeup. The Costas family, the Wilsons, and Missy and her father trooped to the waiting bus. Barb sent Nick a text, and when they pulled up, he was waiting outside the school with Robbie.

"The Home is really slick," Robbie said to Taylor as he took Angela's hand. "Have you been here since it's been finished?" Taylor told him he had, and Robbie led Angela off to show her the labs in the academic center.

"Ready to eat again?" Nick asked. He pulled open the door, and the children ran ahead to find their special friends.

"They are quite at home here, Nick," Taylor noted.

"It's a neat thing to come to Sister Teresa's, Taylor. I feel like I'm taking my children to their grandmother's, and I guess I am."

A dinner bell called them all to the cafeteria, and the boys clamored again for Ian to pray. His sea-green eyes twinkled as he once again said the blessing, first in Irish and then in English, but in the Catholic manner of his childhood. Mother Joanna joined them for dinner, mildly chastening Nick and Ian for leaving the Mother Church but adding her thanks that they hadn't left the family of God.

Nick had suggested they sit among the students this time, and they did. The Hispanic children brought their arms up against Missy's and Alice's, fascinated with the different shades of brown, and asked them about their Native American heritage. None of the Anglo children were as fair as Ian, although a few showed him their freckles. Leroy and the few other black boys laughed at them all for being "honkies."

"Watch your language," Nick cautioned him. But his eyes twinkled as he pulled Leroy into a playful headlock.

"Man, he used to do that to me all the time," Robbie told Leroy. "I had to outgrow him!"

"You didn't have to get all that big to do that, Robbie," one of the older, taller boys said.

"Nick is the biggest man I know," Robbie replied. The boy knew exactly what he meant by that.

After dinner and vespers, the boys wanted to show the new ladies their dorms. They toured them and met back in the library, where Missy and Ian taught the boys a few songs. The boys were appreciative but wanted Brother Nick to lead them in some familiar hymns. Nick shrugged, deferring to the talented O'Malleys, as he usually did in all things musical. But these were his boys, so he did lead them. "You couldn't get him to sing with you, Missy?" Ian asked her.

"No luck at all, Da." When Nick started in the wrong key, he appealed to Missy, and she sat on a stool beside him, pitching it to a perfect G and singing along. Nick explained to the boys that Missy had a rare gift—perfect pitch—and several of them turned to Angelo. He shrugged. Missy asked Angelo for several major keys, and he sang them accurately. Then she moved to minor keys. She turned to Nick. "He has a real gift, too, Nick. We must give him lessons. I'll pay for them."

Angelo's eyes shone. "I sang for *Abuela's* mass, Brother Nick," he said proudly.

Nick hugged him. "I know, and I heard you did an excellent job! Mrs. Hastings, from the nursing home, told me you sounded like an angel."

"It was the only gift I had to give, but thank you for sending the flowers, Nick."

"You sent a nice note, too, Angelo, and that was very polite," Nick reminded him.

"Gosh, Angelo, that was the best gift ever. Like the little drummer boy, you gave your gift to God, for your grandma," Ella said.

He smiled shyly. "I guess."

Missy dropped her hand on his shoulder. "God has given you a gift. Don't fool around with it as I did for too many years. You must give it back to Him and let Him use it." Angelo turned solemn brown eyes to her. "Promise?" she asked.

Bedtime came, and the boys wanted Nick to say goodnight. He sent Barb an apologetic look and followed them upstairs, telling her to go on back to the hotel, he'd be there later. He moved up and down the rows of beds, praying with each of the younger lads after promising the older ones he'd be up in their dorm the next night.

Arriving at the hotel by taxi, Nick stumbled as he got into the elevator. He let himself into the quiet suite and found everyone asleep. After giving his teeth an insufficient brushing, he fell into bed beside Barb. She mumbled and teasingly reached for him in a halfhearted gesture, and he growled, "Leave me alone, you insatiable woman!" Chuckling, she turned her back to him.

* * *

The next day was Good Friday. Only Nick and Ian were comfortable with the Stations of the Cross, but the others were moved by the reverent ceremony and thoughtfully mediated along with their Catholic brothers and sisters. Some of the Protestant boys did, too, but others opted out and remained in the dorm, watching an Easter film under the supervision of Mr. Redding. Nick had provided a bus for the teachers so that they could take the Protestant boys to services, and they went every Sunday to service and to youth group, or to children's programs on Wednesday nights. Everyone at Sister Teresa's had come to appreciate and accept different ways of finding peace with God, and, as Madre said, "That's what it's all about anyway, isn't it?"

Easter was a bit of a problem, but Nick went to sunrise services with the Protestants and hurried back to the cathedral for mass with the Catholics. Once again, community churches provided an excellent holiday feast afterward. Missy patted her tummy, exclaiming that she was afraid she'd gained five pounds because all they did was eat.

On Monday, Missy taught the boys a bit of music theory, Ian gave piano lessons, and Alice and Angela gave an impromptu class in first aid. Robbie and Nick looked at the school's sound system and made some notes about improvements to make. Taylor and Nick met with Mother Joanna to review the financial situation. Nick wrote a large check from the foundation, and he, Ian, and Taylor each gave generous personal donations. They would be adding four new boys soon. God had been faithful.

Meanwhile, Dr. Marshall had found a plastic surgeon who would donate his services for Angelo's surgeries, though Angelo had already had several skin grafts. "How do they look?" Mother Joanna asked, knowing Angelo would have shown his twisted body to Nick.

"Better," Nick said, "but he's got a long way to go. He told me it was painful, but he could already tell it would be worth it." Nick didn't add that the boy had told him there weren't many women like Sister Barb, who would love his scars. "The best thing he told me is that he's working on forgiving his mother. Apparently, Father Victor is helping him with that."

"They meet once a week, usually in the library," Mother Joanna said, knowing Nick was overprotective of the school's reputation because of the Catholic Church's abuse scandals.

"Father Victor talked to me about it," Nick said. "I trust him."

"He's a godly man," the nun replied, "and he always leaves the door open and has one of us nearby. We try to use all caution to protect the boys and the Home."

"Thank you for not being angry with me, Madre."

"You are wise, Nick," she said. "As always, we will hate to see your precious family leave us."

"My heart is torn. But the Skype helps."

"The boys look forward to weekly devotions," Mother Joanna said.

"Does the time difference make it difficult for you? We could move it to an hour earlier."

"That would crowd dinner time. It's fine. Barb and I have the kids down when we Skype. It works out well."

That night, Nick stayed with the older boys. Sitting on the edge of Hank's bed, Nick was pleased to hear him begin their prayer, after he reached for Nick's hand and held it firmly in his own. "Jesus is real, Brother Nick. When I opened my heart, He came in and cleaned house!" He looked down. "The man I killed—remember, I told you."

"I remember," Nick said, squeezing his hand.

"He would've killed my mother. I was only twelve, but I grabbed his pistol out of his hand and shot him." He shuddered, and Nick drew him into an embrace. "The police said she would have died if he'd hit her one more time, but she said I killed the man she loved, and she kicked me into the streets. I didn't go to jail, but they sent me here. It's a good place, Brother Nick. Thank you."

Nick asked Hank about his mother. The last Hank had heard she was still on drugs, still prostituting, and living with first one man and then another. As always, Nick didn't fill the empty spaces with vain words. He listened, squeezed the boy's hand, and waited.

"Pastor Williams says nothing is impossible with God," Hank whispered.

"Let me tell you about my mother, Sister Teresa," Nick said, and he shared his mother's story. Hank hesitantly asked if he could see Nick's back. Several nearby boys covertly stared as Nick lifted his shirt. "I'll tell you about the love of a godly wife, who healed my scars," Nick said. He shared how Barb had kissed each one and wept over them. "Her tears fell on my scars and healed them."

"But they are still there, Nick. I see them," one boy said.

"But *I* don't," he said. "Not anymore." He stood and looked around. "We all have scars, boys—some inside, some outside. But they don't have to define us. Do you understand? You are who *God* says you are—not who your mother says you are, and not who Satan says you are. Learn what God says about you. You are not worthless. You're precious to Him, engraved on the hands He stretched out on the Cross for us. You are worth the death of His Son. Let's pray."

Nick prayed the boys would learn the Word of God and believe what God says about them so that they'd grow up to be men of God. Then he stood, putting his hands on a few of the heads bowed around him—curly silky heads, black curly heads, and coarse blond heads. But all *his* boys—God's boys. "I love you, boys."

"We love you, too, Brother Nick," he heard, along with requests for him to come back soon.

"We will," Nick assured them. "In the meantime, you live in my heart, every one of you."

CHAPTER 30

The Last Piece

NICK WAS DOZING ON the plane, and Barb settled on the seat beside him. Taylor lowered himself by Adelaide, directly across from them. He winked at Barb. "Nick will be thrilled, Taylor," she said in an undertone.

Nick opened one lazy eye and asked, "What will I be thrilled about, *amada*?"

Taylor quickly said, "I've ordered room service to be brought up as soon as we get checked in in Sacramento: chicken fingers and macaroni and cheese for the kids, and fish with wild rice and grilled vegetables for us."

"That's a thrill, Taylor, thanks," Nick responded dryly.

"It may not be a thrill to you, Nick Jo Costas, but it's a thrill to me not to have to haul those irritable kids to a restaurant," Barb said.

"If you're thrilled, I'm thrilled, baby. If Mama ain't happy, nobody's happy." He reached for her hand and let his one eye drift back shut.

Holding his thumb to his ear and his pinky finger to his mouth, in the shape of a phone, Taylor pointed to the back of the plane and stood. He had to go do what he told Nick he'd done, so Nick wouldn't be suspicious. Adelaide shook her head and smiled at Barb, who made a swiping motion over her forehead with her free hand.

A few minutes later, Taylor sat down again, picked up a copy of the day's *Wall Street Journal*, shook it out, and began to read to the pleasant clatter of his wife's knitting needles. Occasionally, he'd read something aloud to her, and they'd discuss it. Sometimes Barb looked up from her book and joined in, and other times she didn't.

Before long, they were landing. Barb heard Ella tell Robbie that they couldn't be landing yet, it had not been long enough, and his quiet response that it wasn't a long trip from Los Angeles to Sacramento. "Not like flying all the way across the country to West Virginia," he told her.

Nick heaved himself up and peered out the window. He flew all the time now, but he was still like a kid at landings and takeoffs. He loved to watch the cars and trucks get bigger and bigger or smaller and smaller. He put his arm around Barb and pulled her close, kissing her neck. "Not much of a nap," he complained good-naturedly, and he began to gather things up.

"Rosa, keep your seat belt on," Ella said in the back.

Rosa whined, and Nick called back, "Rosa, mind your big sister. You hear me?"

A sigh. "Yes, Papa." Click.

The pilot instructed them that they could remove their seat belts shortly but asked that they please keep them on until they had reached a complete stop at the terminal.

"See, Rosa?" Ella said. "I told you."

Soon, they were standing and ready to descend the plane's stairs. Their luggage would await them at the bus. Traveling with Taylor Wilson was traveling in style.

"You should have watched *Princess Diaries* with us, Papa," Ella scolded him.

"Gosh, I wonder how it ends? I've only seen it ten thousand times," Nick said. "Oops, forgot my hat." He reached into the overhead bin to get the Lakers ball cap the boys had presented to him. He went down the stairs first, holding out his hand to help Barb and lifting each girl down.

Robbie carried Michael, who stretched out his hands. Nick tried to take him, but he pushed him aside and said, "I want Ganpa Taylor." Coming down behind Angela, Taylor told Michael he was coming and swung him into his arms when he stepped down.

Alan said, "He knows a good grandfather when he sees one," and reached back to give Adelaide a hand.

Taylor pointed to a side door in the terminal. "We can go right through there to the bus."

"Whatcha reading, Barb?" Missy asked. Barb showed her. "Good?"

"Max Lucado hasn't written a bad book yet," Barb said, and she promised to pass it on.

Alice asked about their suitcases, and Adelaide assured her they'd be on the bus.

As they drove to the hotel, Nick noticed Barb smiling. "Looking forward to these ladies' workshops, Barb?"

"Hmm? Oh, not especially. They'll be okay. I like to talk to ladies. I feel sorry for them, though, because nobody has a husband as good as mine."

Slipping an arm around her waist, he said, "You bring out the best in me." He raised his eyebrows. When they got to the bus, he waved his hand. "You first. I'll hang back and enjoy the view as you go up those stairs." He laughed, and he laughed even harder when she exaggerated the wiggle of her hips. "You're asking for trouble, lady," he told her.

"Promise?" she answered, with a teasing smile.

Taylor chuckled. "You see why everyone loves their workshop, Missy?"

"I can imagine. The only one naughtier than Nick is my dad," she said. Before Ian could respond, she said, "Don't say it, Daddy. I know. 'There's nothing naughty about a man lovin' his wife now, lassie.' You don't have to say it." Ian laughed and put his hands around Alice's waist to lift her into the bus.

"I can get in, Ian," Alice said.

"Sure an' that's true, me love, but I like to have ya in me hands, ya know?"

Angela looked at Robbie, and they shared a smile as he took her hand.

When they reached the hotel, the girls asked Nick if they could go straight to the restaurant. Barb immediately pointed to the elevator. "No, we're going right upstairs!"

Nick thought she was being unfair, but they had a rule that they would stand behind one another when it came to the children, so he steered the girls to the elevator. "Do you have the room keys, Taylor?" he asked.

Michael was wiggling to get down now, and he ran to the elevator to push the button. He pushed the down button, so Robbie quickly pushed the up one. Both elevators arrived at once, and he steered his little brother to the up one. "What floor?" Robbie asked.

"Seven," Taylor said. "Room 715. It will be to the left when we get off."

"I forgot we had dinner ordered," Nick said. He was pushing his card key into their room next door when Taylor motioned him over.

"In here, Nick," Taylor instructed him. "Dinner's in the living room." Nick wanted to wash up, but Taylor seemed almost impatient, rare for him. Nick shrugged and complied. Taylor held the door and waved him in first. Puzzled, Nick looked in the room and saw a Hispanic group—a family—already there.

"We have the wrong room, Taylor. We're walking in on some folks."

The man of the family smiled, and Nick felt a rush of pure love. Flipping through the files in his brain, he tried to check off his memories. The stout, muscular man approached him, patting his midsection. "I've put on a few pounds since you knew me as a rookie cop, eh, Nickie?"

"Oh my God! Jesús! Honey, it's Jesús. Thank you, God!" Nick threw his arms around his rescuer from long ago, laughing and crying. The two men embraced as only Latinos can, and Jesús broke away first to introduce his family: his wife Isabella, his oldest son, Nick, and another son and two daughters. He explained that the others couldn't be there.

Nick Morales stepped forward and shook Nick Costas's hand. "So, this is the man—my big brother, that he named me after. Nice to meet you."

Isabella's plump fingers caught Nick's hand, and her round face creased into at least a thousand lines. "And I thank you for my husband, who married me because of you." She glanced at Jesús with a benevolent smile.

"This is true," Jesús confirmed. "I tried to adopt you, Nickie. I begged for you. But they said no because I was not married. I went to church every day and lit candles to find a wife, and one day, she was there beside me. I married her right away, but when I returned to the welfare office, they still said no. You were settled, they said, and they would not disturb the placement. When I read your book, I was angry! Nickie, I am sorry for what happened to you."

Nick turned to see his children staring at them. He introduced them to the kind man who had taken Papa to the hospital when he was a little boy, only one year older than Michael.

Michael stared. "Jesus? *Éste es* Jesus?"

Jesús laughed. "No, not Jesucristo, Michael. My mama, she named me Jesús. I have much to live up to, no? I have to be good all the time." Nick explained to his son, and the boy's puzzled frown relaxed. Then Nick introduced his boss and Taylor.

"Taylor, I already know," Jesús responded. "He set this up."

Nick looked at Taylor and then at a beaming Barb. "You knew, Barb?"

"I told you you'd be thrilled," she said. Nick's mouth dropped open. For perhaps the first time since she had known him, he had no words. But then she remembered that day in the shower when he could only cry.

The carts of food arrived, and the waiters hastily set up folding tables and chairs for the crowd. Some of Jesús's family begged off to go to work or home to their own families. His fifteen-year-old daughter eyed Alan and attempted to sit next to him, but he politely pushed in her chair and went to another table with the little children. Robbie and Angela joined her table, explaining that he had a serious girlfriend, and her face fell.

Jesús told Nick that he was now an instructor with the state police academy, and Isabella expressed her relief that he was no longer on the streets. She told them that they gave him this job after he had been shot a third time. "He has many medals," she said with pride.

"No, *mi amor*, this is not necessary," Jesús said, and he turned the topic to the upcoming conference. "We will come in the evenings," he promised.

After Jesús and the rest of his family left, Barb hustled the girls to the tub. While she dressed them, Nick got in the shower with Michael. He came out in his pajamas, with Michael wrapped in a towel. The light glistened on both of their dark heads. Handing Michael to his mother, Nick sat between his daughters on the bed and told them of the night long ago when Jesús had helped him say goodbye to his mother.

"Why did your mama have to go, Papa? Where did she go?" Ella asked.

Nick told them the devil had chained her in the evil of drugs. "She was very sick, and her boyfriend had hurt Papa so badly that he had to go to the hospital, and Jesús rode in the ambulance with me. He gave me food when I was hungry and took care of me when I was sick. Jesús has many rewards for him, girls."

"How long were you in the hospital, Papa?" Ella continued.

"Many months—about five or six months. I had several operations."

"Did she come see you, Papa?" Rosa asked.

"My mama?" Rosa nodded. "No, she went to prison. Mamas aren't supposed to let people hurt their children. And she didn't feed me like Mommy feeds you good food to make you grow strong."

"*Abuela* was in prison? But she was a nun!" Rosa said.

"Drugs make you do bad things. When she was in prison, she asked Jesus to come into her heart, and He took the drugs away from her. When she got out, she had to work, so she went to the Convent of the Angels and asked for a job. Then she became a nun. Jesus is a miracle-worker, no?"

Barb sat in a chair with Michael and watched her daughters' faces as they learned the story of their father's childhood. "That is sad, Papa," Ella said. "But that's why you wanted to build the Home, isn't it? For little boys like you?"

"I have prayed for many years for the little boys like me. Even before I knew how to pray, I thought about them. And God has blessed us and answered my prayers. Now," Nick patted the bed, "it is very late, and we must sleep, yes?" The girls scooted under the covers. Nick knelt beside them and thanked God for his family.

Rosa had fallen asleep, but Ella opened her eyes and looked at her father. She laid her hand gently on his head. She had a new understanding of why he loved his family like he did. Feeling her hand of blessing, Nick looked up at her. "I'm glad God gave you a family, Papa, and I'm very glad it was us. And you chose me to be your little girl. I'm Ella Marie Westfall-Costas." Her fingers wiped the corners of his eyes. "I love you." She threw her arms around his neck.

Barb watched them as she tucked Michael into the other bed. She leaned over Ella's bed and whispered. "We got the good end of that deal, didn't we, baby?" Ella loosened her hold. "Go to sleep now blessed-girl. Daddy and I will be in the other bedroom." Leaving the bathroom light on, she snapped off the bedside lamp and left the room, and Nick followed.

Nick was uncharacteristically quiet as he prepared for bed. He stretched out on the bed, his hands under his head, and Barb crawled in beside him. She had learned from him and didn't overpower his thinking time with chatter. She reached up for their lamp and rested beside him. He moved, gathering her into his arms, and made sweet love to her, without a word. She ran her fingers lightly over his scars, knowing each one by heart, and they fell asleep in each other's arms.

* * *

Barb got up silently the next morning, creeping into the living room with her Bible. She read Jesus's sayings about feeding the hungry, clothing the naked, and caring for the sick. She prayed for Jesús, thanking God he'd been there for her husband those many years ago and speaking blessings on him.

Alan wandered in and asked, "You all right, Mom?"

"That was quite a night, wasn't it?" she asked.

"Must have been neat for Nick, huh?" Alan sat beside her on the sofa

"It was. He said it was like the last missing piece of his childhood falling into place."

"His life would've been a lot different if Jesús had adopted him."

"Maybe we never would've met, though," she said.

"That's true, I guess. I'm really glad we have Nick, Mom. Robbie never would have made it without him, and I wouldn't have been the guy I am either."

Barb took her son's hand. Alan prayed for Nick, for Jesús, and for the Home. He thanked God for Ian, Mike, and Taylor. "Thank you, God, for this father you gave us, and help us to be godly men, to make him proud."

"Oh, he is proud, Alan. He's very proud of you and Robbie. The morning you called from Vail, Robbie had called him Dad, and then you did. He went into the bedroom and cried."

"I told him I didn't remember my dad very well—vague images, occasional picture-memories. But he had always been there for me. I know it was hard for you and Nonna when Dad died, but God was good to us to give us Nick."

"Are you talking about me?" Nick said as he walked into the room.

"We're talking about Jesús and how cool it is that he found you again after all those years. He read your book, huh?" Alan asked.

"Yes. And he contacted Taylor. They set this up, but your mother was in on it. 'Thrilled' is hardly the word. I was astounded, overcome, and blessed beyond measure. He has a sweet family, doesn't he? Imagine naming his son Nick. I didn't recognize him right away, but as soon as he said 'Nickie,' the years fled away." Nick dropped down beside Barb. Curling her feet underneath her, she leaned into his chest, and his arms circled her.

Alan stood, glancing at his watch. "I'm meeting Robbie and Angela for breakfast in fifteen minutes. We've booked a tour of the state capitol." A few minutes later, he walked through the room with a wave and let himself out the door.

"You think the kids will sleep awhile, Barb?"

"I do. We were up late talking. They had a lot to absorb."

Nick slipped his hand under her shirt and teased her breasts. "Wanna make a little noise? You were mighty quiet last night." Taking her by the hand, he led her into the bedroom and locked the door behind them. Soon, he had to put a hand over Barb's mouth, and he laughed.

They stayed in bed until they heard the kids up. The toilet flushed, and the girls talked together. The parents pulled on their clothes. Barb went into Michael's bedroom to get him. He was sitting up and rubbing his eyes. "Pee-pee, Mommy," he said.

"Come on." Barb offered him her hand, and he skipped beside her.

Soon, they had the children dressed, and as they were leaving for the restaurant, Taylor came out of his and Adelaide's room on the other side of the living room. "Adelaide had a bad night. Her arthritis is acting up," Taylor informed them. "Mind if I join you?" Michael took Taylor's hand, and they walked ahead.

After they ate, the girls and Michael threw pennies in a fountain on the other side of a black iron half-fence while the grown-ups talked over another cup of coffee and watched them. "I couldn't come up with much for this small-group workshop, Taylor," Barb said. "I thought I'd say a few things about I Peter 3's 'without a word,' but other than that I came up empty. Maybe I Corinthians 7, about our bodies belonging to one another. But anything else?"

"I want this to be a free forum where women can ask you questions. We've restricted enrollment to ten women, so you can have one on one. Dan Murphy listened to your workshop, by the way. He loved it, but he suggested you make a remark about respecting one another's boundaries. We can't impose on our spouses anything that makes them uncomfortable."

"Duly noted, Taylor. Love does not insist on its own way, right?" Nick said. "Remember that, you demanding woman," he teased Barb. She and Taylor both laughed. And Nick and Barb added a few remarks to their workshop.

CHAPTER 31

A Word to the Wives

B ARB ENTERED HER FIRST solo workshop, whispering a prayer for God's help. She greeted the intimate gathering of ten ladies, and each woman introduced herself. Barb read to them from I Peter 3:1–4, God's Word Translation:

> Some husbands may not obey God's word. Their wives could win these men for Jesus Christ, by the way they live without saying anything. Their husbands would see how pure and reverent their lives are. Wives must not let their beauty be something external. Beauty doesn't come from hairstyles, gold jewelry, or clothes. Rather, beauty is something internal that can't be destroyed. Beauty expresses itself in a gentle and quiet attitude which God considers precious.

She closed her Bible and explained to them how Nick looks at many different translations, and he taught her to explore the different facets and nuances by doing the same. She elaborated on the verses a bit and then turned them to I Corinthians 7. She reminded them that withholding sex from men was an ungodly choice and drove many men into sexual impurity.

A woman raised her hand. "I understand, and I respond when my husband asks me for sex, but how many times should we have sex?"

"We are not under the law, but under grace," Barb said. "We are led by the Spirit. I have no rule that says 'Thou shalt have sex once a week, or a month, or twice a week.' That's between the two of you—what you want, what you need, and what he wants and needs."

"But he wants sex three times a week! I have two toddlers, and I'm exhausted. Can I say no if he asks too much of me?"

Barb felt a slow blush mounting up her neck and spreading to her cheeks and cursed her fair complexion for the millionth time. She cleared her throat. "Again, we don't have a law on this. But God created the sexual relationship. It can be the glue that holds marriages together, especially for those of us who know it's sacred and holy and reserved for marriage."

She continued: "As women, sometimes we see 'pleasing our man' as a 'duty.' But God intended it for us as well. In fact, the only part of a body that is solely reserved for sexual pleasure, with no other function, is ours, ladies. We should enjoy this tremendous gift, and if you don't, you need to figure out why.

"Nick has prepared a list of some excellent books. Take your time and tell your husband what you want. Tell him if you're worn out and strike a bargain: if he'll read to the kids and let you soak in a bubble bath, you'll make it worth his while. And you will rest better after you make love. I have a friend who says, 'I sleep so good, after.' That's true. Also, products are available on store shelves that will enhance your lovemaking.

"To encourage our son before his wedding, Nick told him sex is like every other physical activity, it gets better with practice—so keep making it better. Sometimes . . ." Barb closed her eyes, begging the Holy Spirit to help her out. She cleared her throat. "Uh, sometimes we've been known to have sex three times in a day."

"You can *do* that?" the attendee asked. "Doesn't it annoy you?"

Barb's blush deepened. "Um, living with Nick is like spontaneous combustion. He's a passionate man. He's passionate about God, and his kids, and the boys at Sister Teresa's Home. And he's passionate about me. Nick took this dry desert of a church-lady and started a prairie fire. Sometimes, he makes me beg." *God, did I really say that?*

Several of the women were laughing, and one spoke up. "My husband saw Nick looking at you and said, 'Look at that guy! He's undressing her with his eyes.' He didn't know you were a couple. I told him you were his wife, and he said it was a good thing because if any man looked at me like that, he'd punch his lights out."

"Yes, well, he does that—it's quite unnerving, but exciting, too." Then she told them about the day he kept whispering 'later' all day until, when he finally got to the hotel, she was more than ready.

Another woman raised her hand. "I have the opposite problem. My husband is reserved. He grew up in a strait-laced home, and sometimes we'll go for two weeks without sex. I find myself getting irritable. I need it more than he does. What can I do?"

Barb was glad she chose a roundtable discussion for this group. She really needed to sit, and she thanked God for the chair beneath her. "I've heard it said that, spiritually, women are like tinder," she began, "and men are logs, slower to catch fire. Usually, sexually, that is the opposite. Men are visual and ready quicker than we are. But, since your husband is reserved, you must be the tinder. I suggest you choose an appropriate moment and tell him what you told me. It could be he doesn't want to be too demanding. Maybe he got the idea women don't like it.

"Read the book *The Five Love Languages*. I bet your language is touch. Our men don't read touchy-feely books, but we need to study. You need to learn his love language. I bet his is acts of service. We women can read these books and give our guys the condensed version. Put the kids down early or send them to their grandparents. And then stimulate him. Call him at work and tell him you've set the candles out in the bedroom. Heighten his anticipation, like Nick did mine, whispering, 'later' throughout the day. Make your bedroom inviting and romantic. Touch him in the places he loves—discover those places. Tell him you want him. Wear something that turns him on visually, or wear nothing. That usually does it."

A chorus of agreements rose in the room, along with a lot of laughter. The rest of the time flew by, and Barb distributed the bibliography Nick had drawn up for their workshop, exhorting them to read some of the books with an open mind and be willing to experiment a little. She remembered Dr. Murphy's suggestion and quickly added, "But never be forced into anything that makes you uncomfortable. Tell him how you feel and respond quickly to what you do like—and you need to tell him that, too. We think they should already know, but you must tell him when it feels good, where it feels good, and if it hurts. Don't shut him out or get mad.

"Our daughter-in-law thought it wasn't ladylike to make any noise. Boy, would I be in trouble! Then she found out her little cries of pleasure turned her husband on. The marriage bed is undefiled, ladies. Read 'Song of Solomon' and go home, or upstairs tonight, and enjoy." The girls crowded around her when they walked down the hall, giggling and chattering excitedly, and they thanked her profusely.

Nick watched Barb, waiting until he saw her looking around. "Looks like you did okay. I bet we'll have some happy husbands praising you to the skies tonight."

She put her arm around his waist, hooking her thumb into his waistband. "I hope so. I told some of those secrets you told Ella not to tell."

Nick laughed. "I have no secrets, baby. Everybody knows I love you like crazy." She told him about what the woman in the workshop said about how he looked at her, and he thought that was funny. "I do, you know," Nick said, sweeping his eyes down her body, resting them on her breasts, checking out her hips, and admiring it all.

"You're telling me? I feel like I'm stark naked when you look at me like that," she whispered furiously. "Stop it!"

Right there, in the middle of the hall, with people on both sides of them, Nick took Barb in his arms and rested his forehead on hers. "You'll have to stop looking this beautiful then." He smiled with infinite tenderness and absolute devotion. "Your hazel eyes bewitch me, and your long, elegant neck . . ." He groaned. "Do you have a tape of this workshop?"

"No! It's not a public workshop. It's for real women with real problems." Her eyes were shooting fire.

"You're giving me a problem, Barb. I'm so hard I'm in pain here." Nick stopped beside a water fountain and stuck his head in the cold water.

"Maybe we'd better go grab a bite," Barb suggested.

"I'm up for that. My place or yours?"

Barb giggled. "You are impossible."

"Oh, you meant food? We could get some food. Missy's in the restaurant with the kids. She told me to come get you." Nick took her hand, and they veered to where their children were.

Adelaide found Barb there and asked her plans for the rest of the day. Barb opened the schedule and read some of the events that interested her. "Could you repeat your women's workshop?" Adelaide asked. "We have fifty more women who want to attend."

"Oh, no. It wouldn't work for fifty. A dozen, max," Barb said.

"Taylor said to hold it to ten, but could we do two more?" Adelaide suggested. "We'll do the ones who signed up first and stop at thirty." Barb agreed. "We'll let you see the evaluations. The women were definitely helped. I noticed we've had to add a repeat of Nick's class with you as well."

Barb took a deep breath. "God being my Helper, Adelaide." She did another small group that afternoon and two more the next day. In one gathering, a woman said she was being abused at home, and Barb linked her to Dr. Dan Murphy, setting up a meeting after she and the other women gathered around her and prayed. Barb and Nick did their joint workshop that afternoon and the next morning, and each time it was unique and lots of fun.

Nick also produced the worship times for Missy and Ian and planned to do their evening concert as well. Tim surprised Missy by flying in, and the crowd was delighted when she sang "Lost in Your Eyes" while they danced together. On a whim, Tim had brought all the videos of that song that they had in stock. They sold out completely and had to leave a sign-up sheet for people who didn't get a copy to order it.

At the final night's concert, Nick caved to the many requests, agreeing to sing "Hymn to Him"—the song from *My Fair Lady* that he sang for the workshops. With his top hat and cane, he had the gathering laughing and stomping. Robbie was producing.

The next day, the entire group went to the airport on the bus, parting ways as the Wilsons walked to the small plane and the West Virginia crowd climbed the stairs to Taylor's big jet. Nick, Barb, and the younger children changed places with Robbie and Angela, sitting in the back so they could watch *The Princess Diaries* for the ten thousand and first time. Nick heard his adult children having a lively discussion at the front, and he longed to join them. But instead, he looked down at his precious girls beside him and cuddled them close. Michael sat off to himself, his knees up in front of him, and he worked the keys on his iPod, playing some game with little boy intensity.

Eventually, they all fell asleep, and Nick and Barb did move to the front. Nick pulled an envelope out of his computer case and opened it up. Two checks fell out. Laughing, he handed one to Barb. "Taylor doesn't trust me, I guess. This one's for you."

"You're quite the speaker, Mom. I heard lots of ladies talking about your workshop," Alan said.

"I did, too, when I had the kids at the pool yesterday," Angela said. "One of the ladies said she'd never look at sex the same way. But I totally understand it. You're a natural with married stuff. You've helped me, and you helped a lot of them, Barb."

Nick slouched down in his seat, pulling his ball cap down over his eyes. "Lucky husbands!" he exclaimed. Barb threw a pillow at him. He lifted the cap, looked at her, and said, "Just saying." He pulled his hat back down, saying, "Who can find a virtuous woman? For her price is far above rubies. The heart of her husband doth safely trust in her, so that he shall have no need of spoil. She will do him good and not evil all the days of her life." Nick put his feet up on the footrest in front of him. "That's Proverbs 31:10–12, Barb."

From the Publisher

Thank You from the Publisher

Van Rye Publishing, LLC ("VRP") sincerely thanks you for your interest in and purchase of this book.

If you enjoyed this book or found it useful, please consider taking a moment to support the author and get word out to other readers like you by leaving a rating or review of the book at its product page at your favorite online book retailer.

Thank you!

Resources from the Publisher

Van Rye Publishing, LLC ("VRP") offers the following resources to writers and to readers.

For writers who enjoyed this book or found it useful, please consider having VRP edit, format, or fully publish your own book manuscript. You can find out more, and contact the publisher directly, by visiting VRP's website: www.vanryepublishing.com.

For readers who enjoyed this book or found it useful, please consider signing up to have VRP notify you when books like this one are available at a limited-time discounted price, some as low as $0.99. You can sign up to receive such notifications by visiting the following web address: http://eepurl.com/cERow9.

For anyone who enjoyed this book or found it useful, if you have not already done so, please again consider leaving a rating or review of this book at its product page at your favorite online book retailer. These ratings and reviews are themselves extremely valuable resources for writers and for readers like you. VRP hopes you will please take a moment to share your thoughts about this book with others.

Thank you again!

About the Author

CHARLOTTE S. SNEAD holds a Bachelor of Arts in Psychology degree from Duke University and a Master of Social Work degree from the University of North Carolina. OakTara published her first three books: *His Brother's Wife*, in 2012, and *Recovered and Free* and *Invisible Wounds*, in 2014. Charlotte later received Jan-Carol Publishing's Believe and Achieve Award for her novel *A Place to Live*, the first of a scheduled five-book series. While working on the remaining books in the series, she also published her first children's book, *Deano the Dino Goes to the Doctor*, in 2018.

Charlotte married her husband, Dr. Joseph Snead, in 1962. They raised five children and a foster daughter and now proudly grandparent ten boys and one girl. One of their children and four of their grandchildren are adopted. Charlotte was the daughter of a career military officer, who served in WWII, and Dr. Snead served in Vietnam. Their son was a career military officer, so Charlotte has a special place in her heart for our military.

In keeping with Charlotte's strong belief in and celebration of the joys of marriage, family, and writing, she maintains a blog (at www.charlottesnead.com), which has the tagline "Sacred Passion—It's God's Idea." Please feel free to contact her there.